THE JUDGMENT OF THE SWORD...

Milo snapped into wakefulness as a dagger point pricked the flesh just below the right corner of his jaw. Though Mara was weeping, her dagger hand was rock-steady. "Forgive me, Milo, but I *must* know!" she whispered intensely, then pushed the sharp, needle-tipped weapon two inches into his throat and slashed downward.

The initial gush of blood rapidly dwindled to a slow trickle, and what should have been a death wound began to close. Milo's eyes, too, closed and he clenched his teeth, saying between them, "I should have slain you, Mara. Well, now you know! What are you going to do with that knowledge—the knowledge that Milo, the War Chief, bears what your people call the Curse of the Undying?"

GREAT SCIENCE FICTION from SIGNET

- [ ] **CASTAWAYS IN TIME** by Robert Adams. (#AE1474—$2.25)*

- [ ] **SWORDS OF THE HORSECLANS** (Horseclans #2)
  by Robert Adams. (#E9988—$2.50)*

- [ ] **REVENGE OF THE HORSECLANS** (Horseclans #3)
  by Robert Adams. (#AE1431—$2.50)

- [ ] **A CAT OF SILVERY HUE** (Horseclans #4)
  by Robert Adams. (#AE1579—$2.25)*

- [ ] **THE SAVAGE MOUNTAINS** (Horseclans #5)
  by Robert Adams. (#AJ1589—$1.95)

- [ ] **THE PATRIMONY** (Horseclans #6)
  by Robert Adams. (#AE1238—$2.25)*

- [ ] **HORSECLANS ODYSSEY** (Horseclans #7)
  by Robert Adams. (#E9744—$2.75)*

- [ ] **THE DEATH OF A LEGEND** (Horseclans #8)
  by Robert Adams. (#AE1126—$2.50)*

- [ ] **KILLBIRD** by Zach Hughes. (#E9263—$1.75)

- [ ] **PRESSURE MAN** by Zach Hughes. (#J9498—$1.95)*

- [ ] **TIME GATE** by John Jakes. (#Y7889—$1.25)

- [ ] **SUN DOGS** by Mark McGarry. (#J9620—$1.95)*

- [ ] **PLANET OF THE APES** by Pierre Boulle. (#E8632—$1.25)

- [ ] **GREYBEARD** by Brian Aldiss. (#E9035—$1.75)

- [ ] **JACK OF SHADOWS** by Roger Zelazny. (#E9370—$1.75)

*Prices slightly higher in Canada

THE
COMING
OF THE
HORSECLANS

———•———•———

A Horseclans Novel

by
Robert Adams

Ⓢ
A SIGNET BOOK
NEW AMERICAN LIBRARY
TIMES MIRROR

COPYRIGHT © 1975, 1982 BY ROBERT ADAMS

Published by arrangement with the author

 SIGNET TRADEMARK REG. U.S. PAT. OFF. AND FOREIGN COUNTRIES
REGISTERED TRADEMARK—MARCA REGISTRADA
HECHO EN CHICAGO, U.S.A.

SIGNET, SIGNET CLASSICS, MENTOR, PLUME, MERIDIAN AND NAL
BOOKS *are published by The New American Library, Inc.,*
1633 Broadway, New York, New York 10019

FIRST SIGNET PRINTING, JULY, 1982

1 2 3 4 5 6 7 8 9

PRINTED IN THE UNITED STATES OF AMERICA

To Christopher Stasheff and Graham Diamond, respected colleagues and good friends; to Robert and Verna Boos, *alte Kameraden;* to John Estren; to the late, lamented Harvey Shild; and to Pamela Crippen, who is made of sugar and spice and everything nice.

AUTHOR'S INTRODUCTION

The following tale is a fantasy, pure and simple. It is a flight of sheer imagination. It contains no hidden meanings and none should be read into it; none of the sociological, economic, political, religious, or racial "messages," with which far too many modern novels abound, are herein contained. *The Coming of the Horseclans* is, rather, intended for the enjoyment of any man or woman who has ever felt a twinge of that atavistic urge to draw a yard of sharp, flashing steel and with a wild war cry recklessly spur a vicious stallion against impossible odds.

If I must further categorize, I suppose this effort falls among the sci-fi/fantasy stories which are woven about a post-cataclysmic age, far in our future. In this case, the story is set in the twenty-seventh century. The world with which we are dealing is one still submerged in the barbarism into which it was plunged some six hundred years prior to the detailed events, following a succession of man-made and natural disasters which extirpated whole nations and races of mankind.

For the scholars and just plain curious: Yes, the language of the Blackhairs or Ehleenee *is* Greek. I have, indeed, indulged in a bit of literary license with regard to spelling, both in that language and in Mehrikan or English. I tender no apologies.

—Robert Adams

PROLOGUE I

"And, in His time, the God shall come again,
From the south, upon a horse of gold,
To meet the Kindred camped upon the plain,
Or so our Sacred Ancestors were told . . ."
                —From *The Prophecy of the Return*

The big man came ashore at the ancient port of Mazatlán, from off a merchantman out of the equally ancient port of Callao, far to the south. The men of the ship professed little sure knowledge of their former passenger, save that he was a proven and deadly warrior, certainly noble-born, though none seemed quite certain of the country of his origin.

This man, who gave his name as Maylo de Morré, stood a head and a handsbreadth above even the tallest of the men of the mountains who, themselves, towered over the men of the lowlands and coast. His hair was strippled with gray, but most of it was as black as their own, though not so coarse, and his hair, spadebeard and moustachios were cut and fashioned in the style of noblemen of the far-southern lands.

Silver he possessed, and *gold*, as well, but no man thought of taking it from him by force, not after they saw his smooth, effortless movements or looked but once into those brooding, dark-brown eyes. At his trim waist were shortsword, dirk and knife, another knife was tucked into the top of his right boot and the wire-wound leather hilt of a well-kept, antique saber jutted up over his left shoulder.

After he had secured lodgings in the best inn of the upper

town, his first stop was at the forge of Mazatlán's only armor-smith, where he stripped for measurements and ordered a thigh-length shirt of double-link chainmail, paying half the quoted cost in advance in strange, foreign, but pure, gold coins. And that night the smith told all the tavern of his customer's hard, spare, flat-muscled body, covered from head to foot by a veritable network of crosshatched lines denoting old scars—battle wounds, for certain, the smith opined.

The next morning, Morré sought out the town agent for old Don Humberto del Valle de Castillo y de las Vegas and shortly the two were seen to ride out toward the local nobleman's *estancia*. When they returned the next day, the Don himself rode with them, trailed by ten of his lancers, and Morré was astride one of the fine war-stallions which it was the Don's business and pleasure to breed and train. This stallion was of a chestnut hue that shone like fine gold, with mane and tail that seemed silvery ripples in the brisk breeze blowing in from the sea.

Two lancers fetched the stranger's effects from the inn and, for the next month, he resided at Don Humberto's townhouse as a clearly honored guest. He no longer visited the shops; rather, uniformed lancers summoned and escorted the various artisans to the mansion—the saddler, the bootmaker, the best of the tailors, a merchant who was ordered to bring with him several of the rare and hideously expensive but immensely powerful hornbows made by horse-nomads far and far to the north and east, and the armorer.

Julio, the saddler, had to confer with the goldsmith, Pedro, since some of the decorations the foreign nobleman wanted on his saddle and harness were beyond the skills of a provincial worker of leather. And the bootmaker, José, had to have words with Diego, the armorer, if the boots he was to construct were to be properly fitted with thin sheets of steel and panels of light mail.

The tailor, Gustavo, was nearly ecstatic, seeing great future profits from the new and unique designs of clothing this great nobleman had brought from oversea. His only outside need was to haggle with the tanner, Anselmo, for the extra-fine grade of leather to line the esteemed gentleman's riding breeches.

Sergio Gomez—who was a bastard half-brother of the Don and had, himself, done a bit of soldiering before bringing several years' worth of loot back to the town of his birth and setting himself up as a merchant—could talk of nothing save Don Maylo's horsemanship, bowmanship and skill with lance and saber.

Sitting in the smoky tavern with his pint-cup of milk-white *pulque* before him on the knife-scarred board and eager ears hanging upon his words, old Sergio puffed at a thin, black cigarro and opined, "*Muchachos*, I certify, el Senor Maylo de Morré is *un hombre formidable*. With either lance or saber, he is more than a match for any *caballero* I have ever seen fight . . . and I have seen many, in my day.

"But with the bow, now," he whistled softly, "I tell you, it smacks of wizardry. Within minutes after he had selected the bow of his choice and strung it to his satisfaction, he was plunking arrows into a bale of straw with such speed and ac- curacy as to make my poor old head to spin.

"Then that splendid palamino stallion came trotting over, though no one had called him and the Senor had not even looked in that direction. The Senor hooked a full arrowcase to his belt and was up on the stallion with bow in hand in the blinking of an eye, without either saddle or reins or even a bare halter.

"He rode far out, then came back at a hard gallop, guiding the stallion Senor Dios alone knows how, since both hands were busy with the bow. *Muchachos*, he started loosing shafts at a hundred meters or better from that bale of straw, and here to tell you is this one that not one of the dozen shafts he loosed was outside a space I could cover with my palm and fingers.

"*That* would be good shooting from a firm stand at fifty meters. But from a galloping, barebacked horse at a hundred? Angel Gonzales, Don Humberto's sergeant, is himself a bow- master and has, as we all know, won many, many gold pesos in competition, and he told me that there can be no man in all the Four Kingdoms of Mexico with such skill."

The merchant took a long draught of his *pulque*, puffed his cigarro back to life, then lowered his voice conspiratorily. "Don Humberto avows that the Senor Malyo de Morré is but a noble traveler from somewhere in the Associated Duchies of Chile, who is passing through on a leisurely trip; but Angel opines that he is none other than one of the famous *Defen- sores Argentinos*, on loan to our Emperor from the Emperor of the Argentinas and traveling secretly, incognito and in a most roundabout route to meet with his new master."

Of course, all of them were wrong. Maylo de Morré was much less than they thought, but far more than they could imagine.

The long, difficult and dangerous journey across the Sierra Madre Occidentalis to the Grand Duchy of Chihuahua was accomplished—through the good offices of Don Humberto, who seemed to have highly placed friends and/or relatives at the courts of all four kings and of the Emperor, as well—in company with a heavily guarded caravan which had wound down from the Emperor's alternate capital at Guadalajara and was proceeding slowly up the coast roads, making frequent stops so that the merchants might offer their wares and the attached imperial officers could collect the yearly taxes from the various local officers, such as Don Humberto.

Despite the numerous and well-armed guards, Don Humberto would not hear of his guest departing with less than a full squad of his own lancer-bodyguards, a quartet of servants, and a fully equipped and provided pack-train to afford the estimable Conde Maylo de Morré security and civilized comforts on the long trek over the mountains. Don Humberto had never been able to obliquely wheedle—for of course gentlemen did not demand or even inquire about unoffered personal information from other gentlemen; it would have been most impolite—any particulars of el Senor's true origin, nationality, family or rank from him. But he had proclaimed him a count so that his "rank" would match that of the commander of the caravan, who then would treat el Senor as an equal. The old Don felt that it was the least he could do to repay his guest for the many hours of pleasure his tales of the lands and peoples and their singular customs and mores had brought him here in his isolated and provincial little backwater of empire.

For his own part, Don Ramón, Conde-Imperial de Guanajuato and Colonel-General of the Imperial Tax Service, had not needed old Don Humberto's assurances. He knew a well-bred man when he saw one—the air of relaxed self-assurance, the strict observance of the courtesies and proprieties, the matchless seat which made a single creature of him and his fine destrier, the easy and natural assumption of command, like a hand slipping into an old and well-worn glove. Indeed, Don Ramón suspected that this foreign "Conde" had deliberately misled the aged Humberto, that his true rank was likely several notches higher, and throughout the first two legs of the journey, he deferred to his guest as he would have to his own overlord, el Principe de los Numeros. High nobles were often wont to travel incognito—this Don Ramón knew well from his years in and around the imperial court—and while he diligently played the game and always addressed the foreigner by his *nombre de guerra* and his assumed title, he never failed to treat him and see that he was treated like a prince of the imperial house.

The ambuscade was sprung in a rock-walled pass, high in the sierras. While rocks crashed about them, throwing off knife-sharp splinters, and arrows hummed their deadly song, while horses and mules and men screamed, whips cracked and the confusion of those in authority was reflected in their torrent of often contradictory orders, Don Ramón caught a glimpse of Conde Maylo.

Despite his evident fear—his rolling eyes and distended nostrils—the palomino stallion stood still as a statue, while his noble rider calmly uncased and strung his hornbow. Behind him, his ten lances tried hard to emulate him, their efforts frustrated partially by less biddable mounts. Only the short, scarfaced sergeant managed to get his mount under sufficient control to allow him to ready his own bow and follow his lord when that worthy moved at an easy walk up into the pass.

When he was where he wished to be, the Conde once more brought his horse to a rigid halt. With rocks bouncing about them and arrows occasionally caroming off their helmets, the sergeant and his lord commenced—before Ramón's half-disbelieving eyes—such a demonstration of superior archery as not even the ancient rocks could ever before have witnessed.

Soon, the falling rocks had been completely replaced by falling, screaming bodies, and after a good dozen of the bandit archers had hurtled, dead or dying, to the floor of the pass or had dropped their bows to sink back against the rock walls, shrieking in agony and clutching at the feathered shafts which had skewered various portions of their anatomies, their so-far living and whole comrades faded back among the boulders.

So it was that, when the heavily-armed and mounted element of bushwhackers struck the head of the column, they found not a shattered, disorganized and demoralized party to slaughter and plunder at leisure, but rather a rock-hard line of disciplined troops.

Even before they came into physical contact with the waiting soldiery and gentry—almost all of whom should have been down, crushed by rocks or stuck full of arrows—volley on well-aimed volley of shafts rose up in a hissing cloud from the rear ranks to wreak havoc and death amongst the attackers.

Those who had set and activated the ambuscade were not soldiers but hit-and-run banditti, so they could not have been faulted for breaking and running immediately they saw their leaders hacked by sabers and broadswords, lifted writhing from their saddles on dripping lancepoints or hurled to death amid the stamping hooves by blow of ax or mace. Run, the survivors did and pursued they were. Very few escaped alive, nor were any prisoners taken, though several dozen heads were.

Few of the captured horses were of much account, so they were simply stripped of their ratty gear and turned loose. Those which looked as if they might bring a price or a reward were added to the packtrain, loaded with bags of bandit-heads and bundles of captured weapons, valuable for the worked metal.

For the rest, a few pieces of jewelry were taken from the corpses and a scant handful of gold and silver coin were garnered, as well as two battered, antique helmets and an assortment of armrings of brass, copper and iron. None of the robbers had possessed boots or armor of any description or even decent clothing, only rags, rope sandals and jackets of stiff, smelly, ill-cured hide sewn with strips and discs of horn and bone.

Ramón had noted, despite the confusion of the melee, that Morré's skill with his exotic saber was superior to that of most swordsmen if not quite the equal of his astounding talent with the hornbow; on the lance he could render no judgment, since his guest's shaft had splintered on the first shock. But he was satisfied that this Don Maylo de Morré was a most competent warrior, by any standards, as well as a natural and accomplished field commander.

And all of this simply deepened the mystery, in the Conde-Imperial's mind.

While men were sent to climb the crags to detach the heads of those ambushers who had not fallen from their perches—for each bandit head would bring half a peso in silver upon delivery to the proper authority—Ramón circulated, taking stock of his own casualties. That was when he saw Morré, leading his golden chestnut down the rocky defile, with young Don Gaspar de Garrigo reeling in the saddle and the stocky archer-sergeant with the scarred, pocked face straddling the animal's broad rump and gripping the high cantle. From both men, steady trickles of blood dripped down to streak the stallion's glossy hide.

After his aides and other hurriedly summoned men had lifted down the swooning *hidalgo* and the agonized and creatively cursing sergeant, Ramón offered his own, sweat-soaked scarf to "Conde" Maylo, who was dabbing at the blood streaks on his destrier's flanks.

"No, thank you, Count Ramón," croaked Morré from a dry throat. "The only thing that will really help El Dorado, here, is a good wash. I'd settle for a pint of cool wine . . . or even a bare mouthful of stale water, right now."

Ramón proffered the miraculously unbroken saddle-bottle. "Brandy-water, my lord, the best I fear I can do until we get on about a mile and set up camp."

After a long, long pull at the flask, Morré said, "A mile, in those wagons, over these rocks? The young knight will likely be dead when we get there. Why not camp here? That riff-raff, what's left of them, won't be back."

"My lord's pardon, please," said Ramón. "But this is not my first such trip. I know these mountains. This pass doubles as a seasonal riverbed. If my lord will regard those water-marks"—he indicated discolorations at least twelve feet high on the rock walls of the gap—"in this season, a storm could blow in from the west at any moment. But a mile beyond this place there is a fine plateau, with a spring and grass and a few trees.

"As for Don Gaspar, he is a tough *hombre*. And your ser-geant, well, he looks to be the consistency of boiled leather. But I shall see that they are constantly attended and well-padded."

In camp, Ramón and Morré watched the gypsy horse leech-cum-physician—all they now had, as the master physi-cian of the Conde-Imperial's staff had been brained by a boulder early on in the ambush—fumble and blunder his way through a wound-closure, nearly burning himself with the cautery.

Sergeant Angel Gonzales, whose deep wounds in thigh and upper arm assured him next place in line, had also been ob-

serving the less than efficient performance. Raising his good
arm to attract his lord's attention, he said, laconically, "Don
Maylo, if it please you, I be a old sojer and I've survived
right many wounds and camp fevers and I think I'd as lief
take my chances with dying of blood-losing or the black rot
as put my flesh neath the iron of that *faraon fastidioso*. Like
as not, he'd miss his pass at my thigh and sear off my man-
parts."

Morré smiled reassuringly down at his follower. "His lack
of skill is not calculated to breed confidence, is it, Angel?
Would you trust my hand guiding that cautery more?"

The sergeant's ugly head bobbed vigorously. "For a surety,
Don Maylo. But . . . your pardon, my lord. My lord has
burned wounds before?"

"I, too, am an old soldier, Angel." He said, gravely, "Yes,
I have closed many a wound, over the years. And," he added
with a grin to lessen the palpable tension, "never once have I
toasted valuable organs . . . by accident."

With Angel and a couple of other lancers behind him,
Morré and the men attending to the brazier and the dead
physician's other instruments proceeded with Ramón to his
tent, wherein waited Don Gaspar de Garrigo.

At Morré's direction, the young knight was lifted off the
camp bed and onto a sheet of oilskin spread on the earth. To
Ramón's questioning look, he answered, "That bed has too
much give to it, Count Ramón, and we need above all things
a firm surface beneath him. Have your men get his breeks off
and his linens as well. When the iron burns his flesh, his body
will release its water and probably its dung, too. You saw
that, outside, there."

Morré reflected silently that chances were good the boy
would die of lockjaw—tetanus infection—no matter what was
done for him. "Short of," he thought, "tetanus toxoid and an-
tibiotics, but this poor lad was born five or six hundred years
too late for such medical sophistication."

A crude spear—really just an old knife-blade riveted to a
shaft—had been jammed completely through the calf of the
right leg, two thicknesses of boottop-leather, the tough, quilted saddle-skirt and deeply enough into the horse's body to
kill him, outright. Then Don Gaspar had suffered the ill-for-
tune to lie pinned beneath the dead horse until Morré had
chanced across him. Likely, the horse's body fluid had seeped
into the man's wound.

But Morré resolved to do the best he could with the primitive tools at hand. He sought through the bag of instruments until he found what he assumed was an irrigation instrument—a bulb of gut attached to a copper tube—then rinsed it inside and out with brandy from Ramón's seemingly inexhaustible stock. He poured another quart bottle of the fiery beverage into a small camp-kettle, added half the measure of clear, cold spring-water and nodded to the waiting lancers who knelt to pinion the half-conscious knight into immobility.

Filling the bulb with the liquid, Morré scraped away the clots at either end of the wound and, disregarding the fresh flow of blood, thrust the nozzle of the copper tube into one end, pressed the gory flesh tight about it and gave the bulb a powerful squeeze. Diluted blood squirted out of the opposite opening.

And Don Gaspar, his raw flesh subjected to the bite of the brandy, came to full, screaming, thrashing consciousness. He was an exceedingly strong young man and the six lancers were hard-put to hold him down, much less still, so before he proceeded with his treatment, Morré called for three or four more men.

But such was the pain of the second flushing of the penetrating stab that the *hidalgo* again lapsed into an unconscious state, though still he moaned and thrashed fitfully. When the wound was as clean as he felt he could get it, Morré took a thick strip of tooth-scarred rawhide from the physician's bag, swished it about in undiluted brandy, then placed it between Don Gaspar's jaws, securing it with an attached strap around the patient's head.

While one of his helpers sopped up the fluids—blood, brandy, water, serum, sweat and urine—from the oilskin, Morré looked to the cauteries in the glowing brazier, selected one and wrapped a bit of wet hide around the shaft.

"All right, *hombres,* turn the senor over, then hold him as if your lives depended on it. Put your weight on him. You, there, sit you on his buttocks. Pablo, take your best grip on that knee. If your hands slip, I swear I'll burn them for you."

The patient had the misfortune to regain consciousness bare seconds before Morré was ready. Ramón knelt, gently dabbed the younger man's brow with a bit of wet sponge and softly admonished, "Be brave, now, Gaspar. Remember the honor of your *casa.* Set your teeth into the *pera de agonía*

and implore Nuestra Senora that She grant you strength. Don
Maylo is most skilled and it will be done quickly."

It was. Morré lifted the pale-pink-glowing cautery from its
nest of coals, blew on it once to remove any bits of ash, took
careful aim, then laid it firmly upon the entry wound, holding
it while he counted slowly to five. He tried vainly to stop his
nose to the nauseating stench of broiling flesh, his ears to the
gasps and whining moans of his patient.

Morré returned the cautery to the brazier and examined
his handiwork, critically, while Don Gaspar relaxed, sobbing
despite himself, and a lancer cleaned his buttocks and legs of
what had come when his anal sphincter failed. Ramón, himself, sponged away the mucus which had gushed from the tormented man's nostrils, all the while softly praising his bravery
and self-discipline. Morré decided he could hardly have done
a better job and, as he turned again to the brazier, hoped that
the second and last burning would go as well.

After that day, if Morré had revealed himself to truly be a
pretender to the throne of the Emperor of the Four Kingdoms and in league with El Diablo, himself, atop it all, not a
noble or man of the tax train but would have raised his banner and his warcry, and Conde-Imperial Ramón would have
been first.

During the lengthy stay of the caravan in Ciudad Chihuahua, Ramón saw to it that his newfound friend, "Conde"
Maylo de Morré, was feted and honored by his cousin,
Duque-Grande Alberto. The shrewd Conde-Imperial also arranged an exhibition of archery so that his tales of Morré's
expertise might be believed in future days, and further took
advantage of the day to realize more than a few golden pesos
by confidently backing Morré against any and all local con-
tenders.

The way of the tax train now lay south—through the
grand-duchy of Durango and so back to Guadalajara and the
imperial court—and Ramón tried every argument and entice-
ment he could muster to attempt to persuade Morré to accompany him, rather than following his announced course
north, through the inhospitable and bandit-infested desert to
Ciudad Juarez and El Paso del Norte. But it was all in vain.
Morré was determined. The best that Ramón and his cousin,
Duque-Grande Alberto, were able to accomplish was to convince their honored guest that he should delay his departure a

couple more weeks and ride north in company with a detachment of replacement troops bound for Fortaleza Bienaventuranza, just north of the river which separated the sister cities.

At one of the informal dinners a week or so prior to Ramón's scheduled departure, the subject of old Don Humberto, lord of Mazatlán, came up in conversation.

"Ay, poor Umbo," sighed the Duque-Grande, dabbing at his beard and flaring moustachios with a linen napkin, "our two fathers were old comrades, you know, and he and I soldiered together forty years ago, both of us young ensigns in the Dragon Regiment. Ah, those were brave days!"

Morré, looking every inch the hidalgo in his silks and tooled leathers and sparkling jewels, set down his goblet of chased silver and asked, "You said, 'poor Umbo,' my lord duke. May one inquire why? During the month I guested with him, Don Humberto seemed happy enough to me, and Ramón, here, tells me that the old man is a favorite of his overlord, loved by his people and much respected at the imperial court. He takes much pride in the horses he breeds, and rightly so. My own El Dorado is one of the finest and best-trained mounts I have ever straddled."

"Alas," answered the Duque-Grande, "those horses are all that Umbo has left, these days. All four of his fine sons were slain while fighting bravely for the Emperor in Yucatán, these twenty years agone. Then the great plague which decimated the Four Mexicos three years later took his entire household—his wife, Doña Ana, his three young, unmarried daughters, the widows of two of his sons and all his grandchildren.

"When he dies, there will be none of his *casa* to swear the oaths and take over the fief. The overlord will have to take the oaths from some outsider and then there will be trouble in Mazatlán . . . mayhap, much trouble. There often is when one *casa* replaces another, especially a native other, on a fief. Good old Umbo knows this too, and you can be certain the knowledge grieves him, for he is a good man, a good lord and loves his lands and people."

Morré shrugged. "It seems a problem simply enough solved, my lord. He appears a lusty man, even yet, so surely he has a bastard or six living nearby. Why does he not just recognize a likely man of his siring as legitimate? In his position, I would do such."

The Duque-Grande loudly cracked a knuckle. "Other lands, other customs, Conde Maylo. Yes, Umbo has many bastards of both sexes and ranging in age from mere toddlers to not many years his junior. And not just in his homeland, either—he always was *mucho* hombre. But, Conde Maylo, in the Mexicos, a commonborn bastard cannot so easily be legitimatized, not if lands and succession are involved.

"Umbo could recognize every bastard of his *casa* in all of Mazatlán, but he would not be allowed to name any of them heir to imperial fiefs. To inherit lands, obligations and privileges, a man must be born to the *hidalguía* or, failing that, be a formally-invested *caballero*, elevated for conspicuous bravery in the service of the Emperor."

Morré stared into the dark-purple depths of his wine, for a moment, a smile flickering at the corners of his mouth. He was privy to some knowledge to which these two noblemen were not, and it had required time and cunning to set them up so perfectly for consummation of his plan.

"My lord Duque-Grande, if a commoner soldier should take his stand over a fallen knight and fight long and hard, sustaining grave wounds himself, to protect that knight from a horde of foemen, would that be considered grounds for his elevation in rank?"

The Duque-Grande nodded vigorously. "Of a certainty, but at least two noblemen must witness the act."

Morré went on. "You claim friendship of old with Don Humberto and you recognize his predicament. Were you presented a bastard of his who had the requisite noble witnesses to stand for him, would you undertake the investiture?"

"Why, of course, Conde Maylo!" snapped the Duque-Grande. "I should be more than overjoyed were it only possible for me to do such for my old comrade."

Then, Morré told his secret.

Angel Gonzales, sometime sergeant of lances, was knighted in the spacious chapel of the grand-ducal residence by Duque-Grande Alberto, assisted by Conde-Imperial Ramón. The Duque-Grande's gift to the new *caballero* was impressive in the extreme—a fully-trained destrier and all equipage. The Conde-Imperial gave a fine, thigh-length hauberk, mail leggings and a helmet.

Young Don Gaspar, whose life Angel's courage and ferociousness had saved, presented a beautifully wrought dagger-belt of interwoven chains and plaques of bronze and steel, a splendid dirk, eating knife and skewer (with matching hilts) and the gold-washed spurs which he buckled onto the new *caballero*, himself.

Morré proffered the finest broadsword that many of the assembled throng of nobles had ever seen. Duque-Grande Alberto had truly hated to part with the magnificent weapon, but Conde Maylo had readily paid its full value—in honest-weight, unclipped gold pieces—and he had known to whom its buyer would present it.

From the noblemen of the grand-duchy came an oaken battlelance and a triple-bullhide target, rimmed and bossed in iron. The noblewomen gave a silken pennon and two sets of fine plumes—one for his helmet, one for his horse's headgear. Both the target and the embroidered pennon were executed with his device—suggested by Morré—a drawn bow, silver, with an arrow nocked, gold, on a field, black; the plumes reflected the colors of the arms—black, gold and silver.

Throughout the solemn proceedings, Morré had to refrain from looking at Angel's face, lest he burst out laughing. Ever since the moment three days ago when then-Sergeant Gonzales had been summoned to the formal proceedings at the palace, before the Duque-Grande himself and heard himself praised to the very skies by Conde-Imperial Ramón, Conde Maylo, Don Gaspar and all the other *hidalgos* of the tax train, the poor, humble soldier's expression had been that of a man just kicked in the head by a pack mule.

And throughout the long, formal dinner which followed the investiture and elevation, he simply sat, obviously bemused, at his place of honor on the Duque-Grande's right. Morré, who flanked the new *caballero*, had to constantly remind him to eat and drink.

Most of the night before his train's departure, Conde Ramón spent with Morré and several bottles of the Duque-Grande's best brandy. As the empties accumulated, he suddenly leaned across the low table and spoke in a hoarse whisper.

"Since first we met in Mazatlán, my lord and friend, Maylo, I have known what you are, though I played your game by the rules you laid down. But in the time since that meeting, we have, together, seen both life and death and shared many a bottle. Now we must take separate roads, for you ride north and it is my bounden duty to ride south with the morrow's dawning. It well may be that we two never shall meet and drink and talk again.

"As you know, by now, I am a man who never fails to render due honor to those whom Senor Dios has seen fit to place above me, for I hold this to be the only right and proper way for any man of any station to live his life. But, please, my friend Don Maylo, try to forgive the impertinence of my great curiosity. On this last night, can you not tell me your true rank and allegiance, on my word of honor that none other ever shall hear it from my lips?"

Conde Maylo smiled. "Very well, Don Ramón. I really am a chief of the northern horse-nomads. I am six hundred years old and I have spent the last two hundred years roaming the world in search of a fabled island whereon men never age or die."

Ramón stared at him for a long moment, open-mouthed and goggle-eyed. Then he sank back into his chair, chuckling and shaking his head, ruefully.

"For a second, there, you almost had me believing you, Don Maylo; your forbearance, please, but you are a convincing liar, when you wish to be. Very well, my friend, it was a most courteous refusal and gave me a good laugh, in the bargain. I shall not again pry into matters which must not concern me.

"Come, then, we have two full bottles left."

The dawn leavetaking was emotional in the extreme. Tears streamed from Don Ramón's black eyes as he clapped his arms about Don Maylo in a fierce *abrazo*. Between strangled sobs, he said, "My dear friend, I assure you that I never shall forget you and ever shall I pray for your continued health and welfare. If ever your travels lead you to the Condado of Guanajuato, be you assured of a welcome in keeping with your station and my sincere love and respect for you.

"In regard to the other matter, immediately I have discharged my duty to the Emperor and to my overlord, I shall dispatch Don Gaspar and an escort to Don Humberto at Mazatlán, to advise him of the elevation and investiture of his son, Don Angel Gonzales. By the time Don Angel returns to Mazatlán, no doubt he will be legitimate in the eyes of the law.

"Don Angel gained much respect in the eyes of the *hidalguía*, hereabouts, when he refused to accompany me back south. His decision to carry out the orders of Don

Humberto, despite his elevation, and see you safely to your destination was both proper and honorable. He will make a good *caballero* . . . and our Four Kingdoms stand always much in need of such men."

In all times, all lands and among all peoples, military operations very seldom proceed on schedule, and the northernmost kingdom of the Four Mexicos, circa 2550 A.D., proved no exception to the norm. The last contingent of replacements for the fortress on the Rio Grande marched into Ciudad Chihuahua two full weeks after their supposed date of departure from that city and yet another fortnight elapsed before the column finally formed up just beyond the north gate of the city and, with brilliantly clad and equipped *hidalgo* officers on glossy, prancing horses in the lead, followed by a troop of lancers and one of dragoons, three hundred pikemen and crossbowmen marching to the beat of their massed drums, a long, rumbling train of heavy wagons and a final troop of lancers, they were on the road.

Capitán Don Jorge de las Torres was pleased and flattered with his guests—one a new-made *caballero* of about his own age and the other a somewhat mysterious foreign nobleman. He and his lancers escorted these convoys three or four times each year and, after the first year or so, they became boring, routine and tedious. Therefore, he eagerly anticipated this novel element added to the journey.

There was seldom even the brief excitement of a raid or an ambush. For all that the barren land through which they passed swarmed with ruffians of every description and for all that it was well known that among his wagons was the three-month payroll of the northern garrison and that of the government officials of the sister-cities, not to mention stocks of food, wines, clothing, equipment and special consignments of luxury-items, few banditti were willing to take on three hundred infantry and nearly a hundred horsemen.

The captain was not a born *hidalgo*, though he had lucked into a marriage with a born *hidalga*, so his children would all be hereditary nobles; he had become a *caballero* in the same way as had Angel—well-witnessed bravery during the wars which had ended the brief secession of the Kingdom of Yucatán some twenty years earlier. He knew that he probably would die still a captain, as he could never seem to accumulate the funds necessary to purchase a higher rank, not with a household to maintain, sons to arm and outfit and daughters to decently dower. But soldiering was the only trade he owned and he had no option but to pursue it.

His taste and meager purse did not run to fine brandies, but rather to raw tequila and mescal, though he was unstintingly lavish to his guests and officers with what little he did have. He and Don Angel seemed cut of the same bolt—they thought similarly about almost all topics, they spoke the same language and both were more than a little wary of the young *hidalgos* who were Don Jorge's lieutenants—so they quickly became fast friends.

The winding road across the desert—blisteringly hot by day, bitterly cold by night—measured almost five hundred kilometers from the north gate of Ciudad Chihuahua to the south gate of Ciudad Juarez, usually a two-week journey. But this trip proved anything but usual.

Three days out, a wagon axle broke just as the day's march was commencing. Then the axles of two more gave way that afternoon. Nor was there anything for it but to halt the entire column while sweating, blaspheming drivers and infantrymen offloaded the vehicles, jacked them up and set about fitting on spare axles. While one of the afternoon crews was gathering flattish rocks to help brace the jack, a sergeant of infantry was bitten in the cheek by a huge rattlesnake and died within minutes of fear-induced heart failure. And that day was only the beginning.

Two days further on, the point galloped back to report the discovery of a battlefield. With Don Maylo, Don Angel and his handful of lancers, plus a couple of squads of his own, Captain de las Torres followed the point back to where the other scouts waited.

The sight was grim enough. The bare-picked bones of at least thirty men and a dozen horses lay in and around a shallow depression. No weapons, equipment of man or horse or even boots were left, but such bits of stained, ragged, sunbleached cloth as remained caused the bandy-legged captain to frown, squint and purse his chapped lips.

"Lancers and dragoons, a mixed troop of them," he said softly to Dons Maylo and Angel and the lieutenant of scouts, Don Esteban. "Either from La Forteleza or from Fuerte Media, surely, but in either case, why in hell were they bound south? To meet us? Why?"

But the grinning skulls about his feet could give no answer.

The column's marching order was immediately tightened and van- and rear-guards were reinforced, two echelons of flank riders were set out to pace the advance, infantry marched and cavalry rode in full gear with ready weapons. The perimeters of night camps were tightly patrolled by alert sentries walking overlapping posts. But the train reached the halfway point, Fuerte Media, without incident.

The low, adobe houses surrounding the desert fort were almost deserted, all the inhabitants being packed within the strong walls, apparently with all their livestock and personal possessions. No room remained for the wagons and horses or even for more than a bare handful of the men of the column, so Captain de las Torres disgustedly billeted both men and animals in the empty homes, blocked the one street and the interstices between the houses with his wagons and ordered a strong guard while he went to confer with the fort commander.

With the formalities completed amid a chorus of chattering men and women, screaming, scurrying children, the ceaseless lowing of cattle, the barking of dogs and the hubbub attending the sudden onslaught of one burro stallion against another, Captain Juan Alvarez led his three visitors to his office, where a reddish hen sat in the middle of his cluttered desk. With a wave of a short, pudgy arm, the commander sent the fowl fluttering and scolding out the window, leaving a brown egg behind.

When all had been seated and served with half-liter mugs of tepid *pulque*, the short, stout, florid infantry officer gave what little information he had, most of it secondhand.

"It was a fortnight ago, Don Jorge, that Major Don Vicente rode south with his mixed troop, all that were left, he averred, of the cavalry contingents of La Fortaleza."

"A little over a troop?" snapped Don Jorge, incredulously. "Out of six troops of lancers and two of dragoons?"

Alvarez just shrugged his shoulders, spreading his hands, palms upward, over his bulging belly. "Senor, I relate only that which was told to me. Don Vincente said that the peoples of the wastes had banded together and were attacking anyone who tried to either enter or leave the cities or the fortress. Worse, they were creeping under the very walls by night, loosing fire-arrows into the cities or killing the wall guards and scaling the walls to loot and rape and murder, to set fires and destroy food stocks."

The commander raised his mug and gulped noisily, then went on. "In the beginning, lancers were dispatched every time these outrages occurred, but losses were so heavy, what with ambushes in the dark, that the Commandante forbade any more night patrols, no matter how serious the matter. Instead, he sent infantrymen to reinforce the wall- and gate-guards."

Don Jorge nodded. "The wisest decision, of course. But how, by the four-and-twenty balls of the Twelve Apostles, could over three hundred cavalry have been lost in a few piddling skirmishes?"

"They were not so lost, Don Jorge," stated Alvarez. "They were killed in a battle. Raiders had gotten into the northern city one night and opened the north gate to admit scores of their ilk; the guards had fought all night long to hold the citadel and the wall towers, perforce leaving the poor citizens to their terrible fates at the bloody hands of the barbarian butchers.

"With the dawn, the brazen swine commenced to troop out of the blazing city, laden with loot of every description, mules, horses and livestock and even female captives. When this dreadful sight was seen through long-glasses from the walls of the fortress, the Commandante himself had all of the cavalry assembled and led them out in pursuit of the reavers."

The fat officer's voice dropped almost to a whisper. "Within sight of the fortress, a thousand or more men rose up from hiding places or rode out of arroyos and completely surrounded the Commandante and his men, piercing dozens, scores with clouds of arrows, like fish in a barrel, before closing with lances, spears, sabers and axes.

"Three officers and twenty-nine men fought their way back to where the wall archers in the fortress could cover them, and those were the men commanded by Major Don Vicente when he passed through here, bound to report the disaster to El Duque-Grande at Ciudad Chihuahua. The good God rest his soul, he was a gallant *caballero*." The fat man signed himself, reverently.

Captain de las Torres and Don Angel also crossed themselves, then the captain asked, "And that is the reason why your fort is so overcrowded, eh?"

The commander had again been applying himself to the mug of *pulque*. Hurriedly lowering it, he shook his head vigorously. "No, Don Jorge, the night after Don Vicente and his men had ridden onward, many, many fires were seen in the hills to the northwest. The next morning, several scores of riders were seen no more than a half mile away, riding south. That was when I felt it would be best if the families of my garrison and the other folk of the village came within the fort."

"And these hombres, when did they ride back?" demanded Captain Jorge.

"For all that any of us knows," replied the plump officer, "the *bastardos* are still in the south, or out there in the hills."

Captain de las Torres's tone betokened both exasperation and disgust. "You have not at least scouted out the flanking hills, Captain Alvarez?"

The officer leaned as far over his desk as his belly would permit. "Captain Don Jorge, as you know, my garrison includes one squad of lancers. What could ten men do against so many? Call me coward if you will, but I thought it better to simply wait, without risking my men's lives, until either your train or a relief column from Ciudad Chihuahua reached us."

Captain de las Torres sighed. "No, I'll not name you coward, overcautious, perhaps, but . . . hell, who can say what I might have done in your place. Well, assign a man of your squad to each of my patrols and I'll have the hills scouted out today.

"For tomorrow, hmmm." He sat for a moment or two pulling at his spade beard. "I think it might be better if you, your garrison and all these civilians marched on to La Fortaleza with my column. A force of hostile men as large as that mentioned by the late Don Vicente could overrun this dungheap within hours. You'll all be safer, and your troops will be of more value, at La Fortaleza, than huddling here, so overcrowded that you'll likely all die of a fever if the enemy doesn't get you first."

Later, as the captain, Dons Maylo and Angel and two of de las Torres's lieutenants sat about a round, knife-scarred table in the main room of what had been the village cantina, now requisitioned for their headquarters, the train commander stated bluntly, "This whole business is so fantastic as to smack of downright impossibility—save that I've known Fat Juanito for many a year and, while he has many vices, lying is not one of them. But all the same, never within the memory of man have the riffraff, bandits and skulkers combined into a force of such numbers. Usually, they spend more time fighting each other than they do attempting to prey on us, on our columns. And to attack *walled cities* and annihilate a reinforced squadron in open battle, such a thing would be called an impossibility by any officer who heard of it. Yet, we all know that they . . . that *someone* wiped out a troop, at least.

"We could, of course, go back to Ciudad Chihuahua and march back with a relief column, but it is probable that our men and our supplies are now desperately needed by the folk to the north. Possibly another officer might decide it best to stay here, at Fuerte Media, send dispatch riders back to Ciudad Chihuahua and hope for the best; but I feel that this place is now untenable, for many reasons.

"No, *senores*, it is my intention that we march north in the morning, with Captain Alvarez's garrison and their dependents, all supplies and military materiel and such stock as can easily be transported or driven. This is my decision. However, I am always open to suggestion."

So saying, he leaned back in a creaky chair and sipped at a measure of mescal, his black eyes roving from one to the other of his companions.

Teniente Gregorio, slender, foppish and always keenly conscious that he was an *hidalgo*—Don Maylo's clearest recollection of the eighteen-year-old junior officer during the march was of his two-day sulk after Captain de las Torres countermanded his order to have the men laboring to repair the wagons whipped in order to speed their progress—lisped, "Capitán, I agree that we should take most of the garrison of the *fuerte*, but why should we burden ourselves with this useless gaggle of women, children, pigs and chickens? They probably lack decent transport and will slow our advance to a crawl, robbing us of such little maneuverability as we now have."

De las Torres set down his cuplet and leaned forward. "Teniente, even with your limited military experience, you must be aware that Fuerte Media would not withstand any really determined enemy for a day, even with a full garrison. For us to strip the best part of the garrison and then march away would be to condemn those left behind to the uncertain mercies of an enemy, and I, for one, could not do so coldly callous a thing. Besides, just how dependable would our impressed troops be, knowing that their families had been left behind unprotected, eh?"

Teniente Gregorio's handsome face twisted as if to spit out something distasteful. "*Pah*! The Capitán should have been a priest. Such soft sentimentality is not for soldiers." He looked at the other men for approval. Don Maylo's face was a blank, Don Angel looked cool and wary, the other junior officer, however, allowed the ghost of a smile to flit momentarily over his full lips, and this was enough to fuel further remarks from Gregorio.

"Besides, these so-called soldiers, from their gross commander on downward, are nothing but ignorant *peones*. They will fight when told to, or the gibbet and the whip will reward their insubordination. Were you wise, you'd leave old Capitán de Puerco behind. He's too fat to march, and no doubt he'd quickly wear out a horse." He grinned.

De las Torres did not grin. The other lieutenant took one look at that glowering countenance, shivered and applied himself to his tipple.

"Teniente Gregorio," grated the captain from between clenched teeth, "has treated us all to the philosophy gleaned of his vast experience at soldiering. Just how long have you been in uniform, Teniente, all of six months? Eight? An entire *year*?

"Know you this, you pompous puppy, the man you name 'pig' is, for all his recent gain of girth, more man than you likely will live to be. Juan Alvarez was fighting in Yucatán when you knew not enough to wipe the milk—in which, I piss!—of your mother from your mouth."

The young fop knocked over his chair, stood on his spread feet, his hand upon his saberhilt, his face crimson. "I . . . I'll not take such from lowborn scum like you, de las Torres. Draw your blade!"

A lazy smile on his lips, de las Torres arose and lifted the baldric supporting his scabbarded broadsword over his head. "Teniente Patricio, your saber, *por favor*. My good sword is both longer and heavier than most sabers, and I would not have men say that I took unfair advantage of our exquisite and hot-tempered young *compañero*. So, take you my weapon in exchange, and bar and guard the door."

De las Torres took the hilt of the saber in his big, horny hand, quickly found its balance and swung it experimentally a few times, then tested various areas of the keen edge on a calloused thumb, before releasing the hilt long enough to fit the saber-knot around his wrist with great care.

At this last, the impatiently waiting Gregorio barked a harsh, scornful laugh. "Dear Capitán, do you fear that your clumsy, peon's paw will lose its grip?"

"Don't try to teach your grandmother how to suck eggs," muttered the captain, scuffing his bootsoles in the straw on the floor. Then, to Dons Maylo and Angel: "This is no concern of yours, *senores*. It is a matter of discipline in my command. And unless I miss my guess, it bears overtones of class conflict and personal animosity on the part of *el rey de los maricónes*, yonder."

His face working with rage, the younger man stamped forward, his saber blade swept downward in a bluish blur; but the captain simply sidestepped and the edge rang on the stone-hard dirt floor. De las Torres could easily have slain the raging officer then, and all present knew it. All he did, however, was to sink less than an inch of blade into the teniente's flat buttock.

"Puppy, mine," he laughed, "mastery of the light sword does not automatically confer mastery of the saber or the broadsword, you know."

Hurling his blade about in a wide swing at his tormentor, the young man swayed, off balance, when that rage-driven swing again failed to connect. And, again, his opponent deliberately passed up a chance to end the duel in a permanent and deadly manner, only pricking the teniente's other buttock.

"Baseborn peon coward!" snarled the young *hidalgo*. "Why do you run away? A gentleman or a real man of any kind would stand and fight, blade to blade."

The captain only smiled his infuriating smile of condescension. "What would you know of fighting, puppy? By the way you handle yours, one unknowing would think a saber was used for sickling grain or chopping wood."

Recovering his balance at last, the slender youth stamped forward and lunged at the captain's lower belly and crotch. The middle-aged officer, still smiling, sidestepped yet again and, rather than sinking his blade into the exposed body, flicked a quarter-inch off the top rim of an ear with a twist of the wrist.

"Nor, puppy, is the saber used for spearing fish," he admonished, in such tone as might be used to a backward child.

Then, more conversationally, "To allow your anger to surface in a sword fight—or in any other kind of fight, for that matter—is to drive reason and elementary caution from the mind . . . usually, just a few moments before life leaves the body."

All at once, the teniente made as if to thrust again, then abruptly changed the movement to a backhanded upward slash at the captain's chin and throat. For the first time, their two blades met in a ringing clangor as de las Torres beat down the opposing saber.

His smile was no longer mocking and his voice not quite so bantering. "Now, Gregorio, that was better. You're beginning to let your mind fight, as well as your body." He did not pink his foe, this time.

For ten minutes more, the captain parried increasingly shrewd lunges, thrusts and cuts and slashes, always on the defensive, never using his obvious opportunities to maim or kill the younger man.

Finally, when the teniente was panting, gasping, streaked and soaked with sweat, and his swordwork was become slower and less accurate, the captain put a quick end to it by sending the teniente's blade flying out of the tired, slackened grip, to clatter into a corner. Teniente Gregorio, suddenly white as fresh curds, fumbled off his soft, velvet cap with one trembling hand while signing himself with the other, then he stood immobile, his lips moving in his final prayers and his eyes fixed upon the gleaming blade in his captain's hand.

The captain grinned. "Now, young sir, you can appreciate the value of the saber-knot, eh? But stop troubling the saints, Gregorio, I have no intention of killing you today."

"But . . . I would've meant to . . . kill . . . you . . . Capitán," panted the junior officer.

The smile became gentle. "There never was any danger of that, lad. I was a saber-master before you were born. You see, even we *campesinos* can master the sword if you take us early enough and give us good, patient teachers."

The young man's gaze dropped and his pale face reddened again. "I . . . I should not have . . . I insulted you, Capitán, and you . . . no man has control of his birth. I should be . . . Should I consider myself under arrest for my insubordination?"

De las Torres stepped forward and threw his left arm about the young officer's shoulders in a bone-cracking hug. "Lord love you, no, lad! We'll likely have to fight our way up

to La Fortaleza and I'll need every sword, lance and bow.
You go back there to the well and draw up a bucket or two
of water and wash yourself. We don't want the men to think
we've been fighting among ourselves, do we? Bad, very bad,
for their morale, you know."

When the two tenientes had left, the one to help the other,
de las Torres mopped his own slightly damp brow, *whuuffed*
a couple of times, then downed the rest of his cup of mescal,
before addressing the foreign Conde and Don Angel.

"It's an old story, *senores*. These lads come into my command thinking that because they are born to the *hidalguía*
their dung doesn't stink the same as any other man's. One
session of sabers brought this one down to size. Sometimes it
takes two or even three. Occasionally, God help me, I have
to kill one."

Don Angel's brow wrinkled. "Is there not danger in killing
the sons of *hombres ricos*, Don Jorge? Even for one of your
rank?"

"Not really, Don Angel, no," answered the captain, so-
berly. "Both army and Empire value my services. Mine is
basically a seasoning command, both for troopers and officers, and I turn out a good product, a fact well-known to
those in authority."

Don Esteban Fernandez was, as his captain's children
would be, half-*hidalgo*, son of an *hidalga* mother and a commoner father who had been knighted thirty years before. He
was a senior lieutenant, in his early twenties, de las Torres's
executive officer and his only officer with combat experience.
During most of the march up from the south, he had commanded the scouts and, at de las Torres's order, had headed
the patrols of the hills surrounding Fuerte Media.

The broad-shouldered young man strode into the temporary headquarters, covered with dust and stinking of man-
sweat and horse-sweat. After sketching the briefest of salutes,
he sank into one of the chairs and, ignoring the cups, drank
long and deeply from one of the bottles, before commencing
his report in a tired voice.

"Capitán, there are no *bandidos* within two miles on any
flank of the *fuerte*. . . . Not now, but they have been
damned recently. There were two camps, one to the east and
one to the west, a total for both of eighty to one hundred

mounted men, plus twenty or thirty head of spare horses, possibly a small *remuda*, possibly pack animals."

"Or possibly," put in the captain, "those horses of Don Vicente's command not killed in the massacre."

The dusty officer nodded once, brusquely, then went on. "They camped there at least a week, living mostly on wild game from the looks of it, but they must've brought their own water, because we could find no springs or wells up there. They moved out, north, either last night or early this morning, merging into a single column just out of sight of the *fuerte*."

De las Torres nodded. "Then they'll be waiting for us, up ahead, somewhere. There were no tracks leading back south, Esteban?"

Lowering the bottle from his lips, the officer sighed. "No, Capitán, I checked carefully. All the *malditos* rode north."

The captain nodded again. "A clear message, then. If we turn about, we'll be allowed to go in peace. If we march on toward La Fortaleza, we'll have to fight.

"All right, Esteban, choose four men who know the country, put them up on the best and freshest horses you can find. Give them both written and oral messages to the Duque-Grande, telling his grace what has occurred with our column, what Capitán Juan told of and what I intend. Send them out in twos; if they are attacked, one is to stay and fight, one is to ride on. *Comprendes?*"

Teniente Gregorio had been right about one thing. The addition of the dependents and other civilians to the column slowed the march to a snail's pace, and keeping the heterogenous elements closed up to a defensible unit was a constant and nerve-fraying task for the officers and noncoms. But it was done. The scouts often reported fresh sign and occasional sightings of distant riders, but they were allowed to proceed for more than a week without interference from the enemy.

It was during an unofficial conference in his tent, the ninth night out of Fuerte Media, that Capitán Don Jorge told his assembled staff and guests, "Senores, Don Esteban and I discussed a matter this afternoon with several of the lancers from the command of Capitán Alvarez and we now think we know what these *bastardos* are up to, where they likely intend to hit us. If you gentlemen will help to anchor this."

Taking a tightly rolled parchment map from its case of

oiled leather, he spread it out on the camp table. "We are here." He used his long dirk for a pointer. "Tomorrow morning we should pass through the ruins of a small village that dates to the time before the Plagues of God. It has not been inhabited since then—for one thing, the *campesinos* all swear that it is haunted, for another and more practical reason, there is no longer any reliable source of water thereabouts. But some of the walls are still standing and it would make a marvelous site for an ambush.

"But if we are not struck there"—his dirk point moved on—"there is this deep, narrow arroyo, a kilometer northwest, you see."

"The Capitán has a plan to deal with these murderous scum?" asked Teniente Gregorio, respectfully.

When the column formed and rode out the next morning, an observer would have had to have been extremely close to note that quite a few of the "lancers" and "dragoons" were actually civilians, some of them women, mounted on spare horses and mules, decked out in uniforms and armor from the wagons and spare lances brought from Fuerte Media.

Guided by men from Capitán Juan Alvarez's lancer squad and by amateur copies of Don Jorge's map, forty picked men, commanded by Don Esteban and Gregorio, had quit the camp in the dead of night and now were resting in hiding places just outside the ancient ruins of the abandoned village. With them were Dons Maylo and Angel, their arming-men and six lancers.

Widely scattered in arcs on both sides of the road, the watchers could clearly pick out the knots of men squatting in the concealment offered by the half-tumbled walls. As no horses were in evidence, it was apparent that there must be more men somewhere nearby keeping the animals out of sight.

The rocks which hid Don Maylo were still cool from the frigid night, but the rising sun already was giving promise of the ovenlike atmosphere that presently would envelop the desert and all it contained. Most of the inhabitants of this sun-blasted terrain were, perforce, creatures of the night, and were either already in their cool burrows and dens or would soon be there.

Don Maylo's keen peripheral vision detected a movement far to his left, and as he watched, a small desert cat—his companions would have called it a *jaguarundi*—crossed the space between the line of soldiers and the ruins in a series of swift rushes from one bit of concealment to the next, aided by the color of her coat—a brownish-tannish-gray, almost the same shade and texture as the rocks and pebbly clay.

Knowing from times long past that many felines were telepathic, Don Maylo sent his powerful mind ranging out. "Was the hunting good last night, cat-sister?"

But it clearly was not the small cat that answered him. The answer came on a beam of thought as powerful as his own, if not more so. It shocked him to the very core of his being, for he knew of old that power, knew that the mindspeaker could be nothing other than one of the prairie cats of the Horseclans far to the north, beyond the still-distant river called Rio Grande.

"The hunting never is really good in this place Sacred Sun seeks to destroy, as any Cat well knows. But . . . your mind, it is not of Cat, it . . . You are a two-leg! How do you speak the speech of Cats, Two-leg? Two-legs in this place do not speak to us, they only kill us, as they killed our mother and our brothers. Unless . . . ?"

Another, equally powerful mind entered the "conversation." "Unless, sister mine, this be one of the *good* two-legs, of whom our mother spoke so often. Do you ride from the north, from the lands of tall grasses and good hunting, Two-leg? Are cats and horses your kindred, then?"

"Yes, cat-sisters, my stallion is my dear brother," replied Don Maylo. "Cats, too, once were my kindred, but in the many years since I left the lands of tall grasses, all those cat-kindred with whom I hunted plump deer and swift saber-horns and the fierce rams of the high plains have surely gone to Wind. But I would gladly be brother to two cat-sisters."

"If truly you be who and what you say," said the first cat, suspiciously, "then promise us The Promise."

Don Maylo did not need to ask what promise, for he had framed the words of that ancient pledge himself, to the first clans-born generation of prairiecats.

"I will care for you when you are nursing and for your kittens, should you be slain. I will send you quickly to Wind when age has dimmed your eyes and dulled your teeth."

Then, Don Maylo felt his very skin prickle under the great wash of long-bottled emotion that swept into his mind from those two feline minds. "They are the proper words, the Promise that binds cat and two-leg, one to the other. Since the time when the Undying Uncle rode among His children, the clans. Leave your mind open, Brother, and we shall come to you."

"*NO!*" Don Maylo beamed forcefully. "No, cat-sisters. I am with two-legs who are not as am I. They cannot speak with you and would consider you dangerous animals and kill you.

"I am near to the ruined Dirtmen-place. There will soon be a battle here. Is your den near to this place?"

"Yes, cat-brother, a short run, no more," was the reply.

"Then den up until Sacred Sun goes to rest, sisters. I shall try to come to you tonight."

"You could never find our den, brother," one of the cats projected, assuredly.

"No," agreed Don Maylo, "probably not. So one of you must keep your mind open and ranging in this direction from . . . say moonrise to moonset. That way, we can make contact and you two can come to me. But be sure to broadbeam soothingly, as you come, for my stallion is not Horseclans-bred."

The dark-yellow moon rose clear and full over the still, chill desert landscape. From horizon to horizon, the black velvet of the night sky was bespangled with an untold myriad of twinkling stars. Within a small arroyo half a mile from the camp of the caravan Don Maylo's golden stallion, still saddled but bridleless, lazily wandered, browsing halfheartedly on the few rough plants, stamping and whuffling now and again at the tiny, scuttling creatures of the night.

On a ledge six feet up one wall sat Don Maylo, himself. Pressed close to either side, and reveling in the carresses of his strong, gentle hands as much as in the rapport of their three joined minds, sat the cat-sisters—big as jaguars of the far south they were in body, but with longer legs, legs made for the run rather than the short charge; their heads were as large as his own—larger, the cuspids of the upper jaws equipped with yellow-white fangs a good four inches long, their big, amber eyes glinting with intelligence.

They had opened their minds, their memories, to this new and so-satisfying brother, so that he now knew the story of how two three-year-old female prairiecats found themselves immured in this all but waterless place so far from their natural habitat. It was a tale of a raid-in-force by the warriors and cats of three southerly-ranging Horseclans, of a great and bloody battle somewhere in this desert and of a wounded cat crawling off from a stricken field to recover in a den found among the rocks. She bore the litter she had been carrying there, weaned the two males and two females and taught them to hunt the small, elusive game. She also filled them with tales of the Horseclans—of men who could speak with, were the very brothers of, prairiecats.

Finally, when the kittens were large enough to travel long distances, the little family set out northward, toward the lands of the mother's birth. But disaster had struck at the wide, shallow river. Yelling men on horses had fought and slain and skinned the mother and both the brothers, who had bravely held the foe that the two sisters might win free. In the years since, the two cats had roamed, becoming creatures of the desert nights, avoiding men, their places and the river that barred their way north to the fabled lands of tall grasses and plentiful game and men who were brothers not foes.

They still went by the kitten-names which their long-dead mother had given them, Mousesqueak and Skinkkiller. Though neither was fat—their diet and life did not allow for the accumulation of adipose tissue—Mousesqueak had grown to be slightly larger than her sister, perhaps one hundred and fifteen kilos. But the smaller cat did most of the speaking for the two and seemed to have the better memory, as well.

Skinkkiller asked, "Brother, how went your battle? I see that neither claw nor fang gashed your hide."

"It was no real battle, sisters," Maylo replied. "It was a slaughter. The ambushers were themselves ambushed, caught in the meshes of their own trap and either arrowed or ridden down before they could reach their horses."

"And so, now that your battle is done, brother, will you not lead us—my sister and me—back to the lands favored by Sacred Sun and Wind?" asked Mousesqueak, plaintively.

Don Maylo had given much thought to that very matter. To take the two cats among the folk of the caravan would be very sticky, to say the least. The destination of that caravan, Ciudad Juarez and the other city and the fortress, were really much farther west than he had intended going—he had originally intended crossing the Rio Grande somewhere near its confluence with the Rio San Francisco, then riding due north through the area which had been, hundreds of years ago, the

State of Texas—but the friendships of first Conde Ramón and then Don Angel had kept him.

This was as good a time and place as any to part company with the column, and the loss of his one sword would not overly weaken the force. According to the information tortured out of the few survivors of the ambushers, the shaky alliance of *bandido* bands had already broken apart, and the couple of hundred annihilated by them yesterday morning had been the last large or really well-armed group. Nor had he aught to worry about in setting off alone, not with his advance scouted by, his flanks and rear guarded by, the two formidable cats.

Back in camp, he took Don Angel aside and spoke in low tones. "Well, old friend, the time has come when our trails must part. No, allow me to finish."

From under his hauberk, he drew his worn, sweatstained moneybelt and proffered it. "This will be of no use to me whence I am now bound, Angel. Give one *onza* to each of our men and two *onzas* to the families of the two who were slain. The rest is yours, about forty *onzas*, or so."

The bandylegged sergeant-become-knight weighed the dark leather belt in one hand. "*Con su permiso*, Don Maylo, I am rich enough." He flexed a leg so that his horny fingers might tap the gilt spurs on his bootheels, meaningfully. "I shall give two *onzas* to each of our *muchachos* and bear four to the wives of the dead, the rest I shall 'lose' to Don Jorge at the dicecup, one night soon. Then he can afford to purchase a higher rank and better life.

"But as for you, surely you will need escort across this dangerous land. One lone man cannot . . ."

Don Maylo shook his head, smiling. "I shall not be alone, not exactly. Which brings us to my last request of you. Have our men take three of the best of the captured horses and fit them with packsaddles. On one, pack water for three men and three horses for a week, jerked meat, cheese and dried figs, my sleeping robes and two cases of arrows. Oh, and see if you can find me a wolfspear. You may have my lance in trade for it. Take my shield, as well, it's too heavy. Bring me a lancer's target instead, and a light horseman's axe."

As dawn paled the eastern sky, Don Angel rode out of camp, leading the three captured horses to the agreed point of rendezvous. Don Maylo met him at the mouth of the small arroyo on foot, but Angel could not greet him, for something was making the four horses fractious. After a few moments, however, they quieted as if by magic.

"All those things you asked are packed on the one horse, Don Maylo, as well as two fifty-kilo bags of grain, a pan, a stewpot, some clothing from your chest, some dried chilis, garlic and salt. The two bottles of mescal are from Don Jorge, who wishes you a safe journey, but respects your wish for an unannounced departure. Capitán Alvarez sends his best wishes and four dozen *cigarros*.

"But, please, Don Maylo, Don Humberto's—my father's—injunction was to see you safe to your journey's end or to the border of Mexico, whichever came first. The *muchachos* stand ready, even now. Cannot we guard you as far as the border?"

The tall man shook his head. "Thank you, Angel, but no. And fear not for my safety. I shall have better guards than a full troop of lancers could be."

"Then," insisted the short man, "may I not at least meet these, your new companions?"

Don Maylo smiled. "Very well, Angel, but leave your sword and dirk here, please."

Treading at Don Maylo's heels, Angel first saw the golden-chestnut stallion, pulling at a bit of tough scrub. Then, he spotted the two cats, sitting erect on the ledge above.

His eyes never left the huge predators as he slowly laid a hand on his companion's arm, saying in a low voice, "Don Maylo, there are a pair of monstrous cats crouched on a ledge just above your stallion. If we back up carefully, perhaps we can get my bow and . . ."

"No," said Maylo. "They will do us no harm, Angel. They are my friends and will be my companions on the rest of my journey."

"This two-leg you call 'brother' stinks of fear, fear and hate. He would slay both of us if he could," stated Skinkkiller.

"He was unprepared," Maylo mindspoke. "He had thought to see other two-legs, not you. Come down and greet him in friendship."

On a day when the river lay not to their north but far to the south, Skinkkiller's excited mindspeak ranged Don Maylo. "A *cat* lies just ahead, brother, a *male* cat, bigger even than Mousesqueak, he is! And a young two-leg male with a spear sits a small horse just beyond. And the vale beyond them is full of the blatting food-beasts with white, curly fur."

"Mindcall the male cat, sister. Tell him that a man of the Horseclans approaches." The man on the golden horse said, "Tell him that the man is Milo, of the Clan Morai."

Blind Hari then struck upon the strings of his telling-harp those notes which signaled the conclusion of a tale. "And, in the following season, did I first meet Milo of Morai. With the spring thaw, we two quitted the winter camp of Clan Morguhn and rode north, together with the young cat whom he had found in the desert of the south, Skinkkiller. By then, she had been war-trained and blooded and bore the name Elkkiller. And she was the mother of the mighty and much lamented Horsekiller, who led the Clan of the Cats to these new lands.

"This tale is ended, my children."

PROLOGUE II

Out from the caves, onto arid earth, the Kindred trod.
There, were they found by the one Undying God.
He did teach the Kindred all of life and the Law,
How the Horse to ride, how the bow to draw,
Work of iron, work of leather, work of bone,
Work of wood, work of fire with steel and stone,
Did teach of how to mindspeak Horse and Cat.
Three hundreds years and more he did remain,
And leaving, promised One would come again,
To lead the clans whose honor bore no stain
Back to the sea, their City to regain.
> —Chorus of *The Prophecy of the Return*

After two hundred years of roaming over most of a strange, altered world, I came back to the area from which I had begun my fruitless quest, the high plains of what had once been the United States of America. Search as I might, I had been unable to find that fabled isle, said to be peopled exclusively by men and women like myself.

Near the headwaters of the Red River, I rode into the camp of Clan Morguhn. They had summered in the mountains and were moving toward the Llano Estacado to meet with other clans and establish a winter camp. I represented myself as a clanless man, dropping vague references to a mysterious plague which had wiped out my clan-of-birth, and I was granted the hospitality of Chief Djimi's tent.

We wintered at a bend of the Brazos River, along with

four other kindred clans. As the river was beginning to swell with spring snow-melt, our camp became host to Blind Hari Krooguh, the tribal bard. He remained with us until New-grass-time. When the clans dispersed, both he and I rode north with Clan Ohlszuhn. From that day to this, he has ever remained near to me and we have become the closest of friends.

It was the exercise of his not inconsiderable powers which prevented the tribe from separating three years after my return, following the Tenth Year Council and feasts. Bidding the chiefs into yet another sitting, he introduced me. As sole survivor of my clan, I was automatically Morai of Morai, their peer. He recounted the manner of my arrival, sang the entire "The Prophecy of the Return," then pointed out the host of similarities between my coming and the verses of that ancient song. The upshot was that I was acclaimed War Chief of the tribe. The clans began to prepare for the long awaited return to the Sacred Sea, to rebuild their Holy City, Ehlai.

From my travels, I knew better than to attempt a trek to the true place of origin of their ancestors, what had been southern California. The worldwide seismic disturbances of some three hundred years before had tumbled most of that nuclear-scarred area into the Pacific Ocean. Therefore, I led them east. . . .

—From the *Journal of Milo Morai*

1

Ax and saber, spear and bow.
See the craven Dirtmen go.
Ride them down, lay them low.
Each and every maiden catch,
Put fiery torch to bone-dry thatch.
From Dirtmen shoulders, heads detach.
               —Horseclan Riding Song

The farmers were big men. They outnumbered the small contingent of nomad raiders by more than two-to-one and they fought with desperation, but it was the desperation of hopelessness and this counted against them. Also against them were the facts that their opponents had been born in the saddle and had cut their teeth on their sabers and axes. Their cuirasses of boiled leather turned aside the agriculturists' hastily snatched weapons. Besides, most of the farmers were drunk.

The arrow-volley which preceded the first charge had dropped more than a dozen of the olive-skinned dancers. Most of the remainder fell, as had the ripe grain whose harvest they had been celebrating, beneath the keen edges of the riders' steel or the churning hoofs and ravening teeth of their mounts.

Cut off and alone, a flashily dressed, beefy man swung a poleax with such force that it severed the foreleg of a passing horse. But he dropped his well-used weapon and staggered back, clutching at the coils of his intestines which spilled through the abdominal slash dealt him by the crippled horse's wiry, towheaded rider. Another second found the nomad

35

kneeling by his victim, choking on his own blood, an arrow transfixing his throat.

As Milo Morai jerked his saber free from the body of his latest opponent, a hunting arrow caromed off the side of his spiked helmet. Glancing in the direction whence the shaft had come, he saw the archer shoot the towheaded man. He urged his palomino stallion, Steeltooth, toward the gangling teenager, who loosed one more shaft at Milo, dropped his longbow, and turned to run. Milo leaned from his saddlelike kak and, with a single slash of his heavy saber, sent the boy's wide-eyed head spinning from his body. The headless trunk, spouting twin cataracts of blood, ran several more yards before it fell, twitching and jerking, to the firelit dust of the village square.

After the riders' third sweep across the village, nearly all the Dirtmen lay dead or dying in the bloody, hoof-churned mud of the dancing ground. Only one point of resistance remained: A knot of six or eight farmers, plus two men whose garb, armor, and fighting skill attested them professional soldiers, had formed a semi-circle, their backs to the front wall of the headman's house. They were holding their own; in the space before them lay the bodies of four nomads and one horse.

The riders were drawing up to charge yet again, but Milo pulled a shinbone whistle from within his cuirass and blew the signal to halt, then nudged Steeltooth over to the bunched raiders.

"Arrows," he said shortly. "No honor to be gained by allowing scum like this to send more of you to Wind's Home. Drop all but the money-fighters."

Grinning, three of the horsemen uncased their short hornbows. When the last of the farmers had been felled, Milo toed Steeltooth to a point midway between his riders and the two armored soldiers, each armed with a three-foot broadsword and a long, wide-bladed dirk.

"*Meelahteh Ehleeneekos?*" Milo inquired. "Or can you speak Mehrikan?"

The bigger of the two, a man a couple of inches taller than Milo, couched his answer in a drawled, very slurred dialect of the second tongue. "I talk 'em both, you murderin' son of a bitch, you!"

Milo's white teeth flashed startlingly against the background of his weathered face as he smiled his approval of the defiant words.

"You're a brave man, soldier. Are you free-fighters? If so, I've always employment for men with guts."

Raising his head, snorting his scorn, the big man stated, "Yes, I'm a free-fighter, but I'd fight for the Witch King first. Besides, we are sworn bodyguards to the Lady Mara of Pohtohmas."

"So be it," Milo declared, turning the stallion and riding back to his nomads. As he approached, two of the archers raised their bows, but he waved them down. He mindspoke Steeltooth and the big horse sank onto his muscular haunches. Milo stepped from his mount and unslung his iron-rimmed shield, then he stalked toward the soldiers.

When he was closer, he waved his blood-smeared saber at the arrow-quilled bodies of the farmers, saying, "They were treacherous Dirtmen and deserved no better than they received. You two, I'll grant a soldier's death. Singly or both together against me, you choose."

Side by side, the two swordsmen attacked. While fending off the larger with his shield, Milo first feinted at the smaller's exposed face, then brought the back edge of his saber up into the unarmored crotch, recovering with a vicious drawcut. The smaller man let go both sword and dirk and dropped, screaming and clutching at his mutilated masculinity.

The larger man was an excellent swordsman, but Milo had had superiority when the soldier's grandfather's grandfather's great-grandfather had been but a whining babe. After a brief flurry of stroke and counterstroke, he found an opening and rammed the center spike of his shield through the mercenary's eye into his brain. Then a quick signal brought a mercy-arrow to end the sufferings of the smaller man.

After they had fired the emptied stables, Milo galloped ahead of the procession of captured animals—horses, mules and a huge, twenty-five-hand Northorse gelding. House by house, the larger element of the raiding party had rooted out the surviving villagers and herded them into the body-littered, blood-splotched square. As he approached, Milo could hear the women keening over their dead.

The woman caught Milo's eye the moment he reined in beside the men who were guarding the huddle of prisoners. Although obviously of the same race as the people around her, she constituted a distillation of their good physical qualities, unpolluted by any of the bad. Her features were fine-boned and her light-olive skin, flawless. Her eyes were black and slightly almond-shaped; black, too, was her long, thick hair, so black that the flaring torches gave it bluish tints. Her hands were narrow and long-fingered, her body slim-hipped and graceful. She was quite small for an adult woman of her race, standing but a bare finger over fifteen hands, but the proud upthrusting of her well-formed breasts made it clear that she was no child.

Holding Steeltooth's head high (the war horse would bite any human he could get his teeth to unless that human looked and smelled like a nomad), Milo rode over to the small, dark woman. Lounging in his kak, he studied her for a long moment. She met his gaze, no fear in her eyes or her bearing, only hate and ill-suppressed anger.

Suddenly Milo grinned, commenting in Old Mehrikan, "Mad as hops, aren't you, you little vixen? You'd be highly dangerous to bed, probably claw my eyes out, if you couldn't lay hand to a knife. But for all of it, I think you'll be worth the effort."

He mindspoke the horse and, once more, the golden animal sank onto his haunches. Standing astride the glossy steed, Milo curtly beckoned her. *"Ehlahteh thoh!"* he commanded, then repeated himself in Old Mehrikan, "Come here, woman!"

By way of answer, she quickly stooped, her right hand going to the top of one of her felt traveling boots. When she straightened, the torchlight glinted on the steel blade of a small dagger. Still unspeaking, she launched herself directly at Milo. But she had reckoned without Steeltooth. As she came within range, the killer's big, yellow teeth clacked, missing her by but half a fingerbreadth. Shocked, she swerved, planted her foot in a slimy puddle of congealing blood. The foot shot from under her, and she fell heavily . . . directly under the head of the palomino stallion!

Steeltooth felt well served. His head darted down with the speed of a swooping falcon and it required all of Milo's strength to halt that deadly lunge.

In falling, the little woman had lost her knife. She lay, supported on hip and elbow, immediately in front of Steeltooth's huge, chisellike incisors. Her wide eyes had become even wider. She, who had shown no fear of Milo or the other nomads, was quite obviously terrified of the blood-hungry horse.

Milo spoke in a low, calm voice. "Do not attempt to rise, woman, that would put you in range of him, despite the reins. It's only my strength against his, for he has no bit. Do exactly as I say and you have a chance. If you understand me, blink three times, rapidly."

Her long, sooty lashes flicked once, twice, thrice, and he went on. "Now roll onto your belly, *very* slowly . . . Good. Keep your head and your rump down, use your arms to drag yourself to me. If you try to go the other way, he'll think you're fleeing from him, and I'll not be able to hold him; so come here, but do it slowly, very slowly."

She followed his instructions and, at length, lay at his right, her fine clothing filthy with dust and grime and well smeared with the blood through which she had had to crawl. Wordlessly, she obeyed his gesture and, when she was mounted before him, he eased up on the reins and signaled the horse to rise. Once erect, the palomino looked about for the small two-leg he had almost had, but it was nowhere to be seen, although its scent was still present. He shook his head and stamped, snorting his disgust.

Milo had one of his raiders bind the captive and place her in the cargo-pannier of the Northorse, while he saw to the systematic looting of the village. Custom required that a slave be returned for each man killed or seriously wounded, so he selected seven of the strongest-looking girls, then two more for Clan Kahrtuh. When these had been bound and lashed to kak or packsaddle, when the Northorse and mules had been loaded with loot and the weapons and armor of the dead, when the corpses of the slain Kindred had been placed beside Djimi Kahrtuh's mutilated body, Milo allowed shifts of raiders to "test" the remaining Dirtwomen and thus decide which of them they wished to take with them.

While the shrill pleas and sobbing screams of outrage and pain attested to the strenuous activity of the first shift, Milo and the others herded the laden animals to the outskirts of the village. When the third shift had chosen and its well-raped choices were tied across packsaddle or crupper, the remaining villagers—old men, children, and old or ugly or crippled women—were chased far into the stubbled fields. Then, beginning with the headman's house where lay their late comrades and the two dead soldiers, they fired every structure in the village—sparing not even the privies.

The cross was the only thing of wood left standing, that

same cross on which they had found the body of their scout.
Onto the bloodstreaked timbers, they bound the cadaver of
the village headman. Standing on his kak, Milo gripped a
handful of the stripped body's hair and held its head erect.
One of the archers then drove an arrow through eye and
brain and skull, pinning the head to the upright.

Milo hung a weatherproof case on the jutting arrow. It
contained a roll of parchment on which he had printed a
message in three languages—Ehleeneekos, Horseclan
Mehrikan, and the trade language, Old Mehrikan: *This Dirtman and his pack took a man of the Kahrtuh Clan by guile
and murdered him by torture. Dirtman, behold and be
warned! The cost of the life of one Horseclansman is a village and every man in it! By the hand of Milo Morai, War
Chief of the Tribe-that-will-return-to-the-Sacred-Sea.*

2

*Man and Cat and Horse are Kindred, one,
'Neath high domain of Wind and Sword and Sun.*
　　　　　　　　—From *The Couplets of the Law*

The party had not been riding more than an hour when a
savage storm struck. The windy gusts came horizontally, the
rain accompanied by peasize hailstones which rang on helmets like sling missiles. But Milo led his men on despite the
dark and storm, glad of them, in fact. For they were but a
small group and uncomfortably near to the High Lord's capital, with its well-armed soldiery, and the sheets of water
would surely wash away the traces of their passage, making
things more difficult for the patrols that were certain to be after them by daybreak, if not already. Burdened as they were,
they could look forward to at least twenty hours of travel.

From their present position, it was some fifty miles to the
tribe's sprawling encampment around the hilltop town which
the Ehleenee called Theesispolis, and nearly every one of
those miles lay through little-known, hostile country.

Throughout the rest of the night, Milo drove them on west-ward. When it became too light to travel safely and the rain slackened, they found a dense copse and made a cold camp. After the animals were all fed and picketed, the captive women were untied and, under close guard, allowed to eat and attend their bodies' needs. Then the strongest of the men cold-fitted an iron cuff to each woman's right ankle, the cuffs bearing the mark of the clan to whom the slave-woman now belonged. Threading an iron chain through the cuffs, the raiders picketed their captives on the other side of the clearing from the horseline, and the first shift of sleepers flopped down and were soon snoring despite soggy earth and wet clothing. A group of equal size watched over them, the slaves and the horses, while the other third guarded the perimeter of the copse and watched for signs of pursuit. All were seasoned warriors, old hands at raiding.

Milo's cuff was of hardened silver rather than iron, and he fitted it to his captive himself. Then, taking a leathern flask and a brace of small horncups from among his gear, he poured out measures of a clear liquid and offered one to the dark woman, who stared at it for a moment before accepting. She watched him toss down his own and attempted to follow suit; gasping, spluttering, choking, her eyes streaming, she dropped the cup. Milo laughed until he was forced to hold his sides.

When she had regained her powers of speech, she angrily demanded, "What in hell is that stuff?"

"Distilled grain mash," Milo answered smilingly. "When you're accustomed to it, you'll find it quite pleasing. We call it 'water of life.'"

At his instruction, she sipped her refilled cup, deciding af-ter a moment that she could truly learn to enjoy the fluid.

While packing flask and cups away, Milo regarded her closely. "Two sleep warmer than one, woman. Give me your word you'll not try to escape and I'll not chain you with the others."

She shrugged. "Where could I go? I've no idea where we are and only the vaguest idea in which direction Kehnooryos Atheenahs lies. You or one of your barbarians will probably rape me shortly, but at least you've not tried to kill me. My next captor might not be so merciful." Reaching down, she tapped a fingernail against the silver ring. "I suppose this means I'm now your clan's slave. Am I allowed to ask your name and the name of your clan, Master?"

"My name is Milo Morai. I am clanless as a War Chief must be; that way, there's less chance that he'll play favorites."

"I guess you expect me to feel honored that my master is so important a man." She gave him a hard, cold stare before continuing. "Well, I don't feel honored. All that I feel is relief. You see, I have some knowledge of your disgusting customs, barbarian. I'm relieved that, clanless as you say you are, you're the only man to whom I'll have to submit. At least, I'll not be the common property of half a hundred of your stinking Kinsmen. You are a strong and handsome man and, for what you are, you seem kind. Perhaps I can come to enjoy coupling with you. Time will tell."

He shook his head brusquely. "Sorry to disillusion you, but you're no common Dirtwoman to be taken for slave or bedwarmer. For you, I'll expect a ransom."

It was the woman's turn to shake her head. "There's no one to ransom me, Master. I, too, have no family; they are all long dead. As for my own wealth, my jewels were the bulk of it, and your raiders have them all now. No, my master, slave-woman or concubine is the only use that Mara of Pohtohmas can ever be to you."

"So, you take another female, Friend Milo. For your kind, she is unugly. Perhaps this one will present you with kittens." The mindspeak wakened Milo and he sat up. A great, gray form loomed at his right. It sat in the classic feline posture, tail curled to cover forepaws. Milo reached out to gently scratch the underside of the lower jaw, between the wicked points of the long cuspids. Venting a rumbling purr, the cat extended his massive head to enable Milo to scratch the throat as well.

"You know how to please, don't you, Friend Milo?" The thought was clearer now that Milo was awake and they were in physical contact.

"What have you been up to, Horsekiller?" asked Milo silently. "There's still some blood at the left corner of your mouth, you know. Man blood?"

"Thanks for telling me." The creature raised one huge paw, licked it, and began to wash his face, while he thought-conversed with Milo.

"No, not your kind, Friend Milo. Understand, I've no ob-
jection to killing them, but the mere thought of having to actually *eat* one makes me gag; you wouldn't believe how awful
they taste. No, the cub and I shared a small deer." He had
finished his ablutions, but now extended his big pink tongue
again, licking his furry lips in memory of the gastronomic
pleasure. "Delicious. The cub killed it."

"*Cub!*" The thought was faint with distance. "I'm no cub!
You may be Cat Chief and you may be older, but if you insult me so another time, this will be a day of claws."

"Cub, you are!" thought Horsekiller. "You are barely
larger than your mother. Be impudent and you'll have
toothprints on your haunches. I've nipped you before and I
can do it again. Bear that in mind."

The thought was closer now, stronger. "You and what clan
of two-legs, Mousekiller?"

Aloud, the Cat Chief ripped out a muted snarl. Every
horse and mule on the picket line commenced to whinny and
pull at the moorings, eyes rolling white.

"Easy, old friend, easy," thought Milo. "Can't you see that
your son is teasing you? The clanshorses know you, but the
others over there don't. Look what your snarl did. For Sun's
sake, let them know you've a full belly, before they
stampede."

Obediently, the big animal stood and slowly strolled toward
the picket line, beaming soothing thoughts ahead of him.
Milo sensed Steeltooth and others of the clanshorses greeting
the wanderer.

The huddled girl had not moved, and, thinking her yet
asleep, Milo began to draw on his short boots. However,
when he chanced to glance down, he could see that her eyes
were wide open and fixed on the massive bulk of the cat, who
was now working his way along the picket line, touching
noses with each animal unacquainted with him.

"Master," she whispered, "what is that? It's as big as . . .
as a *pony!*"

Milo smiled reassuringly, squatted, and patted her grubby
hand. "His name, in speech, would be Horsekiller. He's a
prairiecat, Chief of the Cat Clan and an old friend. You've
not seen him earlier because he and one of his sons have
been scouting our rear to determine the numbers, speed, and
route of the pursuit. When he's done mindspeaking the new
animals, I'll introduce you."

Mara's brow wrinkled. "I have heard of these prairiecats. Is it true that you barb . . . uhh, nomads can really converse with them?"

"Quite true," Milo nodded. "He and I were just discussing, among other things, you; he feels that, for a human female, you are not unattractive and will throw healthy kittens. I agree."

"Naturally." Horsekiller projected his thought as he ambled back to Milo, picking a path among the sleeping raiders. "Any intelligent creature would agree with me, Friend War Chief. I don't know what it is to be wrong."

"Nor," came the other thought which was now quite near, "what it is to be modest."

Milo mindspoke. "Horsekiller, can you reach this female's mind?"

After a moment, the cat replied, "Only the surface, Friend Milo. She has a mind-shield. I've touched but one other like it and . . . ahhh, pardon me." The Cat Chief stalked around Milo to Mara. He licked the little woman's hand, then crouched and laid his big head in her lap. The cat's demeanor was one of adoration, nothing less. Milo was shocked; he had never seen the Cat Chief behave so toward any two-leg.

"Friend Milo," Horsekiller chided him, "you have not yet mounted this female. You should. She wants you to." He had not personalized the transmission and Mara flushed.

So, thought Milo to himself, she *can* mindspeak; now I wonder. . . .

But Horsekiller went on. "Ah, you foolish two-legs, sometimes I wonder how I can bear to be around you. You waste so much of your lives. Life should be lived, Friend Milo, not frittered away on trivialities."

"My, my," thought Milo, "Horsekiller is become a philosopher in his old age."

The Cat Chief ignored the sarcasm. "Were you truly wise, Friend Milo, you would push this female onto her belly and sink your teeth into her neck and enter her body and . . . ahhhh . . . there are few things so enjoyable." The cat sighed. "It is on a plane with crouching in the snow on a crackling cold morning and feeling hot, fragrant blood spurt onto your nose as you tear your first mouthful from a new-killed fawn; or catching delicious little mice on a flower covered prairie under a warm, spring sky; or . . ."

Milo chuckled aloud, then mindspoke. "Horsekiller, you're a hedonist."

"He's a dirty old cat!" announced the third mindspeaker. "All he can think of is eating and making kittens, and then he wonders that I fail to respect him."

Horsekiller's ears went back in folds against his brawny neck and smoldering anger purged his mind of sensuality. Prairiecats were every bit as hot-blooded and quick-tempered as the human clansmen, this Milo knew well. And the last thing needed at this juncture was a spitting, squalling cat fight, so Milo quickly interjected, "We're still in the land of the Blackhairs, with much danger behind and ahead. Horsekiller, as Cat Chief, you know better than to carry family squabbles on a raid."

Then he turned to the "smaller" cat—the cub weighed over 150 pounds, and his paws, larger even than his sire's, attested to the fact that he had yet to fill out. "Stop harassing your chief, Swimmer, or you'll be eating cold beef on herd-guard with your fellow kittens, until your mental maturity matches your physical. Understood?"

"I was only teasing." The yellow-brown cat sulked. "Can't I have *any* fun, Friend War Chief?"

"On a raid? No, definitely not, Swimmer," Milo affirmed. "Unless you want your pelt pegged out for curing behind some Blackhair's cabin."

The young cat shuddered. "Stop, please! I'll regurgitate all that fine venison. That was an obscene thing to suggest."

"But true, nonetheless," put in Horsekiller. "It is said that the king of the Blackhairs has his seat of ruling covered by a large robe made of pelts of prairiecats."

Swimmer shuddered again. "He must be a monster."

"No, Swimmer, just of another race. Few of his people can communicate with your kind. To them you are just animals—dangerous animals."

Deeply shaken, the adolescent feline crouched close to Milo, who stroked his head soothingly. "Are two-leg Blackhairs pursuing us, Horsekiller?"

"Yes, Friend Milo, but it will be night before they are near to this place."

"How many two-legs?"

"As many as a clan—males and females and cubs. Some on horses, some on two-wheels. Far behind them are many clans without horses, but they and the two-wheels are a long run south of this place on the flat-way."

So, Milo mused, it's as I thought. The chariots and the infantry are sticking to the road—what was Route 250, six hundred years ago. Even so, it may be a tight race. Laden with the loot and the slaves, we'll be hard put to outrun their cavalry. What I should do is dump the packs and the women here, but if I did, there'd be hell to pay. The men fought hard and well for this booty and won't give it up easily.

"Horsekiller, if you leave now, how long will it take you to reach Tribe Camp?"

"One of your time periods, maybe less."

"Then go. Go fast, both of you. Horsekiller, go to Lord Bili of Esmith. Tell him that I said to ride at once with all his males and as many others as he can gather quickly. Then leave Swimmer to guide them. As for you, gather the Cats— as many as are not on duty—get them battle-armed, and speed back to me. Damn that cavalry! Why couldn't they have stayed on the road as well?"

3

Clanswomen shall be taught the skills of war,
To draw bow and to cast the spear afar;
For valiant woman, valiant horse, and valiant man
Do live and die in honor of their clan.
                    —From *The Couplets of the Law*

As the two giant cats sped westward, Milo strode among the sleepers, nudging them into wakefulness. Few words were required; the worry on his face said enough. Those who had removed their cuirasses re-donned them, then slapped saddles to horses. Once Steeltooth was saddled and accoutered, Milo assisted with the captured animals. With amazing speed, the little column was again underway, the captives' wrists lashed to pommel or packsaddle—all, save Mara; for some reason, Milo believed her, didn't think that she would try to escape.

She rode beside him, astride dead Djimi Kahrtuh's horse, her long hair stuffed under the late scout's peaked helmet.

This time they bore southwest toward the road. On it, they would make far better time than cross-country and, now, speed was more important than concealment. It had been a 50-50 chance that all the pursuers would adhere to the road, in which case Milo might have swung wide to the north and missed the pursuit entirely. Dropping to the tail, he urged the riders on. He had lost his gamble, but had no intention of losing more than that.

It had been midday when they struck camp. The sun was low on the horizon when Milo sighted his objective. About three hundred years after what Milo thought of as the Two-Day War, there had been an earthquake of considerable proportions somewhere in the Eastern Ocean. This section of the piedmont, though not visited by the tidal waves which had devastated the seaboard, had been racked by sympathetic quakes. Now a result of this geologic turmoil confronted them—a sixty-foot-high upthrust of earth and rock and ancient asphalt shards, thickly grown with trees and undergrowth. The original path of the road bisected its hundred yard length, and the Sea-invaders had laid their replacement road under its thickly forested southern brow.

Milo waited until his party had rounded it before he halted them.

"Kindred, Blackhair cavalry rides close behind. After them are war-carts and spearmen. Just before we rode again, I sent Horsekiller and Swimmer to fetch help from the tribe, but it will take time for them to reach us. Saving this booty means much to you who fought for it and more to the clans of our Kindred who died. Therefore, some must continue west, while the others of us delay the Blackhairs. Since we will not be enough to fight them sword-to-sword, I shall only take the bow-masters. The others leave your quivers behind. Now, ride!" Milo turned and led his nine bow-masters into the forest that fringed the hill. They had ridden but twenty yards when the pitch abruptly mounted, too steep for the horses. Mentally enjoining their steeds to silence, the nomads dismounted, took their bows and quivers, and started to pick a way to the slope which overlay the road.

Burdened with several extra arrow cases, Milo was about to follow his men, when he heard two riders galloping from the west. He quickly nocked a shaft and crouched just below the hill. Careless of the low-hanging branches, Mara clattered into view, close-pursued by one of the booty-guard nomads, his saber out.

Milo stood and Mara leaped from her mount and raced to stand before him.

"What in hell . . . ?" he began.

Flushed and panting, the girl stood with Djimi Kahrtuh's cased bow in her hand. "Please, Master, let me stay with you. I'm a good archer and I've no love for the Ehleenee—Blackhairs, you call them. If I am to be one of your women, let me fight beside you, as clanswomen do. Please allow me to stay."

"Horses! Many horses near, galloping." Steeltooth's thought beamed out.

"Oh, all right," Milo said in exasperation. "It's too late to send you back now. Brother." He addressed the mounted clansman. "Go back to your duty and tell them to ride like the wind!"

Walking over to Mara's trembling, blowing horse, Milo untied the bundle of Djimi Kahrtuh's weapons and gear from behind the kak. Fortunately, the nomad had been small, even for his race, and his armor was a fair fit for Mara.

"Can you use a sword, too, woman-of-surprises?"

Mara nodded briskly. "If it becomes necessary, Master."

So he slung the Kahrtuh-crested baldric over one of her shoulders and the strap of an arrow case over the other. "Give me the bow, Mara. I'll string it for you."

She drew back. "*I* am capable of stringing my own bow, Master, thank you."

"Then do so, woman, and come on. Leave the case here. You'll not need it up there."

Urged on by repeated thought-messages from Steeltooth, he placed his men just in time. He'd only just hunkered down when three scale-armored scouts galloped into view, the setting sun glinting from their lance points and oiled, black beards.

Beside him, Mara whispered, "*Kahtahfrahktoee, the Mahvroh Ahloghoh*. A Black Horse squadron. Most of them are from the northern lands, only the officers are Ehleenee. They are mercenaries, but hard fighters."

Milo allowed the scouts to pass his position; the two archers around the hill would take care of them. Sure enough, there was soon a twanging of bowstrings and a strangled half-scream, then silence. Milo was sure that the approaching squadron had not heard any sounds, not above the clatter of their own advance.

Four abreast, they swept around the hill, pressing hard, their black horses well lathered. Behind the first troop was a knot of Ehleenee officers, the gold-washed scales of their hauberks sparkling in the setting sun. As the dark-visaged, flashy group came into effective range, Milo placed a bone-tipped shaft in their leader's right eye. At this, other bowstrings twanged around him. Mara's did as well, and, following the shaft, Milo saw it thud into a blue-coated Ehleen's throat—the girl *could* handle a bow at that!

Noisy confusion prevailed as the squadron commander and his staff went down. Horses became difficult to control for Milo and two nomads who were also mindtalkers were—even as they nocked, drew, and released, nocked, drew, and released—beaming warnings of imminent agony and death at the cavalry mounts. When both the first and second troops started to take casualties and the nerve-shattering screams of a wounded horse suddenly rent the air, the van wavered, milling uncertainly. Milo prayed to every god he'd ever heard mentioned that they'd break; panic is contagious, and if these two troops were routed, the entire squadron might be swept back with them.

But such was not to be. The Ehleenee officers might be dead, but at least one effective noncom—always the backbone of any military body—had retained his life and, more importantly, his head. Milo could hear his hoarse bellow rising above the din. He was not shouting Ehleeneekos words, but Southeastern Mehrikan. Milo could understand him easily, as could most of the nomads; the language was not that different from the old Mehrikan of the plains.

"Hol! Hol! Stand firm! Boogluh! Hweanhz the fuggin boogluh?"

All at once a bugle signaled "Fours left." As it repeated the call, other buglers took it up, and—with or without human guidance—the well-drilled horses executed the indicated maneuver. Before the last of the cavalry had cleared the road, Milo saw a large chunky man wheel his mount and, spurring hard, bear toward the hill at a dead run. Though the plates of his scale-mail were of plain, serviceable iron, his helmet decoration was that of a mercenary sergeant-major—the highest rank which a non-Ehleen could hold in the territories of the Sea-invaders. His scar-seamed, weathered face was clearly visible as, heedless of the feathered death all around him, he bore down on that section of road where his officers had died. The horse galloped in on a wide arc and, a second before he reached his objective, the big man kicked free of his stirrups and slid to the off-side of the thundering animal. With his right leg gripping the underside of the horse, his left knee hooked onto the saddle's high cantle, and his left hand locked on the forward strap of the double girth; he leaned down to tear the squadron standard from the dead hand which still held it. Throughout the courageous episode, the only arrows which struck the big man bounced harmlessly off the scales of his well-worn hauberk. As the sergeant regained his seat, he turned and flourished the standard at Milo and his men. If there were any three things the nomads appreciated and respected, they were bravery, defiance and horsemanship; they cheered, shouting their approval of this valiant foe. Nothing but honor—for both individual and clan—could come from the killing of such a man!

Even Milo felt admiration, despite his realization that retrieval of that standard had probably sealed the fates of Mara and his nomads. As he and his companions watched, the squadron rallied and re-formed, its archers dismounting and advancing in a widely spaced line of skirmishers. Just behind them, at the walk, rode a triple-rank of cavalry—lances left behind, shields slung, to free both hands—at least two hundred of them.

"Twenty-to-one," thought Milo. "Good, hard, experienced soldiers, too, with a battlewise mind directing them. None of these showy Ehleenee pantywaists. When the archers are close enough, they will lay down a covering fire and the horsemen will come in under it. They'll ride as far as the horses can go, then they'll dismount and climb up to us. And that will be all. You can't but admire that old bastard, but I wish to hell he *had* been killed!"

At three hundred paces, the archers halted and commenced to arch shafts onto the area occupied by the nomads. But Milo had chosen his position well, if hurriedly, with just this possibility in mind. Realizing that most of their arrows were being stopped or deflected by the overhanging branches of the thick old trees, the skirmishers picked up their quivers and paced closer. When they had halved their original distance, they again halted and their bolts came straight and true, to clatter among the rocks and tree trunks or sink into the rich loam. After a few minutes, they stopped, allowing the cavalry time to canter to a point out of the line of fire. When the bowstrings were twanging again, a bugle call commanded and the canter became a gallop. Abruptly, the two rearmost lines reined up on the opposite side of the road, the foremost continuing on to the foot of the rocky slope, where three men of every four dismounted and ran—zigzagging— up the slope. The moment the horse-holders were out of the way, the second line repeated the first's maneuver. Then the third followed suit and Milo shook his head in wonderment and awe. Gods, there went first-class soldiers. What couldn't *he* do with troops like that?

Sometime within the last twenty years, the original forward face of the south slope had slid down toward the new road, leaving the area on which Milo's nomads were making their stand. Before them was a sheer drop of twenty-odd feet. The soldiers would be able to scale it, but with difficulty. From the foot of the scarp was a thirty-degree, pebble-strewn slope, culminating in a jumble of rocks and smashed and uprooted trees. There was no cover worthy of the name on the pebbly slope, so Milo and his men saved their dwindling supply of arrows until the first line had reached this ready-made deathtrap.

A few of the men in the first line reached the foot of the scarp where they crouched helplessly, safe from the arrow-hail but too few in number to mount a frontal attack against who knew how many Western barbarians. Most of the first wave lay twitching or dead between their line-of-departure and their objective. A few had made it back to the questionable safety of their original position, where they awaited the reinforcement of the second wave.

Atop the scarp, most of the arrowcases were empty and— as the cavalry archers had ceased fire for fear of felling their own—the nomads were scrabbling among the rocks, searching for undamaged shafts to supplement their own meager supply. Then came the second wave and, though they broke it, too, Milo knew with certainty that they'd *not* break the third. He had one arrow, Mara had two, and the others had less than a dozen among them. To save time later, he drew his saber and buried its point in the leafmold within easy reach. Then he turned to Mara.

"You have fought well, Mara. It is not right you should die a slave. Move your leg so that I may reach your ankle."

"Wait, Master." She laid her hand on his arm. "Horsekiller is coming. He and many, many of his kind and . . . and there is a . . . another very near, but . . . but different." Her brow wrinkled.

Milo started. "Do you wish, woman, or do you . . . ?" Then, faint with distance, "I come, Friend Milo. The female's mind is even easier to range than yours. I come with many cats. Swimmer is with Friend Bili, while the young ones and the pregnant or nursing ones guard the camp. The rest are with me. I come."

Milo closed his eyes and devoted every ounce of concentration to the beaming of one word. "Hurry!"

Then, his mind relaxed and receptive, he caught the vague shadow of a thought. Slowly, it gained strength. "The female . . . and the one called Milo . . . you are truly the friends of cats?" The mindspeaker was close.

When Milo affirmed his friendship with the Cat Clans, the mindspeaker went on. "Then, I shall try to aid you. I, too, hate Blackhairs. They killed my kin. I am the last. It is good to mindspeak again. It has been long and I was beginning to become an animal. I am old now, and not so fast as once I was, but what I can do, I will do. Wait."

4

> *Arrow fly far, arrow fly true,*
> *Strike and pierce the foeman through.*
> *Saber, slash, lay open throat.*
> *Dirk-point, stab like tooth of stoat.*
> *Target, guard thy bearer well,*
> *Spear-blade, all before you fell.*
> *Heavy ax, with keen edge, rend.*
> *Helm and cuirass, life defend.*
>
> —Horseclan War Song

Only there was no more time for waiting. The third wave had formed and, leaping the bodies of their predecessors, were pouring up the hazardous slope. Sure of reinforcement, the handful of men at the scarp-foot were already beginning to seek handholds and pull themselves up toward their quarry. Milo loosed his last arrow, dropped the now-useless bow and picked up his heavy saber.

An arrow hissed by his ear and he instinctively ducked. The archers had advanced to the moraine and were once more bringing them under fire. Farther down, at the very lip of the scarp, two of the nomads stood and began to heave at the huge, jagged rock which had been sheltering them. It gave a little, then abruptly slipped from its centuries-old niche, to drop straight down the scarp-face, hurling a couple of climbing soldiers to their deaths and crushing another as it bounced toward the moraine. When it struck the base of the rock wall, two hundred cubic yards of earth and stone dissolved and began to pour after it with frightening speed, taking three nomads and an undeterminable number of soldiers with it. The entire scarp quivered and Milo started to call his surviving men to quit it, but at that moment, the first cavalryman pulled himself over the rim, almost directly before Milo and Mara.

She struck first and, as the bearded trooper parried her blow, Milo severed the man's right arm, just below the elbow. Holding the bloody stump and screaming, the soldier turned and stepped into space. When he struck the ground, his screams ceased. Then it was a maelstrom of hack and slash and thrust, of kicking the faces which came into view and stamping the hands, feeling the bones crunch under the boot heels.

For a moment, there was respite, even from arrows, for the archers had run out and had to send back to the horselines for more. While Milo and Mara and the four surviving nomads watched helplessly, their attackers reformed behind the moraine and a troop-strength contingent separated from the distant squadron to trot toward the scene of conflict. Meantime, the unemployed archers occupied themselves by dragging or carrying the wounded that lay on the slope back beyond the moraine.

After a brief pause to get their breath, Milo and the others hastily scrounged for arrows, being rewarded with a score of relatively undamaged shafts. The nomads thought to save them for the coming attack, until Mio pointed out that, except for those lost in the landslide, all their companions had been slain by those same archers, who were presently busy on the slope and well within range of Horseclan bows. When the archers had fled—leaving fourteen of their number dead or dying on the blood-slimed avenue of attack—Mara sped a shaft which spitted both cheeks of a junior noncom, who had been shouting instructions to the massing survivors of the earlier assaults. At this, they elected to form farther down the embankment, nearer to the horselines, which their reinforcements were quickly approaching.

All at once, the riderless horses commenced to mill and stir, nervously tossing their heads and stamping, their eyes rolling in fear. Then, with a blood-chilling snarl, two hundred pounds of grizzled feline fury launched itself from the lower reaches of the forest and landed atop the nearest cavalry mount. Though the cat attacked the animal viciously, it made no attempt to kill. The screams of the stricken horse panicked the others and, jerking their reins from the grasps of the horse-holders who were trying to remain on their own bucking mounts, they sped to the four winds. Some half-dozen bore through the formation of dismounted men, bowling them over and stamping out lives beneath heedless hoofs. Most of the frantic herd, however, careened into the ordered ranks of the advancing troop. The cat was still riding the leader of this herd and the sight and smell of him was enough to plunge most of the troop's horses into a state of equal panic. Beyond the disordered troop, the cat adroitly turned his gashed and bleeding "mount" and "rode" through them a second time, now headed back toward the road. At the road's edge, a dismounted archer loosed a hurriedly aimed shaft at the cat. It took the horse at the base of the throat and, as the stricken beast stumbled, the cat launched himself onto the stupidly-staring archer, slamming him onto his back as the long, cruel teeth crunched out his face. Bounding from his kill amid a hail of arrows, the cat sailed twenty feet to disappear into the woods from which he had emerged.

"I have done what I could, Cat-friend-called-Milo."

"And well was it done!" replied Milo. "I will care for your kittens and females and vouchsafe you a clean death, when your teeth have dulled and age rests upon you." Milo recited the ancient cat-human alliance formula.

The emotion which was beamed into Milo and Mara brought tears streaming down the girl's dirty cheeks. "Oh, my Friends," the cat mindspoke, "my kittens and my dear females and all my clan are long years dead, murdered by the Blackhairs. Nearly forty Cold-times have come and gone, since I opened my eyes and first saw Sacred Sun. Age already nibbles at me with cold, hateful teeth. Though I shiver far from the plains of pleasant memory, in your mind, Friend Milo, I find the warmth of youth and home. I have no wish to suffer the slow death of an old animal, so, as you have given the words, I shall come up. It is a good death, to die fighting beside cat-friends."

Horsekiller's thought broke in. "I too, have heard, Friend Milo, but there is no need for the old one's death, or for yours. I am just behind the hill where the Blackhair road becomes straight. My clan-brother, Long-Ears, and most of the clan are in a stream bed and have almost reached a spot which will put them behind the Blackhair soldiers. So, you and the brave old one sit and wash yourselves. Now it is my clan's turn to fight the Blackhairs."

Then arrows clacked and hissed again among Milo and the group. The dismounted troops, impatient to get the job done, lumbered up the slope, shouting. On Milo's right, beyond the moraine, a man screamed in pain and terror. There was another scream, in a different voice, then another and another. The arrow rain became an ill-aimed trickle, then ceased altogether. A few of the rearmost assaulters half-turned. Then, bounding over the rocks and bodies which marked the path of the landslide, came Horsekiller and a dozen other cats—snarling and spitting, their boiled-leather armor rattling and their razor-edge toothspurs throwing evil, metallic glints.

As he passed behind one of the troopers, Horsekiller's great head dipped and swung in a smooth, practiced motion. The man yelped and his hauberk's scales struck sparks from the slope as he fell, hamstrung. The cats were outnumbered by more than five-to-one, but their fantastic speed and agility and the unexpectedness of their attack stood them in good stead. Some were content to cripple, as had Horsekiller, others bore individual men to the ground, slashing at arms and legs, at faces and throats. Expecting to have to climb before they fought, the troopers had had their weapons sheathed and their baldrics hitched up and around, so that the swords hung between their shoulder-blades. In the time it took them to awkwardly draw the long swords, they took numerous casualties. Even when the steel was out, men continued to go down beneath tearing fangs and rending claws, for few swordsmen possessed the speed to counter a prairiecat.

The troopers attempted to form a shoulder-to-shoulder defensive semi-circle at the foot of the scarp, but were treated to such a shower of rocks from Milo and the nomads that, in the end, they broke rank to sprint for the moraine. On Milo's left, Horsekiller leaped onto the back of a trooper, crouching over the screaming, struggling man, but unable to make a quick kill because of his armor. Another trooper ran back to bring his saber down on the cat's already-cracked cuirass. Heavy as the blow was, it still failed to break the tough leather, but its force drove Horsekiller down, stunned. Gripping his hilt with both hands, the trooper whirled his blade up for another try. But just as the heavy steel whooshed downward, a bolt of unarmored, brown fury shot from the brush to knock the sword-wielder to his back. His helmet spun off and his attacker sank long cuspids into the top of his skull. Behind the newcomer, Horsekiller straightened up, shook himself, and with a forepaw flipped his own victim over, then, tore out his throat. He and the newcomer exchanged no communication, but raced after the other cats, on the trail of the terrified troopers.

Before the first archers had raced back across the road, the cavalry commander had already started the bulk of the squadron forward. At that distance, he could not discern the cause of his men's withdrawal, but he surmised that his objective had been reinforced. Barely had the serried ranks started forward—four-deep, presenting squadron-front—when the earth behind them erupted Long-Ear and over fifty of his clan. Emitting their horrific battle cries, they sped along the rearmost rank, slashing the horses' haunches or hamstringing them or rearing to sink long claws into men's arms or legs and drag them from the pitching backs of their crazed mounts. As only the rear rank had been attacked, all might have been saved, had the other three ranks turned and dealt with the small band of felines; but these were warhorses, not hunters, and they refused to be turned. Long-Ears had chosen the proper angle of attack and the wind was right, carrying the horrible stink of predators and spilled blood to the quivering nostrils of every equine in the squadron. Those who did not first rid themselves of their human burdens, bore them—impotently sawing tooth-held bits—on a wild gallop for the supposed safety of the road.

The troop which the stranger-cat had stampeded had just more or less re-formed when the fear-mad squadron rode into it, creating a tangled welter of downed men and horses. The screams of man and horse, the sick-soggy impact of flailing hoof on flesh, and the sharp cracks of snapping bones sped the still-erect on their way. But at the road, leaping ahead of the hapless assault troops, came Horsekiller at the head of his furry demons. At that point, Mahvroh Ahloghoh Squadron ceased being a unit! East and west raced a few mounted men and many riderless horses or horseless riders. The Cat Clan converged upon a field covered with discarded lances and smashed saddles and dented helmets. As its center squirmed the screaming, sobbing, writhing tangle of horse-man horror. Around and beyond it, as far as the retreating dust of the widely scattered survivors, lay the dead, dying, or stunned cavalrymen, and among them, others crawled or staggered aimlessly. Efficiently, the cats worked outward from their rallying point, slashing or tearing at any man-thing who moved or showed signs of life.

Milo, Mara, and the four nomads had not seen the rout of the bulk of the *kahtahfrahktoee*, but from the cacophony in the meadow, it had not been difficult to imagine what was taking place. Climbing down, they had picked their way across the unsure footing of the landslide and hurried back to the horses. As soon as the others were mounted, Milo urged them on their way and set about freeing the mounts of those who would not be coming for them. Because his cuirass, which had been split and was dangling, hampered his movements, he sheathed his saber and began removing the useless armor. At the mouth of the trail, Mara sat her fidgeting horse, Steeltooth's reins looped over her right arm.

With a sudden crackling of underbrush, a wild-eyed, helmetless soldier tore into the tiny glade. He had lost his sword, but he gripped a broad dirk in one hairy hand. Bellowing, he raced toward Milo, big boots thud-thudding on the loam.

As he had but one arm free, Milo was unable to protect himself from the snarling, berserk man whose rush knocked him down. With a shout of triumph, the soldier eluded his victim's grasping left hand and plunged a leaf-shaped blade toward the side of his unarmored chest.

In the second required for the trooper to cross to Milo, Mara had dropped Steeltooth's reins, drawn her saber, and spurred after the dirk-man. But even as she swung the blade up, towering over the combatants, she saw that she had arrived too late. The dirk was already hilt-deep in Milo Morai's chest. No man ever survived a wound like that, so the extra impetus of revenge was with the blade which split the soldier's close-cropped skull. As the corpse rolled off Milo's body, the dirk was wrenched out and a flood of frothy blood gushed from the hole it had made. Mara shook her head sadly. For a barbarian, this man had been unusual, and something about him had attracted her. He could have made a few of the long years happier.

While she sat musing, Steeltooth trotted up and shouldered her mount away from Milo's body; now he stood nosing at the inert form. When she dismounted and attempted to approach the motionless body, still half-encased in the shattered cuirass, the big stallion raised his head and bared his sharp teeth, rolling his eyes and stamping a warning. Mara tried to reach the horse's mind, but reason had fled before the necessity of protecting his fallen master. She could discern little movement in Milo's chest, so there appeared to be no good reason for braving the killer-stallion's wrath. Retreating back to her own horse, she mounted and rode down the forest path.

5

And it is meet, the old should teach the young
of how the ax is heft, the saber's swung.
                        —From *The Couplets of the Law*

Most of the east-bound cavalry eventually made it to safety, but the west-bound unfortunates rode directly into Chief Bili

Esmith and his blood-hungry Kindred. A viciously fought, running battle swept back to lap around the western foot of the hill. Mara emerged into it and, before she was aware that a battle was in progress, she found herself engaged in a horseback saber duel with a big mercenary.

Her saber-skill matched her bow-mastery. Lacking the strength needed for a hacking attack, she had become a point-fighter—a skill entirely absent from the repertoires of many opponents she had faced—and, adroitly parrying, she soon saw an opening and spitted the cavalryman's hairy throat. As the man plunged off his horse, something crashed against the backplate of her cuirass and hurled her, too, down amid the stamping hoofs. While Mara struggled to rise, a horse thundered past and a blade rang on her helmet. She dropped back, her head filled with a star-shot red-blackness. At the edge of consciousness, she screamed as a horse stepped on her right hand; then, oblivion took her.

As the darkness cleared from her mind and she opened her eyes, she thought that she saw dead Milo's face swimming before her. Sure that she was hallucinating, she closed her lids again, softly moaning. Then a man's strong arm was around her shoulders, lifting and supporting them, and she felt the rim of a horncup on her lips and her nostrils registered the odor of the raw alcohol. She looked again. The hallucination was still there; then it spoke.

"Drink this, Mara. Do you hear me, woman? Drink it!" Not waiting for compliance, Milo forced open her jaws and poured a measure of the fiery liquid into her mouth. With a gasp she became fully conscious. Milo squatted on his heels beside her, smiling at her reaction to his "restorative."

Her eyes wide, she just stared for a long moment. "But ... but *you're dead!* I *saw* you slain! You ..."

Still smiling, Milo shook his head. "You *thought* you saw me killed, Mara, but the tip of the dirk only tore my shirt and scratched my side—not deeply at that—and. ..."

"No, no!" She shook her head violently. "It ... it went *into* you, to the hilt! There were airbubbles in the blood you bled! Your ... your shirt is still blood-wet. You *must* be dead!"

Instead of replying again, Milo shifted his position and opened his soggy, reddened shirt. While streaks of blood were drying on his smooth, sun-darkened skin, the wound from which they had come was all but closed. Mara's eyes looked upon it and a tingling, prickling chill coursed through her and she *knew*. Then, she *knew!*

But her carefully trained features did not reveal her knowledge. It was not the time or the place for that. Flexing the fingers of her right hand, she said, "It . . . it all happened so dreadfully fast, Master, that . . . And then that stroke I took on my helmet, too. I'm sorry. I had no intention of death-wishing you."

The full moon had all but set before the victorious nomads started their return to the tribe-camp. Tons of armor and weapons and clothing were lashed to the backs of the hundreds of captured horses, who traveled westward, having been reassured by mindspeak that if they were unhappy with the tribe, they would be quickly freed. They were eastern-bred horses and, having always considered themselves and been treated as beasts of burden, being spoken to as an equal by a two-leg was a fascinating novelty and imbued them with a happy, heady feeling of being where they belonged.

Her many travels had put Mara in occasional contact with Horseclans, but she had never before been in a camp of this size. Round about the sacked town, clustered in clan-groups, were well over a thousand wagon-lodges and tents. South of the encampment, watched over by adolescent cats, grazed many thousands of horses. To the north, the cattle and sheep—neither of which species had the intelligence to realize that the prairiecats would not harm them—were guarded by mounted striplings of the various clans, armed with bows and wolf-spears.

Between cattle and camp, half a hundred pubescent boys and girls took turns loosing arrows at a straw-packed mani-kin, under the one good eye of a white-haired but tough-looking old man. Older boys and girls, afoot and mounted, practiced with saber and ax and spear and javelin, learning or polishing their skills under the direction of old or maimed warriors.

In the camp itself, warriors and unmarried girls lazed in the sun, gaming and laughing and talking, caring for their gear or sharpening their weapons, ignoring both the incredible din of camp life and the swarms of flies. Naked children ran screaming among the tents while married women gossiped and slaves bustled about their chores. The arrival of the caravan excited but little notice; returning raiders were too common a sight among these people.

Uphill from the camp, they passed through the charred ruins of the outer town and entered the smashed and sagging gates of the inner town. The cats had deserted them in the camp, loping off to have two-leg friends remove their uncomfortable armor and fang-spurs. In the courtyard of the Citadel, Chief Bili entrusted the bootytrain to the care of one of his sub-chiefs, then he dismounted and needlessly stood at Steeltooth's head while Milo slipped from his kak—it was but a way of rendering homage to the tribe's War Chief. He started to precede his superior into the building, but halted when Milo did.

Mara was still mounted and Milo looked up at her. "Mara, you fought for the tribe and have earned your freedom. Come, I wish the chiefs to hear of your valor, so that the honors and booty you have won will be unquestioned among the clans." Raising his arms, he grasped her slim waist and lifted her down from her mount.

The Citadel complex, through which they threaded their way, had been begun shortly after the Great Quake had leveled what had remained of the ancient city (said to have been a temple of learning in the days when gods had walked the earth). Most of the present structure and the town walls had been fashioned of a lovely gray-green stone, cut from an ancient quarry miles away, and transported here to construct the westernmost outpost of the principality known to Ehleenee as Kehnooryos Ehlas and to most other eastern peoples as Vuhdjinyah. In ancient times, the town had been called Charlottesville; to the Ehleenee, it was Theesispolis; but to the nomads, it was simply the Place-of-Green-Walls.

Green-Walls had been a rich city, a city of commerce with trade routes from the mountains and beyond converging on it. Its garrison had consisted of a squadron of *kahtahfrahktoee* to ride the frontier and guard and police the road; three hundred spearmen to man the gates and the Citadel; three hundred more to perform the function of civil police. In addition, there was the six-hundred-man town levy—every male between the ages of sixteen and sixty had to provide his own equipage and weapons; the quality of the force ran the gamut from fair to worse than useless. When word reached them that an entire tribe of nomads were just the other side of the nearest range of mountains, every man was alerted and a dispatch was posted to the High Lord at Kehnooryos Atheenahs seventy miles southeast.

The High Lord was young and had ascended to power only five years before, but he knew what to do and, as he was already deep in debt, was pleased at the prospect. At irregular intervals over the course of the centuries that the Ehleenee had held this land, Horseclans—one or two at the time—had drifted across the mountains and into his domain. They had always been dealt with in the same way since they were an excellent source of horses, cattle and slaves—the fair-skinned, generally blond or red-haired girls and women and young boys bringing especially high prices from private citizen and brothel-keeper, alike.

High Lord Demetrios had been delighted, an entire tribe of them! Since all slaves were automatically the property of the High Lord, if captured by his troops, he quickly dispatched an army under command of his cousin, Manos, Lord of the West. (After all, being the nominal capital of the Western Lord's lands, Theesispolis *was* Manos' responsibility, though Demetrios privately doubted that the man had visited the primitive little place more than a dozen times in his entire life; and why should he when everything which made life worth the living lay in the city of the High Lord?)

So Lord Manos marched west at the head of some eight thousand men, and High Lord Demetrios sat back and waited for the thousands of slaves whose prices would lift all his financial burdens. "But I'll not glut the market," he thought. "I'll pen them here and only dribble them out a few at the time. That way, I should be able to have a new boy every day for a long, long while, break the little dears in for the brothel-keepers." Closing his bloodshot eyes, he sat back and began to fantasize, smacking his thick lips. Already his hairy hands seemed to be gripping the smooth-skinned body of an untried darling of a blond boy, who screamed and struggled, deliciously. . . . The High Lord shuddered in anticipation.

Lord Manos' army was light on cavalry, so when he marched past Theesispolis, he dragooned the entire *kahtafrahktoee* squadron. Thirty-two of the wealthier citizens, who could afford to maintain chariots and a full panoply, drove out to his column and requested they be allowed a place in his array and a consequent share in the sure rewards of his venture. As all were his theoretical equals—pure Ehleenee of noble lineage—he graciously consented (though he could not, for the life of him, understand why *any* civilized man would deliberately seek the all but unbearable discomfort of a war-camp without direct orders). So he marched on west. The Trade Gap was the only feasible route for the large wagons, so Manos camped his army at its eastern mouth and waited, appropriating the Gap-fort for his headquarters and residence and adding its small garrison to his army.

6

One valiant wolf will attack a guarded herd,
But, even in packs, jackals fear any save a hornless calf.
                                            —Horseclans Proverb

The commander of the Gap-fort was a mercenary with a bar-barian name—Hwil Kuk. Manos did not feel that the man was properly subservient and would not have him around the place, insisting he camp with his men. Kuk was a widower and his 12-year-old son shared his life. When first he laid eyes on the towheaded, blue-eyed boy, Manos lusted for him. He suggested to Kuk that he take the boy back with the army as his page, rear and educate him in the city of the High Lord, make a gentleman of him. Kuk understood; he had served some years in the capital and knew only too well of the unnatural passions of many of the Ehleenee, wealthy ones in particular. Kuk refused politely, saying he had promised the boy's dead mother that they would stay together.

Manos ordered the noncom from his presence and sulked and brooded for three days. On the morning of the fourth, Hwil Kuk—who knew the country and spoke Old Mehrikan fluently—was ordered to take half his command through the Gap. He was to enter the nomads' camp and attempt to esti-mate their numbers, telling the chiefs that their approach had alarmed the Ehleenee and that was why the army had been sent; but, if the tribe came in peace, they were more than welcome to come through the Gap, so long as they continued

north or south and did not tarry in Kehnooryos Ehlas. He
was to take along gifts for the chiefs and spend as much time
as was required to lull them into the trap Manos' men were
preparing.

The night of the fourth day, a detachment of Manos' bodyguard entered the main camp, seized Kuk's son, and bore
him back to the Gap-fort.

Kuk and his party were well received by the Council of
Chiefs, were honored and gifted and assured that, once
through the Gap, the tribe would be bearing south. It had
been prophesied that they would return to the Great Water
whence they had come, but it was unnecessary to proceed in
a straight line. Raids were one thing, but none of the chiefs
was especially keen to come up against an army nearly as
large as the entire tribe.

Feeling a bit like a Judas-goat—for he had truly liked his
hosts and had been made to feel truly at home with them—
Hwil Kuk led his men back into the Gap after two days.
Halfway through, he was met by his second-in-command and
the remainder of the Gap-fort garrison, who were mounted
on stolen horses. When the first, wild rage of his grief over
his son had spent itself, Kuk realized the sure consequences
of returning into the clutches of his son's murderer. He decided to seek again the nomad camp. Once there, he would
tell the chiefs the truth and, if allowed to do so, join with
them. He absolved his men of their oaths to him, bidding
them follow or not, as they wished. All forty followed. Their
pay was far in arrears and they owed the Ehleenee and the
High Lord no service as they were all mercenaries, indigenous to the mountains of the Middle Domain, Karaleenos.
While they served the Ehleenee for gold, they neither liked
nor respected them (for one thing, they felt dispossessed; the
rich piedmont having once belonged to *their* race). They all
respected Hwil Kuk and they had—to a man—loved little
Hwili, Kuk's shamefully murdered son.

Before the Council of Chiefs, Kuk bared his breast. He
freely confessed his duplicity in his earlier dealings with
them, carefully detailing the strengths of the Ehleenee host—
and its weaknesses, chief among which was its inexperienced,
hotheaded commander, the monster Manos. He told, too, of
the preparations for ambushing the tribe as soon as most of it
was through the Gap and massacring its warriors.

"Then," Kuk concluded, "it will be with you as it has been before with other Horseclans. After all the men are dead, your women will be raped to death or sold over the sea to brothels; your maidens will be enslaved as well, to receive the tainted seed of the devilish Ehleenee; and your young boys. . . ." He broke off sharply, tears streaming down his cheeks. Then, clenching his big fists and squaring his shoulders, he forced himself to continue. "Your dear little sons will be sold to brothels, too; but brothels of a different sort, where their immature bodies will sate the dark lusts of the unclean, unnatural beasts who call themselves Ehleenee. I speak of certain knowledge, honorable chieftains—my oath to Sun and Wind and Sword, on it. My own little boy—my Hwili—lies dead on the other side of the Gap, murdered by this same Lord Manos. When I would not give my son to his keeping— knowing him for what he is—he first sent me to lie to you, then had his men to seize the child."

Hwil Kuk hung his head and sunk teeth into lip; blood trickled down his stubbed chin. When he raised his head again, his eyes were screwed shut. His quavering voice was low but penetrating, and his facial muscles twitched with emotion.

"I have been told that my child's screams could be heard through all the camp. Then they suddenly ceased. The next morning, certain of my followers found Hwili's pitiful little corpse, flung onto the fort midden. They washed it and clothed it and . . . and buried it. *Things* had been done to my boy's body, terrible things. His . . . flesh had been torn, and my followers think that Lord Manos, uncaring after his hellish lusts were satisfied, allowed my Hwili to bleed to death."

Then Hwil Kuk's eyes opened and the fire of bloodlusting madness blazed from them. "Chieftains, if you would to the sea—your Great Water—you must fight long and hard. It is that or return to the plains, for, in all the Ehleenee lands, you will meet with the same. You owe me nothing, yet would I ask this of you: If it is your intent to fight, allow me and my followers to swing our swords beside you."

Henri, chief of Clan Kashul, was first to speak. "You claim that you lied before; perhaps you are lying now. What think you, War Chief?"

Knowing the Ehleenee, as he did, Milo believed the man, but only a dramatic vindication would please and convince

these chiefs. He arose and advanced to stand before Hwil
Kuk. He looked into the ex-mercenary's eyes; they met his
unwaveringly.

"Hwil Kuk," said Milo. "Will you submit to the Test of the
Cat?"

Kuk cleared his throat. "I will!" he replied in a firm voice.

Horsekiller, who, as Cat Chief, missed but few meetings of
the council, padded across the tent. On Milo's instructions,
Kuk knelt and placed his head in Horsekiller's widespread
jaws.

"You understand, Hwil Kuk, the cat has the power to read
your thoughts. If this you have said is truth, you have nothing to fear. If not, his jaws will slowly crush your skull." But
even as he spoke, he knew. Through Horsekiller, he too could
enter the grief-stricken man's mind, endure with the cat the
half-madness of Kuk's tortured thoughts. "Enough!" He
mindspoke to Horsekiller.

The big cat gently released his grip and licked Kuk's face
in sympathy. Losing one's kittens was never easy to bear.

Milo took Kuk's arm and raised him to his feet. "Kindred,
this man has spoken truth. He has suffered much and it is
right that he should shed the blood of those who helped to
bring about that suffering. When we fight the Ehleenee, as we
must, he and his men will ride with me. As I am clanless, so
too are they."

"How can we fight?" inquired Gil, Chief of Clan Marshul.
"This man has told us the Ehleenee lord leads between eighty
and ninety hundreds of soldiers. We are forty-two clans, but
our warriors number less than twenty-five hundreds. If we
were able to surprise them, we would have a chance, but having to fight them at the place of their choosing . . ."

"But we won't," replied Milo.

Throughout the course of the next month, Lord Manos was
harassed in every quarter. Demetrios' riders came almost every day with inquiries, commands and, as the month passed
the halfway point, thinly veiled threats. The Theesispolis
kahtahfrahktoee were grumbling; they wanted to get back to
their garrison with its wine shops and bordellos. The army's
mercenaries were grumbling, many of the units not having
been paid for four months. His officers were grumbling, anxious to return to the comforts and civilized delights of the
capital. The bulk of his army was heavy infantry—levied

from the areas lying east and south of the capital, and called out, equipped, and armed by the High Lord—and they were grumbling. Most were peasant farmers and harvest time was near; there was much to do. The barbarians just sat on the other side of the Gap. They grazed their herds on the thick luxuriant grass of the mountain valley, and it seemed as if they never intended to move on, into the fidgeting jaws of Manos' trap.

Manos had waited a week for Kuk to return, then had sent out a dozen cavalrymen under command of a minor noble of Theesispolis, one Herakles, to search and inquire his whereabouts. Lord Herakles possessed a working knowledge of Trade Mehrikan, and he and his men were well received by the nomads. He was informed that Kuk and his men had come, lived with the nomads a few days, and then—after having been joined by another party of equal size—had ridden away south, saying nothing to anyone. Herakles and his men saw but few adult warriors about the camp and, when they asked, were informed that most of the fighters had ridden north on a raid-in-force some three weeks before; there had been no word from the fifteen hundred or so men, but no one seemed alarmed, not really expecting them back for at least another moon. The camp and herds were watched over by old men and young boys—and the grace and beauty of these nomad boys sent the hot blood pounding in Lord Herakles' temples.

His report was pleasing to Lord Manos, who was relieved that the barbarian Kuk would not be back. Head over heels in debt, as were most of the libertine nobles of the capital, Manos had no money for a bloodprice and would have had to have executed Kuk on some contrived charge. Besides, it was not *his* fault anyway! Had the silly little swine not resisted so stubbornly, he'd not have been rent so seriously; he would not have been torn to such an extent that not even the physician and his cauteries could halt the bleeding. Manos did not blame himself. It was the will of the gods, and what was one barbarian boy, more or less. There would always be more of his kind; they tended to breed like rabbits.

During the time of waiting, he amused himself with a trio of peasant boys, kidnapped by his bodyguard which was experienced and skilled at such abductions. None of the three chunky-bodied lads had an iota of the beauty that had attracted him to darling Hwili, but there were compensations.

A mere touch of the whip put an end to their resistance, and once broken in, they proved enjoyable and not one of them had the effrontery to die.

But as the month wore on and Demetrios' messages became more vicious and the grumbling of mercenaries, spearmen and officers became louder, Manos' minions, with their dark hair and coarse features, began to bore him. Their never-ending whining and pleading for their parents, and their bodies' limp acceptance of his usage got on his nerves. He could think only of the wild, spirited, blond and red-haired beauties that Herakles had described in such glowing terms.

The last message Manos received from the High Lord left him shuddering. It described in sickening details what was to be done to him should he delay any longer in securing the slaves, animals and loot for which he and his huge, expensive army had been dispatched. When Manos regained his composure, he sent for Herakles.

That officer's news, upon his return from his second visit to the camp of the nomads, cheered Manos considerably. The warriors were still absent, and furthermore, most of the older men had gone into the western mountains to hunt, expecting to be away for at least three days. The nomads had been made to feel secure, and the rich, sprawling camp was all but defenseless.

That settled it in Manos' mind. At the next dawn, mercenary trumpets brayed and the drums of the Ehleenee rolled. Manos formed his army in the usual Ehleenee march column—*kahtahfrahktoee* in the van, then nobles and officers in their chariots, and then the massed spearmen on an eight-man front in the rear eating dust, their iron-soled sandals squishing the horse-droppings into the interstices of the logs which paved the steep Traderoad of the Gap. Manos took far more men than he felt he'd have need of, leaving a mere six hundred of his least effective spearmen and sixty cavalry to guard camp and fort from the thieving peasants of the area.

Nearly a thousand horsemen, seventy-three chariots, and close to seven thousand spearmen pantingly negotiated the eastern half of the winding Traderoad. The route was incredibly ancient—said to have been used by the creatures who trod these mountains *before* the gods. At noon, the column drew to a halt in a brushy but sparsely wooded area near the crest. Here and there, bits of weathered masonry poked through the sparse soil. One of the mercenary noncoms claimed that they stood atop the ruins of one of the Cities of the Gods. The site, he went on, was called Hwainzbroh by the indigenous peoples.

When the officers had completed their meal, the column again took to the road and started down the western face to the Gap. So cocksure was Manos of the invincibility of his army, that he had vetoed a mercenary leader's suggestion that outriders be posted at van, flanks and rear. It would have required more time to see to such unnecessary details, and Manos was in a hurry. Therefore, when the first fours of the Theesispolis *kahtahfrahktoee* rounded the last curve of a winding cut and came up against a high, road-filling rock slide, disaster set in. Because the officers could not signal with bugles or drums—for fear of causing more rock slides—by the time they got the snakelike column halted, fully nine-tenths of it were solidly jammed into the cut. At the site of the obstruction the troopers were so wedged together that not a single man could dismount, much less go about clearing the road. Screaming threats, shouting imprecations, promising horrible punishments, making vicious use of whips and sword-flats, Manos and the other Ehleenee officers began trying to force the mass of spearmen back; but their efforts were unavailing. The bulk of flesh and bone behind them stopped the infantry's withdrawal as surely as the bulk of rock and earth before had stopped the cavalry's advance.

7

Kindred, list' while I sing of the slaughter,
At the Gap-of-Burning-Men, ere we marched to the Water....
                              —From the Telling-harp of Blind Hari

With his head and face wrapped in bandages, Milo had received Lord Herakles on both visits, and had attended to his guests's accommodations and entertainment. The bandages supposedly covered the terrible injuries he had sustained in an

unexpected encounter with a gigantic Tree Cat. Not only did
the "injuries" explain why he was not in the north with the
tribe's warriors, but Milo felt that Manos' emissary would
probably be less attentive to facial expressions and the
thoughts which bred them when in conversation with a
"blind" man. This proved true, and—through Horsekiller,
who, despite repeated rebuffs, was constantly fawning over
the foppish Ehleen in order to maintain bodily contact, which
made mind-entering easier—Milo was able to glean much
useful information from Lord Herakles. Both he and the cat
had to force themselves to their work, however, for entering
the mind of the perverted man was as nauseating as a swim
in a cesspool.

After the departure of the Ehleen and his party, Milo rode
Steeltooth up the Traderoad. He took only Horsekiller with
him and was gone for three days. When he returned, he informed the chiefs that the Wind, which had guided them
eastward, had spoken to him on the mountain and had told
him how the horde of Ehleenee might be exterminated at but
little cost to His people. The Wind had further informed him
that He had blown His people here for a purpose: In regain-
ing their homeland by the Great Water, they were to free this
land from the evil sway of the Ehleenee who were an abomi-
nation in the sight of the gods. They were to purge the land
of these human monsters and fulfill the ancient prophecy by
rebuilding the paradisical city of their origin, Ehlai, on the
site to which He would guide them.

Milo drew Hwil Kuk aside and explained what he had in
mind, then he and Kuk rode north with a score of Kuk's followers. The pass to which Kuk guided Milo lay about fifteen
miles north of the Gap and Traderoad. Sometime in the dim
past, the path might have been paved, but today it was little
more than a game trail, partially blocked here and there by
old tree-covered rock slides, but Milo, Kuk, and the others
found it passable, and they came down about eleven miles
north of Lord Manos' camp. Milo was satisfied and, on his
return, set every able-bodied member of the tribe to work on
his plan.

After all the officers were hoarse from shouting, their arms
aching from vainly wielding their whips and swords and lance
butts, Manos disgustedly suggested that the spearmen be in-
structed to relay back the order to withdraw from the impass-

able pass. The embarrassed and exasperated officers jumped at the suggestion, and a score of dusty spearmen were given the command simultaneously. It soon sounded as if every one of the thousands of sweaty, iron-clad levymen was shouting over and over again, "Rock slide ahead. Move back. The Lord Manos commands to move back!"

Because of this highly dangerous noise, few were surprised to see rocks fall from the mountains; it was natural that rocks should fall from the frowning cliffs above the compact mass of the column. But then these rocks were followed by more and yet more rocks, and by pots of flaming oil and resin, and by blazing logs, and by sheet after deadly sheet of hissing arrows. What followed could not by any stretch of the term be called a battle—it was a slaughter, a butchery, pure and simple. In the press, few men were able to move their arms even to clutch at the wounds which killed them. They could but scream or croak and die, and even when dead, they could not fall. The din was indescribable, and none who heard it ever forgot the unbelievable sounds of men and horses as their flesh, covered with flaming oil or pitch, crisped and crackled; the shrieks of those men who, while not afire themselves, were suffering unguessable agonies as their bodies slowly roasted in white-hot armor. Some made frantic attempts to climb the smooth rock walls, only to fall back to a comparatively merciful death, impaled on the carpet of spearpoints below. Their cut-off screams but blended with the hellish a cappella and, above it all, crowing exultantly, skirled the warpipes of the Horseclans.

At the outset of the bombardment, those cavalrymen nearest the rock slide pulled themselves onto the barrier, climbed to the top, and dropped from sight. Seeing this, hundreds tried to follow, some dozens made it including a few of the Ehleenee officers—Lord Manos among them—by sliding and crawling and skipping over the packed mass of burning men, over blazing saddles and sizzling horseflesh, dodging the snapping teeth of pain-maddened horses, through the unceasing rain of death. Few of the fugitives bore any sort of weapon when they fell to the far side of the rockslide. Those who did were quickly relieved of them by a detachment of leather-armored women, who soon had all those men fortunate enough to escape the blazing carnage stripped of armor, wrist-bound, yoked in coffles of twenty head and jogging campward, spurred by judicious pricks of saber or wolf-spear.

Twenty mercenary cavalry commanded by a half-Ehleenee junior officer had brought up the rear of the long column of spearmen, acting as file-closers. They and the five or six hundred spearmen who had not been able to wedge into the pass had not known what to make of the confused shouting. But a trained ear is not necessary to fathom the unmistakable. It was not necessary to see the blazing, arrow-quilled men clawing their way out of the pass in order to know what was happening.

Apparently overlooking the fact that the road was impassable, Petros, a half-breed ensign, drew his sword and waved it. "Forward, men! The column's been attacked."

The horsemen didn't even look at him. Realizing that twenty men would not make a particle of difference to the eventual outcome even if they could force a way into the pass, and remembering that their pay was long overdue, they whirled their mounts and galloped back uphill. After a moment of indecision, Petros shrugged, sheathed his sword, and clattered after his command. Behind him—throwing away spears, shields, swords and helmets—raced the remaining few hundreds of the spearlevy. None of them felt that the service due the High Lord included or should include broiling to death for him.

By the time Petros managed to spur his foaming, staggering horse onto the plateau on which rested the site of the ancient city, the twenty mercenaries had already given their God Oaths and were walking their heated horses behind the five hundred hard-eyed, battle-ready Horseclansmen. Petros died well, everyone said so.

When the first fours of the *kahtahfrahktoee* set hoof to the Traderoad, Milo was informed of it by the cats who were scattered at even intervals all along the road leading to the army's encampment area. Then he and Kuk and Kuk's followers guided fifteen hundred nomad warriors over the pass they had scouted. While Manos sat among the ruins of Hwainzbroh, sipping warm wine and cursing everyone and everything in sight, maddened by the discomfort of dust and flies, Milo was pacing Steeltooth among the bodies and wreckage of the Ehleenee camp.

"My lord Milo. . . ." A horseman, one of Kuk's men, galloped up to him. "Lord Milo, please . . . Hwil requests you come to the fort . . . it . . . it's horrible. . . . He wants you should see it. . . ."

The three bloodstreaked little bodies hung by the ankles. Before leaving that morning, Manos had gouged out their eyes, raggedly emasculated them, and left them to bleed to death. Two of the little chests bore the wide mark of a saber thrust. Hwil Kuk's ashen face was tear-tracked, and there was precious little sanity in his eyes.

"I . . . I was searching . . . anything that had been little Hwili's . . . remember him by . . . heard something in here. Oh gods! Two of them were still alive . . . begged me to kill them. I . . . I . . ." His quivering hand fumbled at his sword-hilt. Abruptly, he began to claw at his face, and mouth wide open, the tortured man began to scream mindlessly.

Milo grasped Kuk's shoulder, spun him half-around, and slammed the side of one hard fist behind the screamer's ear. In mid-scream, the ex-mercenary slumped to the floor. Two of his men tenderly carried him out of the chamber of horrors.

Milo mindcalled and Horsekiller responded. Soon he was at the fort and, working together, he and Milo did what they could to ease the mind of Hwil Kuk, tormented almost beyond endurance. When they had finished, they carried him out to a resting place in one of the officer's tents. Awakening in that fort might have undone their therapy, too many memories, good and bad, lodged within its sooty walls.

On the morning of the sixth day after the massacre of the Ehleenee army, as the last wagons of the tribe were toiling up the western grade of the now-cleared Gap, Milo sat Steeltooth, watching the eight hundred-odd survivors of the spear-levy disappear in the distance, trudging the Traderoad toward Theesispolis. Milo had promised these men their freedom at the completion of the hard horrible labor he required of them: clearing the Gap of the debris—mineral, human, animal, and unidentifiable—which clogged it. He had more than kept his word, giving each of the peasants clothing, a knife, a scrip of food for the journey, a waterbag and either a silver coin or a handful of bronze ones, in addition to his freedom. In council, some of the chiefs had grumbled, but Milo had won them over. His reasons were many and sound. The peasants, who had contemplated death or a life of slavery, grasped eagerly at the promise of freedom. Considering the size of the undertaking, they performed the grisly, hideous work quickly and then went to work on the rock slide. Milo was amazed that they could do it at all, for after a couple of hot sunny days, few of the nomads could bear to ride within a mile of the carnal-reek. Aside from this easy method of disposing of the Gap's highly odiferous blockage was the fact that Milo could see and fear what the nomad chiefs, in the beginning at least, could not: the terrible dangers involved in marching so large a number of able-bodied male slaves through their native country. Also to be considered was the propaganda effect. The returning peasants would spread news of the army's disastrous defeat far and wide. Considering mankind's penchant for exaggeration, each of the tribe's hundreds of warriors would, in the telling, become thousands and untold thousands, each man would be eight feet tall, mounted on a Northorse, and cleaving a dozen men at a time with a six-foot saber. Lastly, if the tribe was to conquer and hold this land, they would need to win the confidence and support of the humbler Dirtmen. Cattle and horses could wax fat on grass alone, and the cats could do the same on meat, but men needed a more varied diet which called for farmers and these peasants *were* farmers. They would remember the generosity of the nomads—the clothing and food and money, especially the money. They would remember it and speak of it often and each time they or those they told were abused by the Ehleenee master, they would ponder the thought that some masters might prove less harsh than others.

8

The blood in the streets ran fetlock-deep.
And the flashing sabers did sweep and weep,
Red tears for the Kindred who in death did sleep,
Torn and maimed by the treacherous foe—
Dirtmen, without honor, who reap and who sow
And who fell beneath arrow and hard-swung blow.
                              —From *Revenge at Green-Walls*

The tribe had remained at the eastern outlet of the Gap only for one sleep. The next morning, the tribe—wood-thrifty from their years on the prairies—had laid all their dead on one pyre and, as the Wind bore the souls of their kindred back to His home, the wagons commenced to creak eastward, along the Traderoad to Theesispolis. A migrating tribe does not move fast. It took them five days to come under the walls of that unhappy city, already in dire straits.

It had been well before dark on the day they had been freed that most of the anxious-to-get-home peasants had poured through the outer city. Their richly embroidered accounts of the huge army's annihilation at the hands of the stupendous horde of grim (but just) nomads precipitated such a panic that many families of the outer town had fled east, so many that Simos, governor and commander of the city, had all the remaining citizens herded willy nilly within the walls and barred the gates behind them. Next, he drafted and dispatched a message to the High Lord. He informed the suzerain of the disaster which had befallen the army and gave the names of the only three noblemen to survive the massacre: Lord Manos, Theodoros of Petropolis, and Herakles of Theesispolis—all captives of the barbarians, if not by now slain (though he didn't say so, Simos sincerely hoped the barbarians *had* killed Herakles, slowly; he'd had no use for the arrogant young swine since he'd outbid him for a truly stunning young slave-boy two years before). He gave the facts as he knew them: The barbarian horde numbered in the neighborhood of forty thousand, at least twelve thousand of whom were warriors or maiden-archers, and was moving east along the Traderoad. He went on to point out that Lord Manos had ordered out the Theesispolis *kahtahfrahktoee*, and that squadron had fallen with the army—as too had above thirty Theesispolis aristocrats and their hundred or so retainers. He prayed the High Lord to send reinforcements for his tiny garrison as the levy was ill-trained, ill-armed and unreliable, and the four hundred dependable troops were far too few to adequately defend the Citadel, much less the walls of the city.

Demetrios' answer was prompt. He assured Simos that a relief army would soon be up to him—a patent lie, but Simos

had no way of knowing it—and that the city was to be held
at all costs, pending its arrival. He gently chided Simos' lack
of faith in his citizen-levy, pointing out that the levy had
been the strong spine of Ehleenee arms. With the Theesispolis
levy, beefed up by the civic guard and the remaining nobility,
he went on, he could not imagine so well-situated and forti-
fied a city falling to a band of mere barbarian marauders in
the short time it would require a field army to march from
the capital. He closed with an order. Since all that befell men
lay in the lap of the gods, in the final analysis, the Theesispolis city treasury was to be rushed to Kehnooryos Atheenahs,
along with the valuables of the temples, to be held in trust
until the crisis was ended and Theesispolis was safe again.
Such private citizens as wished were to be allowed to send
their own valuables along and Simos was to give them receipts
in return. Because the road might be unsafe, considering the
present emergency and the massing of troops, the treasure
should be well guarded; three hundred mercenaries should be
sufficient. He closed the letter with lavish promises of honors
and rewards upon the victory of their arms. The moment the
letter was sealed, Demetrios dismissed from his mind all
thought of the lost city and the walking dead men who commanded it and concentrated upon devising ways to raise
money to raise troops to secure his capital.

As soon as the tribe was encamped around the city, Milo
sent two nomads to escort Lord Herakles back to the city of
his birth. The Ehleenee nobleman was to deliver a message
from Milo to the governor; and the nomads, both chiefs'
sons, were to return with the answer. Milo's offer was quite
generous, all things being considered. All soldiers, nobility
and their families were to evacuate the city; where they went
was up to them. All slaves of Horseclan stock and all
weapons and armor must be left behind; all other possessions
were theirs, if they wished to and could transport them. Any
other citizens who wished to leave the city were welcome to
do so and the tribe guaranteed their safety as far as a day's
ride from the capital, as did it guarantee the safety and possessions of those who chose to remain in Theesispolis. As
proof of his and the tribe's good will, Herakles bore a bag
containing the family signets of the thirty-one Theesispolis
nobles slain with the army of Lord Manos. At Lord Herakles'
word, the city gates opened and the Ehleen trotted his horse
through them, followed by the two chiefs' sons, who sat their

horses proudly, fully aware of the gravity and honor of their mission, brave in their best lacquered armor.

Some hours later, one of the gates was gapped sufficiently for the two barefoot, near-nude nomads to be thrust through it, to make their way back to the tribe as best they could. The once-handsome men had been hideously mutilated; one of them had been left his tongue to deliver Lord Simos' reply.

Brought to the council tent, the suffering man relayed what he had been told. Lord Simos did not treat with barbarians. Were the tribe's leaders wise, they would pack their putrid tents, gather their wormy children and haste as fast as their bow legs or spavined horses would take them back to the mountains and swamps where they and all other animals belonged. The High Lord and all his forces were, Simos said, only a short day's march from Theesispolis and would make bloody hash of any barbarians in evidence upon their arrival. As for the city, it was heavily garrisoned and well supplied, and the nomads would attack it at their peril.

"But War Chief," said the senselessly savaged man, "the Ehleenee chief lies. The walls are thinly manned by ones who are not soldiers. Most have no armor and seem unused to the weapons they hold. Those who seized us and did these things to us were true soldiers, but there are very few of them. From what I saw when still I possessed eyes, it did not seem to me that there were more than six hundred fighters in all the city.

"And now, War Chief, we suffer greatly, Hermun and I. Please allow our chiefs to put an end to suffering."

At Milo's nod, the fathers of the two stepped forward, drew sabers and with tears of grief and rage on their cheeks, heart-thrust their agonized sons.

And so the blood-mad tribesmen swept against the city. They burst open the gates and their axes and sabers slashed a bloody course through the screaming mobs of helpless noncombatants. The levymen died under or ran from the arrow-rain which fell upon the walls, so those who scaled them were unopposed. Horseclansmen did not normally slay strong or pretty women or young children, but Theesispolis was a sanguinary exception! On their ride out of the camp, all the nomads had been led past the biers on which rested the bloody, mangled, incomplete remains of the tribe's heralds. Once within the walls, they showed no mercy, regardless of age, sex or station.

While the bulk of the nomads butchered the bulk of the

population, Milo rode with his eight score mercenaries—a total of one hundred twenty troopers who had survived the massacre at the Gap. Having no love for the Ehleenee and an understandable aversion to slavery as well as a yearning for loot
and/or hard money after months of being paid in Ehleenee
promises, they had signed on with Milo and were now being
commanded by Hwil Kuk. With Horsekiller and a score or so
of his clan, they all rode toward the Citadel, to which had
fled most of the nobility and the fleetest "fighters." Atop the
flat roof of the central portion, Lord Simos, Lord Herakles
and four other officers shrieked a sextet series of orders and
counter-orders at soldiers who were straining and fumbling at
something.

Even as Milo turned to inquire, one of Kuk's squadron, a
former noncom of Theesispolis *kahtahfrahktoee,* muttered,
"*Dung!* Greedy and cruel, Lord Simos certainly is, but not
stupid; he should know better than *that.* Those catapults were
useless fifty years ago! All they are now is wormy wood and
rotted ropes and rusted iron, covered with gilt paint. In the
condition those fornicating abortions are in, even if they put
fresh ropes on them and get them to working, they'll be more
dangerous to the crews than they'll be to any fornicating
thing they are aimed at!"

A moment later the man's words were vindicated, as one
of the war-engine's half-wound ropes snapped and the gilded
iron basket's edge virtually decapitated one unfortunate soldier who happened to be leaning over it. As for the other, it
was wound, loaded with a sixty-pound stone, aimed at the
largest visible group of nomads and fired. The arm shot up to
slam into gilt-flakes and splinters and dust against its stop-
timbers; the stone-laden basket never budged! The half-hys-
terical officers were screaming invective at the hapless soldiers
when, preceded by a trio of huge blood-dripping cats, Hwil
Kuk and half his squadron poured up the stairs.

But that had been over five weeks before and, aside from
the empty and frequently charred houses or the all but
deserted streets, the city through which Mara had ridden had
given little indication of the bloodbath which had attended
the end of its Ehleenee phase. The Citadel showed none, as
little fighting had taken place there. The soldiers of the civic
guard, offered a choice between pain and death or freedom
and honorable employment—the promisers being men known

to them, fellow mercenaries—had surrendered almost to a man and they now served with Hwil Kuk's squadron. The only significant fight had taken place in the wing housing the households of the Ehleenee nobility. There, driven to the wall, the hastily armed Ehleenee men and boys belied their effete appearance by fighting with the reckless courage which had earned their ancestors this land centuries before. Though they all died well, die they certainly did, under the businesslike cuts and thrusts of their own former mercenaries. The noble ladies of the ruling race—young, pretty ones, at least—were the only survivors of the taking of Theesispolis (as well as several hundred former slaves who emerged from hiding after the blood-lusting madness had abated and now constituted the first citizens and only full-time occupants of the city). Old or ugly or very young Ehleenee were stripped of their valuables and, along with half a hundred disarmed levymen, hurled out of the Citadel to the tender mercies of the berserk nomads. The mercenaries took full enjoyment of their captives for a week or so, then got good prices for them from the cooled-down nomads.

Keenly aware of how the father of the two dead young nomads must feel, Hwil Kuk saw to it that Lord Simos and the treacherous Herakles were taken alive. At Milo's order, Kuk personally delivered them to the clans of their victims. The chiefs and kinsmen received the two Ehleenee gravely, thanked Kuk graciously, then gave the nobles to the young men's mothers and wives and kinswomen. It was four days before Lord Simos, no longer capable of screaming, croaked his last; the younger and stronger Herakles lived an amazing day and a half longer!

9

In level circle, shall sit the Chiefs,
None the highest, none the least,
For all are equal, Kindred one,
And thus it shall be, till time is done.
        —From The Couplets of the Law

Before the assembled chiefs, in the spacious, lofty chamber
which had been the Citadel's reception and banquet hall,
Milo and Bili recounted the events and tremendous profits of
the village raid and the subsequent battle. They detailed the
names and clans of men killed or maimed so that blood-price
or suffering-price might be properly allotted prior to the
equal division of the spoils among all the clans. Toward the
end of the barrage of comments and questions which marked
the conclusion of the reports of the war chief and Chief Bili,
old Chief Djeri Hahfmun addressed Milo.

"Most-successful-of-all-war-chiefs-in-the-memory-of-all-the
clans-of-men, I will give two hundred cows, two bulls and a
jeweled Ehleenee sword for your slave, yonder."

Milo grasped Mara's arm and drew her forward and told
of the girl's bravery in her first attempt on him, attacking an
armed and armored and mounted man, and her with only a
dagger. The chiefs nodded and muttered approval; they could
understand and appreciate that kind of courage. Then he told
how she, a slave-prisoner, had risked death or injury to ride
back and fight for the tribe, emphasizing her matchless skill
with bow and saber on the hilltop. And the chiefs wondered
aloud if she might not be of Horseclan stock. Then he rendered a vivid account of how she had saved his life, cleaving
a mercenary from crown to chin. And he heard the first of
the comments he had been waiting for.

"If she is not a woman of the Horseclans," announced
Chuk, Chief of Djahnsun, "she *should* be. I say free her!"

But one was not enough, so Milo told of how—armed and
well mounted and with an excellent chance to escape—she
had galloped to add the weight of her sword to Clan Esmith's
hard-fought battle against thrice their numbers of *kahtahfrahktoee*, and had come close to losing her life in that
undertaking.

"Kindred," Milo addressed them. "It is the law that a slave
may not be freed but with approval of all men of the clan.
As it is also the law that the war chief is clanless, but the
kinsman of all the tribe, I must have the approval of you all
to grant this brave woman the freedom she has earned with

courage and with the giving and taking of hard blows for the good of the tribe. What say you, my Kindred?"

"Free her!" All around the circle of chiefs it was the same.

Milo dropped to one knee before Mara—she still clad in the Kahrtr-crested cuirass and baldric, from which hung the well-used saber—and, taking her foot upon his other knee, he slowly removed the silver ring from her trim ankle.

He arose and looked down into her eyes. "You are free, Mara."

Djeri, Chief of Hahfmun, rose from his place and, hitching his gaudy new Ehleenee sword around to make for easier walking, strode smiling to the center of the chamber.

"I for one, Kindred, am glad the woman is a free woman. A man who owned a concubine of such courage and weapons-skill might wake up with a foot of steel in his gullet!" He chuckled good-naturedly. "Djeri of Hahfmun doesn't fancy an end like that, thank you. Since the chit is clanless, I must leave it to the rest of you to set the bride-price. Set it not too low; such a woman has immense value. By my steel, can you imagine the strength and spirit of the colts she'll throw to the honor of Clan Hahfmun?"

Suddenly, Bili of Esmith leaped between Mara and the older chieftain.

"Hold on, kinsman! I have prior claim and besides, you already have three wives. I have only two!"

"Prior claim?" yelped the older chief. "Why I spoke for her before she was freed!"

"Yes, you old goat," affirmed Bili, "prior claim! She has shed blood for the honor of my clan on the field of battle."

"*Goat*, am I?" snarled Chief Djeri, clapping hand to hilt. "You rapist of ewes, gotten by a boar-hog on a dimwitted Dirtwoman slave, if you continue to contest my just claim, *you* will be shedding *your* blood—every worthless drop of the stuff—here on these stones!"

The tempers of Horseclansmen were ever quick, but before either Djeri or Bili could free his blade, Chief Sami of Kahrtuh placed himself between them. To Chief Djeri, he exclaimed, "Sun and Wind and Sword have claim above any other, cannot you see that They have chosen? Look at the crest on her baldric, the style of her armor, the pommel of her saber—all Kahrtuh. Besides, she's a youngish woman and fair, what good would two old jackasses like you do her?

She'll be married to my third son, who will be chief after me."

As one, the weapons of the two original contestants cleared scabbards. Bili aimed a wicked diagonal slash at Sami, who leaped back fumbling for his own hilt, and the heavy blade struck sparks from the polished floor, the well-tempered steel ringing like a bell. Bili's recovery was lightning-quick, but his vicious upthrust was struck aside by Chief Djeri's blade.

"How *dare* you try to kill Chief Sami!" the Hahfmun roared. "I have prior claim to his blood! He was looking at *me* when he spoke his blasphemous lies. Of course, perhaps he meant nought by it; to a Kahrtuh, lying is inborn."

No man, unfamiliar with the life-long fighting-trim of the Horseclansmen, would have believed that men of the ages of Chiefs Sami and Djeri could have moved so fast. Sami's yard of keen steel lashed horizontally from left to right—the classic backhand decapitation stroke—hissing bare millimeters above Djeri's shaven poll and then looping down and across to counter his opponent's disemboweling attempt with such force that both blades were slammed up against the breastplate of Bili's cuirass.

"Enough, children! Enough!" Milo's voice, pitched to battle volume, preceded him as he sprang from the dais. "The tribe is not in sufficient danger, does not have more than enough fighting before it, but that three supposedly wise chieftains . . . pardon, 'brawling brats' . . . must precipitate a three-way blood-feud between clans?"

"But . . ." chorused the three chiefs.

Blind Hari set down his telling-harp, rose from his place, and slowly made his way toward the sounds of rasping breath. He was the oldest tribesman—some said as much as one and one-half hundreds of years had passed since his birth into a clan of which he was the last living member, and the most respected. Genealogist, chronicler, sage and bard he was, and the closest thing to a priest the tribe had. In his day, he had been a mighty warrior, as his scars attested. When Blind Hari spoke—an infrequent occurrence—all men humbly attended him. He spoke now, his old voice firm and grave.

"The war chief is right, my sons, there can be no argument. The Sword's curse lies on men who use Him to draw the blood of Kindred, unasked. My dear sons—Djeri Hahfmun, Sami Kahrtuh, Bili Esmith—each of you is well proven a brave and honorable man, otherwise you would not be chiefs, your birth notwithstanding. This is Law, all know, it needs not retelling. There cannot be cause for any of you to establish your bravery upon the flesh and bone of your Kindred or to wash out thoughtless insults in blood. You have shown all the people the bravery and honor of chieftains-born, now show the equally necessary wisdom and greatness of heart. Let each recall his words and show his love for his Kindred."

The transition was abrupt. Tears appeared on Djeri's scarred and weathered cheeks. He sheathed his sword and opened his arms, extending a hand to each of the other two men. Within seconds, all steel was cased and the three late-combatants were hand-locked, sobbing tearful apologies and renewing vows of brotherhood as they went back to their places in the council circle. All the chiefs were moved; there were few dry eyes among them.

Milo shook his head. The very real powers of this old man had been amazing him for years.

With eerie precision, Blind Hari turned and "gazed" directly into Mara's eyes. To Milo he said, "Go to your accustomed place, War Chief."

Milo did so, shivering despite himself at the force of Blind Hari's will.

Sightless eyes still locked on Mara, the ancient extended one withered hand. "Come here, my child," he commanded gently.

When she stood before him, Blind Hari placed a hand on each side of her face and tilting it, pressed his dry lips to her smooth brow. He was seen to start once, but he held the kiss for a moment longer, then turned back toward the chieftains.

"My sons, it is the Law that a woman of the tribe be not unmarried by her twentieth year and this is right and proper. It is man who chooses her who he will marry; but, though this practice bears the patina of years, it is not Law, it is custom and not truly binding. Right often, in the times of your grandfathers—as I rode from clan to clan—have I seen woman choose man and it is done today. Though her wiles leave him convinced that it was he who chose." He showed his worn teeth in a smile.

"We camp in a hostile land, confronted by evil enemies, my sons. This is not the time for dissension between clans or

tribe-kindred. We have seen dissension and near-bloodshed
bred by adherence to custom. There must not be more.

"Before the council is ended, this woman will choose he
who is to be her husband. In order that she may choose
wisely, each man here shall rise as I call his name. He shall
tell her the number of fighters in his clan and the amount of
the clan's wealth. If he wants her for himself, he shall tell her
the numbers of his wives and concubines and what her place
would be in his tent. If he wants her for a son, he shall tell
her of *all* his marriageable sons and the numbers of wives
and concubines of each. Before he returns to his place, each
man will, before us all, swear his Sword Oath that he and all
his clan will abide by the choice of this woman. When the
times comes, I will set her bride-price, and—never fear, Djeri
Hahfmun—it will be high!"

Blind Hari commenced with the chief at Milo's immediate
right, Fil, Chief of Djordun. When the red-mustachioed chief
had named his assets and sworn and sat down, the man at his
right began and, by the time they had worked around the
circle and Milo too had sworn and resumed his seat, the
Sacred Sun was westering.

Blind Hari kept to his seat, fingering the turning-keys of
his telling-harp, and an odd smile flitted before he spoke.

"Mara of Pohtohmas, how say you? Which of the offered
men will you have? By what clan-name would you be
known?"

"Morai, Wise One. I would be Mara of Morai, wife to
Milo of that name."

10

And, in His time, the God shall come again
From the south, upon a horse of gold
And greet the Kindred, camped upon the plain
Or, so the sacred ancestors were told.
            —From The Prophecy of the Return

Milo snapped into wakefulness, a dagger-point was pricking the flesh, just below the right corner of his jaw. Though Mara was weeping, her dagger-hand was rock-steady.

"Forgive me, Milo, but I *must* know!" she whispered, then pushed the sharp, needle-tipped weapon two inches into his throat and slashed downward.

As his blood gushed from the severed carotid, Milo rolled and lunged, his hands grasping at her slim nude body. But fast as he was, she eluded him, leaping up and back. She just stood there, her eyes locked on the gaping wound she had inflicted.

"*Why*, Mara?"

"Poor Milo," she replied. "Death will come quickly and there will be no more pain if I was wrong, but I don't think that I . . . ahhh!"

The initial gush of blood had rapidly dwindled to a slow trickle and her sigh announced its total cessation as what should have been a death-wound began to close. Milo's eyes, too, closed, and he clenched his teeth, saying between them, "I should have slain you, Mara. You guessed, didn't you, back there, below that hill? Well, now you know! What intend you to do with that knowledge, the knowledge that Milo, the war chief, bears what your people call the Curse of the Undying?"

She did not answer, but he felt her weight return to the Ehleenee bed, and he opened his eyes just as she lowered her face on his and pasted her dark red lips onto his half-open mouth. Both their faces then became shrouded from the world in the blue-black luxuriance of her musk-scented hair.

When she at last raised herself, she was weeping again, but now there was joy in her sloe-black eyes and a whole plethora of inexpressible emotions played over her lovely features as she began to speak.

"What do I want? Why, dear dear Milo, all that I want is you. I wanted you, simply as a man, before I was aware you might be aught else. It has been so very long and I have been so terribly lonely, but . . . you too know of that kind of loneliness, don't you? Now, we are together and we shall never know of that loneliness again, my love."

Milo bolted erect, his every nerve tingling. *"Mara,* you mean . . . you, too . . . ?"

The smile never left her lips or her eyes as, again picking up the bloody dagger, she placed that point which had so recently drunk of Milo's blood in the crook of her left arm. She thrust, slowly; thrust so deeply that steel grated against slender bone and the thick, red richness of her life fluid gushed high, upon the already bloody blade.

Milo jerked a wadded sheet to him and reached for her, but she drew back, still smiling. "Oh no, my Milo. Wait and watch. There is no danger."

Her bloodflow ceased as quickly as had his and, within a half-hour, both their wounds had become only pinkish-red scars.

Blind Hari smiled to himself, humming a snatch of a bard song, as he fitted a new string to his telling-harp. The tribe should succeed to all the prophecies, now—if prophecies, they truly were—with *two* "gods" guiding and directing them.

"And our Holy City, reborn shall be," he sang softly, "Ehlai, washed by Wind, beside the Sun-lit sea."

"Of course," he muttered to himself as he tightened the new string, "Ehlai, if it was ever aught than a paradisical dream, lies far and far from this place; beyond another range of mountains, higher mountains, with snow forever on them. God Milo has convinced all the others that the key word in the 'Bard Song of Prophecy' is wrong, became twisted over the years, but Blind Hari knows better. The march toward the *true* Ehlai should be the path of the *setting,* not the *rising* Sun; but, why should old Hari say aught to gainsay God Milo, for he means the clans no ill. To him, we all—even I, who have seen the coming and going of seven score and seven winters—are yet but his children and he loves us well. He, it was, who succored our ancestors, gave to them the knowledge and skills necessary to sustain life, taught them partnership with cat and horse and instilled in them, those who came after, respect and regard for Brotherhood and Honor and Law.

"And, compared to him . . . and now, her, we are as children. One direction is as another to the tribe, so long as there be rich graze for the herds and good hunting for the cats and fighting and loot for the Kindred; while he has a purpose which none could fault, he seeks his own kind, fellow Gods, of his sacred clan. This is meet, even Gods should sometimes visit with their own, share the cooking fire of their dear Kindred."

Suddenly, a great and agonizing loneliness pervaded the being of the old, old man. He closed his unseeing eyes and sat back, reliving the happy and joyous days of his youth and young manhood—before he lost his sight, found compensatory "powers" and became a bard—riding and hunting and wenching with his clan-brothers.

"It is said," he mused to himself, "that Clan Krooguh came east, along with Clan Buhkuh and a part of the Cat Clan . . . perhaps, somewhere on this land . . . ?"

A thought was beamed into his mind. "Not so, wise Cat-brother. All that this land holds of them is their scattered bones."

"I know not your mind," Hari mindspoke in reply. "How is my brother-cat called?"

"You may call me Old-Cat, Cat-brother. For one of my race, I am nearly as old as are you for yours, and it is meet that the name of my prime—given and borne in honor—should be as dead as my Kindred and yours, for he of that name fled in dishonor, when the treacherous Blackhairs tricked and slew or enslaved all with whom he crossed the mountains. The pelts of his brothers and sisters, of his females and his kittens, adorn the stone tents of the Blackhairs and, if he had been of honor, his would hang among them."

"Not so, Old-Cat," retorted the bard. "Needless death is not necessarily honorable death. If one does not live, how will the dead be avenged, to whom will their killers pay the blood-price?"

"But, he who fled was Cat Chief, wise Cat-brother. He should have died with his clan."

Old Hari sighed. "To allow pursuit of honor to lead one to a certain death, which does not benefit the clan, is the act of a fool, Old-Cat. The clan which has a fool as chief has no chief at all!"

The cat licked at the snow white fur of his muzzle. "Wise Cat-brother, you mindspeak words of comfort to one long years in need of such. If I can but live a bit longer, long enough to wreak vengeance upon the murderers of my kin and yours. . . ."

Hari placed his harp on the floor at his feet and extended a hand. "Come, Old-Cat, let our bodies touch and mayhap I can tell something of what is to come for you."

The cat advanced toward the proffered hand, awed reverence in his mind. "You are older than I'd thought. I know you now, Kin of Power. You are Blind Hari of Krooguh. I'd thought you long years in the Home of Wind, yet still you live. Are you then an Undying God?"

Hari touched the shaggy head, then placed his palms on either side of it. "No, Old-Cat, I am but a man, though an exceedingly old one. By men who have not the Power, the Undying God is called Milo Morai, he is our . . ."

"War chief." The cat finished the thought. "Yes, I fought beside him and your Cat Clan yesterday. We slew many Blackhairs, he and I and the Blackhair-female-who-mind-speaks."

Hari nodded. "She, too, is of the Race of the Undying Gods; and now She is mated to our God. Nought but good for all the clans can come of such a union."

Raising the old cat's head and bending to it, Hari placed his lips just above its eyes. After a long long moment, he sat back and stroked Old-Cat's grizzled neck.

"Never fear, Brother-cat, you will live to revenge your murdered clan. More, you will beget kittens and, when they are as old as you, still will they be filled with pride that their sire—a Cat Chief, of fame and honored memory—bore the name of Dirktooth."

Though barely eleven years, Aldora Ahpoolios' little olive-skinned body was as well developed as that of any Horseclan girl half again her age, and this had saved her life on that terrible day Theesispolis had fallen. Huddled with the other women and girls and boys in the south wing of the Citadel, she had watched in horror as the methodical mercenaries coldly cut down her father—grown so stout that he'd been unable to buckle his hauberk properly—and her uncle and both her brothers. Then rough hands had torn her, screaming, from Aunt Salena—her dead mother's older sister—and she had become the property of Djoh-Sahl, he of the brown beard and the rotten teeth who, when she had told him her age, had wept drunken tears and humbly apologized for having deflowered her; then had traded her for an older woman to a trio of less discriminating soldiers. Aldora could not call to mind one of the men's names; as for their faces and bodies, they all ran together into a one who had brought only a dayless, nightless time of constant pain, shame and terror. When, at the end of the week, she was dragged to the slave mart, stripped and placed for sale, the girl had been certain that the worst must now be over, but she had been wrong.

Her nomad purchaser—Hwahlis Linszee, a natural brother of the chief of Linszee—was not a cruel man, and he treated Aldora as he treated his other two concubines—possibly even a little better, for she was new and novel and as dark as the others were fair. Hwahlis had chosen his wives well and the two women saw to it that the work was equally divided amongst Aldora and the two older bondswomen, one of whom was a girl called Neekohl. Of brown-red hair and blue eyes, she spoke the Trade language with an odd accent and sang strange songs in an unknown tongue and had been taken on a raid in the distant north. The other was a more recent captive, a blond, mountain barbarian named Bertee. Among three, the work was neither long nor hard. Though the food was strange to Aldora, it was plentiful; all shared the contents of a common pot, morning and evening, and if one hungered at other times, milk or curds or jerked meat was always available. The clothing too was strange and rough, but practical and serviceable—a loose shirt which pulled over the head and tucked into a pair of equally loose trousers, tightened by a drawstring, and a pair of ankle-length boots. Aside from the iron cuff on her leg, her alien hair and skin were all that indicated her not to be of the Horseclans.

As Hwahlis took good care of his possessions, he expected good service of them. Still in his prime and lusty, he waited but precious few hours to begin making use of his latest possession—long and strenuous and frequent use. She cried, but that was to be expected, captive females always cried the first few times they were used. Also, the chit seemed to be trying to tell him something, but he spoke no Ehleeneekos and her command of Trade language was almost non-existent, so he ignored her; when she learned Mehrikan, she'd tell him whatever it was. Despite his fascination, Hwahlis lived by clan customs and had never been accused of tight-fistedness. He willingly shared his latest acquisition with his two oldest sons, his brothers, nephews and cousins. None could say he had been denied the sampling of Hwahlis' new Ehleenee girl!

Aldora tried once to kill herself; but apparently she failed to cut her wrist deeply enough, for the blood soon ceased to flow, and she couldn't bring herself to try again. Then, with the onset of her time of the moon, she gained a brief respite.

Several hours after Old-Cat left Hari Krooguh, he lay hidden in tall grass, some hundred yards from the outer-most tents of the encampment. Tired of playing with kittens and cubs not his own, he had loped to this spot to snooze. Beyond, at the foot of a hillock, a small brook chuckled over worn stones between mossy banks; and, under the near bank, he sensed life as he awoke. Hoping to perhaps cozen some unwary wild creature within reach of tooth or claw, he opened his mind.

The unexpected shock caused him to sit up sharply. An inchoate mass of thought-messages smote his receptive senses—a compound of sorrow, fear, shame and helpless resignation; of hopeless terror and abysmal loneliness. These would have been terrible enough for an adult mind, but Old-Cat realized that the sufferer's mind was that of a cub, a female, two-leg cub.

11

Worship Wind and Sun and you need no priests;
And heed well the Law or become as beasts.
　　　　　　　—From *The Couplets of the Law*

Aldora had come to the stream to wash the pouch which one of her master's wives had given her the week before and to change its stuffing of the dry moss that had received her body's discharges. But today, she had found it unnecessary, yesterday's moss being still almost fresh. She knew what that meant, had indeed been dreading it and terror consumed her. Sobbing, death-wishing herself, she was stretched, trembling on the cool moss, when first she heard the firm and gentle voice. At first, it seemed to come from everywhere and nowhere and something about it was as wonderfully soothing as had been her old slave-nurse's, when, as a much younger child, she had awakened from a bad dream. No reassurance was needed; Aldora knew that the strange speaker meant her no harm.

"Why do you fear and mourn, little kitten?"

Aldora raised her tear-streaked face and answered aloud in halting Mehrikan. "You are who? You are where?"

She could sense the tender smile. "No, little female, mouth-speak is wasteful of Wind and only necessary with your two-leg kindred. Open your thoughts to me, my dear."

"M . . . m . . . my thoughts?" stuttered Aldora. "I . . . please, Master . . . how? . . . don't know."

"It will be easier if I touch your head. Wait there; I will come down to you."

Old-Cat heaved himself up and paced to the edge of the narrow valley. As he started down the shady bank in her direction, the girl didn't scream, she simply fainted.

When Aldora awakened, the sun was westering and Old-Cat was licking her face with a tongue wide enough to cover it. But she no longer feared him or any cat, and wondered why ever she had. She no longer feared anyone, in fact. Here, close to Old-Cat, was safety and comfort and . . . and peace.

Then, suddenly, she was *not* safe. The comfort was shattered, the peace fled. The Linszee men would come for her again tonight, and . . . and . . . Aldora whimpered.

The voice called yet another time. "Aaallldorraaa!" It was Beti, Hwahlis Linszee's second wife, and she sounded almost to the top of the bank.

"Aalldorraa, are you down there, girl?"

In weary resignation, Aldora opened her mouth to answer, only to have one of Old-Cat's big paws placed over it.

The cat's thought beamed out, menacing as a drawn bow. "I, Old-Cat, am down here with a female, meddlesome two-leg! Just because your shameless kind have no regard for the privacy of others, will not save your haunches from my teeth. You proceed at your own peril!"

Beti's high soprano laughter pealed out. Then, with obvious amusement, she mindspoke. "Old-Cat, indeed! *That's* an alias, if I ever heard one. Enjoy yourselves, the tribe needs the kittens. Nevertheless, if either of you see a Blackhair slave-girl, chase her back to Clan Linszee. Mind you though, don't hurt her. I don't think she has run away. She's a good girl and probably just asleep somewhere." Hoofs thud-thudded as her mount cantered back toward the camp.

Milo and Mara sat at what had been Lord Simos' council table. Across from them sat Blind Hari, flanked by Old-Cat and Horsekiller. As all were capable of mindspeak, only the rasp of their breathing broke the stillness.

"How long have you known of me?" inquired Milo, still somewhat stunned at Hari's revelation.

The old man smiled. "Almost from the day of your return, God Milo. Though *I* could not see you, others could and I could use their eyes. My father was a young man when you left us, and you were just as he described you to me. Eighteen years agone, God Milo, I tried to read you, then I *knew!* I could but barely see the beginning of your life—lying, as it does, so many hundreds of years in the past—and I could not even sense an end. Who could have such a mind, save a god?"

"Then, you've known for nearly twenty years, Bard Hari. Why have you not spoken before this time? Why wait until now?"

Blind Hari settled himself against the backrest of his chair, regarding Milo's face through Horsekiller's eyes. "Though you, unlike mere men, God Milo, can shield off portions of your mind, I sensed that you knew or suspected my knowledge, yet you said nothing. I am a very old man, God Milo—nearly one and one-half hundreds of winters—and age has vouchsafed me two things: patience and wisdom. How much greater than mine must be the wisdom of one who has lived four times my age and more, who knew birth at a time when all men were as gods? Though but a man, yet could I perceive that—when the time was as it must be—either the God would tell the man or the man would tell the God. That time is now, God Milo."

"And you, Cat-brother?" Milo questioned Horsekiller.

"I have known since kittenhood that your mind was not as other men's, God Milo."

Milo had had more than enough. He slammed one fist upon the tabletop and both cats blinked. "That's sufficient subservience. I'm no Ehleenee, dammit! If you must give me a title, let it be war chief or cat-friend or, better yet, none at all."

"The God speaks, His servants obey," replied Blind Hari

aloud. He was broadly smiling and a hint of gentle sarcasm tinged his over-humble voice.

Mara had been watching and listening, and now her laughter trilled. "You speak with all the conviction of an Ehleenee priest, 'Father' Hari. But you must have a very good reason for disclosing your knowledge at this time. What urgency has impelled you, Man of Powers?"

". . . and so, keeping under the cover of the creek bank, I brought her here, to my cat-brother, Bard Hari."

After Old-Cat had recounted his portion of the table, Milo shrugged. "I lived among the Northern Ehleenee for some years. While mindspeak is rare among their race, it is not unheard of. Over the course of years and centuries, races tend to mingle. I suspect that many who think of themselves as pure embody more than a trace of the blood of the fair races.

"As for the fact that the girl dislikes her lot. . . ." He shrugged again. "Few slaves do, not in the beginning. And you have probably earned her a beating, Old-Cat, by keeping her this long from her owner's clan-camp."

Old-Cat bared his teeth and gave vent to a hair-raising snarl of unadulterated menace.

"The cub has suffered enough! Much more suffering and her thought-mind will depart her little body. She has neither the maturity nor the training to control or prevent such. By my fangs and claws, the two-leg who seeks to hurt her more shall be found intestineless! Beware, Old-Cat makes not false threats!"

"If such is your feeling," replied Milo, "the answer is simple: buy her. I am sure that your personal shares from the Black-Horse battle would be more than enough to pay a fair price for her, and if they are not, borrow from your clan; Chief Horsekiller is both generous and understanding."

"That has been attempted, Friend Milo," interjected Horsekiller. "Clan Linszee refuses to sell her. Chief Rik and his brother, Hwahlis, became quite angry when my emissary, Black-Claw, would not tell him where she was."

Milo grimaced. "*That,* I don't doubt, Cat Chief! Men like not to lose a new and but half-tried female."

Mara turned on him bristling. "Sometimes, you are disgusting, my husband, and I can but wonder that I chose to marry you!"

Hari beamed his thought at her. "It is meet that you

should defend the poor slave, Lady Goddess, for, though she has yet to see her twelfth year . . ."

"What?" Milo shouted aloud. "Has Clan Linszee, then, ceased to honor the Law? Slave girl or clan girl, I set the age of taking at fourteen!"

"And the Law, like all your Law, has proven just and good for clan and tribe." Hari nodded sagely. "Little Aldora—for that is her name, Aldora Ahpoolios—says that she has tried ceaselessly to tell her ravishers her age and beg them to leave off abusing of her body, but she has only a few words of Mehrikan and could speak only in Ehleeneekos. The mercenaries who first raped her understood; but she is quite womanlike for her age, and they convinced her buyer, Hwahlis Linszee, that she was older, I am sure, for Hwahlis is a brave and honorable man and a respecter of the law."

"Then, when he is made aware of truth, he . . ." Milo broke off at the shake of Bard Hari's old head.

"Hwahlis is not the problem, nor is he the Law-defiler, War Chief. It is his brother, Chief Rik of Linszee. He fully understood and took her anyway, often and brutally! She *knows* he understood, for when they were alone once, he spoke to her in her own tongue, told her that as soon as she began to learn to speak Mehrikan, he would have her killed. She did not know the reason for this or why her death should be necessary, but *we* do!

"It has been long and long since a *chief* of the Horseclans has defied the Law. Rik of Linszee must not go unpunished. He knows the extent of his crime and is frightened—Black Claw said that he reeked of fear. Though Hwahlis likes Aldora, he would have sold her; but Rik convinced the clansmen to refuse to sell.

"Also, War Chief and War Chief's wife, there is another thing that you must know: Though Ehleenee-born, this child is of your sacred race, the Race of Gods!"

Horsekiller and Old-Cat strode into the Clan Linszee chief-tent. Chief Rik neither rose in deference to Horsekiller as Cat Chief nor gave greeting. His mindspeak was flat and more than a little hostile. "Well, yet two more flea-factories today! Has the Cat Chief come to return my clan's property that they took away? Where is she?"

"I come," said Horsekiller, trying hard to keep his lip down and his claws in, "to summon you and one of your clansmen, Hwahlis Linszee, to the war chief's stone tent, within Green-Walls. If you refuse to come, Old-Cat and I have orders to hamstring you and drag you there! The council sits and will judge you and your clansmen for deliberate defilement of the Law."

Though obviously stunned by the Pronouncement, Hwahlis was just as puzzled; Rik, on the other hand, paled to ashiness and his hand crept toward his saber-hilt reflexively. His self-admitted guilt gave evidence that all could easily see and, muttering, gripping at Sun-talismans or the hilts of their sacred steel, his clansmen tightened their circle, edging away from him.

Arm cradling his telling-harp, Vinz Linszee, the clan bard, rose and mindspoke Horsekiller. "How speaks Blind Hari, Tribe-Bard and Sage of the Law, on this, Cat Chief?"

The big cat replied with ominous solemnity. "It is he who brings the charge, oh, Clan-Bard."

Bard Vinz hung his head in shame. Such a charge from such a man was dishonor enough; but if, as he suspected from Chief Rik's appearance and behavior, it were adjudged *true*, then the clan could claim no honor, past, present or future.

"Well?" snarled Chief Rik. "Speak up, useless-maker-of-useless-songs. Must I go or do we fight?"

Those clansmen who had been grasping hilts let them go, as if red hot, and hastily averted their eyes from their accused chief.

"You and Hwahlis must go," answered Vinz with as much dignity as he could muster. "Under such a charge, it were further Law-defilement to draw steel against summoners or council."

"And, raper-of-kittens," put in Old-Cat, who had moved quite near to Chief Rik, "if your hand does not depart from your saber hilt quickly, it will depart from your arm immediately!"

At the beginning, Chief Rik denied all: threatening the slave's life, understanding her tongue or speaking to her in it, even having had knowledge of her flesh. He swore sword oath that the charge was false, calling on Sun and Wind to witness his oath's verity, but the Test of the Cat, administered by Horsekiller's delegate, Old-Cat, broke him. As the teeth pierced his scalp and grated on bone, he screamingly admitted his deceptions and the blasphemies with which he had attempted to cover his misdeeds.

Bard Vinz and Hwahlis hung their heads and wept that their chief should so dishonor his clan. All the Linszee warriors were summoned to hear the foresworn man's rerecital of his crimes. When he had finished, Milo rose and addressed the council.

"Kindred, at the fight on the hill, when there were no more arrows in our cases and all seemed lost, two brave men rose amid the foemen's arrow-rain and precipitated a falling of rocks which, though it killed them, stopped the charge of the iron-shirts and preserved their Kindred. Both those valiant ones bore the clan-name of Linszee.

"The heinous misdeeds of Rik, Chief of Linszee, should be broadcast among all the tribe, to the irreparable dishonor of his clan. You Chiefs know what this will mean. As a dishonored clan has no place in the tribe, they will be banished. The Kindred will drive them out of tribe territory, that their dishonored blood may never pollute that of the other clans."

While he had been speaking, the weeping Linszee warriors had begun to voice a low moan. Clan dishonor and banishment from the tribe were the worst things that could befall them. After such, death would be a mercy.

"But, Chiefs," Milo continued, "to save the honor of such a clan as produced the Heroes of the Rock, I ask that the council grant a boon."

Several of the chiefs growled at once. "What would you, War Chief?"

"Allow Rik—who is clan-chief as well as chief malefactor—to personally expiate his clan's dishonor. Allow him to reject his chiefhood, divorce his wives, give up his title to any clan-property, save only some clothing and a little food and a mule. Then allow him to ride away, bearing only dirk and ax and spear, for he has lost, by his blasphemies, the right to bear sword or bow or shield. And let him be declared outlaw, to be slain if ever he returns."

No longer moaning, the Linszee warriors looked up, hope glimmering in their teary eyes; but Rik shattered their hopes.

12

A chief, with two sons,
Gained three more and a daughter.
Two score and two chiefs
The bastard did slaughter.
And the God led the Kindred
To the east, to the Water.
—From *Return of the Undying God*

"No!" Rik shouted hoarsely, his two fists clenched until the knuckles shone as white as his face. "No, no, I'll not go alone. They all are as guilty as I of Law-defilement! Every one of them has had the slave-bitch, too. Let the clan be banished! I'll *not* go alone!"

Where she sat on the dais, between Milo and Aldora, Mara rapidly mindspoke to her mate. "Why don't you just have the lying pig killed and end this business rapidly and permanently, darling?"

"I can't," his answer beamed back to her. "The Law forbids it. To slay a fellow of the Kindred in cold blood is a crime worse than Rik's. Kindred may only be slain on their request or in defense from unprovoked attack. I hate to do what I now must, but . . ."

Aloud, Milo spoke slowly and solemnly. "Sobeit. Chiefs, you must assemble your warriors and all your free-women and all children older than eight winters at the second hour of the Sun tomorrow, that they may see and hear and remember."

Blind Hari came abruptly to his feet. "War Chief, may I be heard?"

Milo nodded and resumed his seat.

"Kindred," began the bard, "from my earliest memory, have I heard of the bravery and honor of Clan Linszee. Though their valor has brought them honor and more honor over the hundreds of years, it has cost them dearly, for honor of clan and tribe has ere meant more to their warriors than limbs or life. These are good memories. They sing well and I have no wish to forget them."

The oldest chief, Djeri of Hahfmun, stood. "But Tribe-Bard, the Law is the Law. You yourself brought the charges and they have—after much false-oathing—been admitted true. The honor of a clan is carried by its chief and, if that chief be not only criminal but craven, the clan must suffer. None here deny that Clan Linszee has long possessed honor, but by the Law-defilement of all the warriors and the perjury of Chief Rik, all the centuries of honor are dissipated. If the chief will not go and bear the dishonor away with him, what is there to do but drive off the clan?"

Hari's reply was quick. "There is this, Chief Djeri: Rik is chief by birth, but, if his father were to declare him ill-got and not a true Linszee, his dishonor would be his alone and not of the clan."

Chief Rik had regained some of his arrogance. He laughed harshly. "You'll grow wings before then, old Dung-face. My father is dead these seven years!"

"Chiefs," asked Hari, "who among us bears the clan-name sacred of prophecy? Who was affirmed 'Father of the Tribe' when we began this march nearly twenty winters past?"

Almost as one the council members murmured, "Milo, Milo of Morai, our war chief, he is 'Father of the Tribe.' "

Hari nodded. "So as 'Father of the Tribe' is he supposed father of the man, Rik."

Milo recognized his cue. "Him called Rik, I declare ill-got! Such a one cannot be of Linszee or any other honorable clan, his attributes are got of dirt; he stinks of swine."

As Milo slowly pronounced the ritualistic words which declared Rik's bastardy, that man commenced to tremble and, when all was said, he screamed, "No, no, what you do is *unnatural!* I . . . I am my father's son!"

Milo shook his head. "I suppose you are, strange man, but none knows who your father might be, or what." He addressed the Linszee warriors. "Kindred, if aught is unnatural, it is that a clan should be without a chief—especially, a clan so ancient and honorable as Linszee. Who is your oldest chief-born?"

Bard Vinz replied, "Hwahlis, brother to . . . to Haenk, who is next oldest."

"Then Kindred," asked Milo, "can any Linszee say good reason why the clan should not have chief-born Hwahlis for the Linszee of Linszees?"

"But," shouted Rik ragingly, "he brought the Ehleenee shoat in the first place, and *he* was first to use her, too!"

"Horseclansmen of true purity of blood," declared Milo shortly, "need not listen to the rantings of a perjured manthing of doubtful lineage. If yonder dog-man yaps again, teach him respect for his betters."

Before the Council of Chiefs, Hwahlis was declared successor to his father, Haenk. The new chief paced the circuit of council, stopping before each chief who then rose to declare his recognition of Chief Hwahlis and to exchange with Hwahlis Sword Oaths and Blood Oaths of brotherhood. Meanwhile some of the Linszee clansmen threw Rik and stripped him of everything which bore the Linszee crest (and everything else of value), so that, at the last, he was left barefoot, wearing his sole possessions—drawers and a badly torn shirt.

The moment that Clan-Bard and Tribe-Bard had finished reciting his genealogy and the more spectacular exploits of his family and his clan and he had been invested with the trappings and insigniae of his new rank, Hwahlis set about his duty as he saw it. Striding to the dais, he took Aldora's small ankle and removed the ownership cuff from it and dropped onto his knees before the wide-eyed Ehleen.

"Child," he said, meeting her eyes steadily, "I have caused you much to suffer and have allowed others to do the same. Your face and your body are good to look upon and we thought you woman, not child. So, being men, we behaved as men will. This is not excuse, only statement.

"For the price of your blood, spilled by me and by my clan, will you accept your freedom as payment?"

Patient and silent, he waited until, in a tremulous voice, the girl answered. "Yes, Master."

Hwahlis shook his head. "Master no more, child. If any be master, it is you, for I and all my clansmen owe you suffering-price. We will send word to your father, your kin, that he and they may come to set the price and collect it. Mine is not a wealthy clan, but all that we have, if necessary, will go to pay your suffering-price. Until your kin and your noble father arrive, our tents are yours. You are Clan Linszee's hon-

ored guest and every clansman and clanswoman is your ...
Why, child, what now, have I done to ..."

Aldora's great mental powers—and later years were to see
just how great they truly were—had been awakened for but a
few hours, yet already could she *feel* the emotions of others
with painful clarity. So sincerely sorry was her former master, such utter goodness of spirit and true repentance did his
mind radiate, that she could not but weep. But what began as
weeping for the soul-agony that Hwahlis was suffering,
merged into weeping for herself, for her aloneness, with no
kin to come for her.

"My ... my f ... father, he ... come ... never," she
sobbed in halting Mehrikan.

Hwahlis took Aldora's tiny hand and patted it, roughly but
gently. "Why, of course, he will, child! What sort of father
would not come a thousand thousand days' ride to fetch his
loved daughter?"

Her eyes closed, she shook her dark head and lapsed into
Ehleeneekos. *"Ohee, ohee, Ahfendiss, ohee. Eeneh nehkrohs,
nehkrohs. Aldora eeneh kohree iss kahniss."*

Seeing Hwahlis' honest ignorance of Aldora's pitiful pro-
testations, Mara leaned down and softly translated. "She says,
'no,' Chief Hwahlis. She says that her father is dead, that she
is nobody's daughter."

The Chief of Linszee thought for only a moment, then he
placed his calloused hand under the girl's chin and raised it.
Gazing deep into her swimming eyes, he said, "Child-I-have-
wronged, you are a daughter without a father. I am a father
without a daughter. It is not meet that children should be
without parents. Would you consent to be a child of my tent
and clan? Aldora, will you be *my* daughter?"

Aldora entered his mind. All that she could find were his
innate goodness and his honest concern for her welfare. She
searched for signs of lust, but there were none. Its place had
been completely usurped by a protective solicitude.

"Oh, Lady Mara," she mindspoke, "what shall I do?"

Having had far wider experience with men and, consequently, trusting their motives even less than Aldora, a part
of Mara's mind had been in Hwahlis' from the beginning.

"He is an honorable man, Aldora, and, for what he is, a
very good and a gentle man. He truly wants to adopt you
and he would be a fine father to you. It is but a question of
whether or not you want a father."

"Well, child," Hwahlis prodded tentatively. "Will you grant my clan the honor of becoming its chief's daughter? Mine?"

"*Pahtehrahs. . . .*" was all that Aldora could get out before the intensity of her emotions closed her throat. Sobbing wildly, she slid from the chair and flung her slender arms around the grizzled chieftain's neck and rested her head on his epaulet, her tears trailing down the shiny leather of his cuirass.

Hers were not the only tears in that place. Horseclans men never sought to restrain their emotions—not among the Kindred, at least—and there were few dry eyes as Hwahlis lifted her easily, cradled her in his thick arms, and strode to the center of the hall.

His own eyes streamed as he declared loudly, "Clan-brothers, Chief-brothers, Cat-brothers, hear me! The slave-child is free! The free-child is *my* daughter and *your* kin! She is as a Linszee-born. She is of the tent of a chief and all shall soon recognize her as such! Next year, she will commence her war-training and, when she is a maiden, she will wear my crest and draw my mother's bow. Let any man who would take her for wife come to me, and let him know that Aldora, daughter of Hwahlis Linszee of Linszee, will be well-dowered by her father and her clan!

"Gairee." He called to the youngest of his two living sons—who, though but eighteen, had already killed three men in single combat—and, after disengaging her arms, handed Aldora to the younger man. "This child is now your sister. Bear your sister to your mother and so inform her and all my tent-dwellers.

"Kahl, Fil, Sami." He addressed those who happened to be sons of Rik, the deposed chief. "You are now *my* sons and will hold the chief-tent and all it contains for my return to the clan-camp.

"Erl, as my eldest son, I declare you sub-chief. See that your clan-brothers, on their return, bid their women to begin preparation of the chief-feast."

Addressing the remainder of the clansmen, he said, "Brothers, you may return to our clan-camp. When the council is ended, your chief will join you." Then he strode over to his place in the circle and seated himself.

When the last of the Linszee men had filed out, Milo commanded, "Let the man of unknown lineage be brought before me."

The two nearest chiefs rose and ungently hustled the all-but-naked former-chief forward, to stand before the dais, clenching and unclenching his fists in his frustrated rage, his face starting to puff as a result of the blows dealt him by his former clansmen.

Shoulders hunched, as if about to spring at Milo, he snarled. "This . . . this thing that you are trying to do is . . . is . . . is. . . . All here know who *I* am, who my father was, know that I . . ."

He got no farther. The hard-swung buffet from the chief on his right split his lips yet again and finished knocking out an already loosened front tooth.

"Silence, bastard! No man gave you leave to speak," said the chief on his left.

Milo treated the disgraced man to a look which bespoke icy contempt. Then he stated, "Though you yap like a cur, and conduct yourself like a swine, yet you are a man. All my Kindred know that there are two kinds of men: true men and Dirtmen. Since you are not the one, you must be the other. So, Dirtman, you shall be served in the same fashion as were the Dirtmen the tribe took at the Ehleenee camp.

"You are wearing all the clothing a Dirtman needs. In addition, you shall receive a silver trade-coin, a knife, a water bottle and a wallet of food. Take them and journey far and fast, for—as you are a Dirtman—you are the enemy of all true men."

Unconsciously, Rik wiped the back of his hand across his bloody chin and looked down at his red-smeared knuckles. With a bellow, he went berserk! All in the blinking of an eye, his right foot lashed—heel foremost—between the legs of the chief who had struck him and, as that man clutched his crotch and doubled in agony, Rik's left forearm smashed the bridge of the other's nose while his right tore saber from its sheath. Before Milo's blade was half-drawn, more than a foot of Rik's weapon was protruding from the war chief's back, just below the shoulder blade! Then, Mara's dirk found the berserker's throat and he released his sword hilt to clutch at his gushing wound and stumble backward, off the dais. Within fractions of seconds, all that lay beneath the dripping sabers of the vengeful chiefs was a bundle of bloody rags and raw bone and hacked flesh.

Panting, the chiefs of the council looked to the dais.

Several dropped their swords! Their war chief, whose last words they had expected to soon hear, was not only still on his feet, but was presently engaged in carefully pulling the sharp saber out of his chest!

The forty-two chiefs were typical specimens of their rugged race. Born to frequent privation and casual violence, they were weaned to weapons-skills and they were a-horse more often than afoot; armed with bow or spear or ax or saber, they knew fear of neither man nor beast. But this . . . this watching of a man, who should be dead, still standing and withdrawing the steel from his heart, was more than unnerving. The sensation evoked by such an unnatural occurrence was *terror*, icy-cold, crawling, nameless terror!

As many appeared on the very verge of precipitate withdrawal—not to say, flight—Blind Hari stood, raised his arms to draw attention to himself, and began to broad-beam a soothing reassurance. Sensing it, Milo and Mara, Horsekiller and Old-Cat added their own efforts.

Then Hari spoke, softly but aloud. "Kindred, my children, draw near and put up your steel. There are great and good tidings for you and your people. For many reasons, the telling of them has long been delayed, but now the time is come that you should know."

13

Horse shall choose and man shall choose.
Be neither, slave nor master. . . .
    —From *The Couplets of the Law*

Later, Milo and Mara and Hari and the two cats were once more closeted in the small meeting chamber. On the table were three drinking cups, an ewer of Ehleenee wine, a slab of cheese and a bowl of wild apples.

As he accepted a hunk of cheese from the point of Hari's knife, Old-Cat mindspoke Milo. "Though she cannot be slain or injured, it is true, do you think it was wise to allow the God-child to return to the people who so ill-used her, God Milo?"

Milo halved an apple, passed one piece to Mara and bit into the other. "I can think of no better nor safer place for her, Old-Cat. My race is *not* completely immune to death, you know; there *do* exist ways to kill us and the Ehleenee have learned them all. I cannot imagine how she managed to live among them undetected, as long as she did. What the Horseclans call God-kinship, the Ehleenee and many other peoples call 'curse'—the Curse of the Undying. They all hate and fear my kind. To them, we are incredibly evil devils, to be sought out and slain slowly and horribly, for we feel pain quite as keenly as do other living creatures.

"No, Old-Cat, of all the many races of man, only among the men of the Horseclans can little Aldora expect life. Since her future lies with them, it were well that she came to know them. It is unfortunate that she had to learn first of the bad of Horsepeople; but let her, now, learn of the good."

After Hari had fulfilled Horsekiller's request for a bit of the sheep-cheese, his hand moved unerringly to his wine cup. While sipping, he mindspoke. "Still, Milo, you might have kept her here. Her mind needs training, if she is to advance to her full powers. Good and well-meaning as they are, what can Hwahlis and his clan provide that we could not?"

Milo concentrated his gaze on the surface of the resinous wine in his cup. "Did you ever sire and rear children, Hari?"

There was a twinge of ancient pain in the bard's mind. "No. When I was a young man, I took as wife a lovely maiden of the Clan Koopuh, one Kairi. In the two years before she conceived of me, she became all things, all that ever I could want or need. When she died a-borning—she and the child together—I never again felt desire for, and never took, another woman—wife nor slave."

While Old-Cat nuzzled Hari's thigh sympathetically, Milo went on. "*You* have never reared a child, Hari, nor has Mara. I *have*, but it was centuries ago and in another world. Aldora is of, and must learn to live in *this* world. For all that she is, she is still a child and she needs the love and guidance and companionship of parents and a family—and she needs them *now*. As for training her mind, that can come later, one thing that my clan never lacks of is *time!*"

One morning about two weeks after the event-filled day of her adoption, Aldora Linszee awakened to the realization that she had never in her life felt happier or more secure. All her icy fears of these people, acquired by dint of the sufferings experienced at their hands, she found to have completely dissipated in the warm glow of the very real and oft demonstrated love which her new family and clan—all members of them—lavished on her; and, thanks to her daily-increasing mental abilities, she was keenly aware of the verity and depth of their feelings.

She had not yet been a year old when one of the contagions, which swept the cities of the Ehleenee every summer (being especially virulent in dry summers), had carried off her mother. So, having been reared almost entirely by slave-women, she had never known what it was to have a mother. Now she had two—Tsheri, Hwahlis' eldest wife, and Beti—on a full-time basis, in addition to every matron in the clan, part-time. Also, there was the eldest of Hwahlis' concubines, Neekohl.

Aldora's natural father had never really *liked* females, considering them a necessary evil. He married and begat only because it was expected of him. After his wife's unmourned death, he devoted very nearly all his waking hours to his minions, his peers, his commercial enterprises and his sons—in descending order. In the few scraps of time he grudgingly allotted to his daughter, he was coldly correct and stiffly formal—even for his tightly controlled and undemonstrative race. He did not like to have to touch females anyway, and if any had ever suggested that he hold or kiss his little girl, he would very probably have vomited.

Hwahlis, on the other hand, was a typical nomad warrior—volatile, uninhibited, emotional, intense. He was open-handedly generous, not only with his personal effects and possessions, but with his love, of which he seemed to have an endless supply. For the first few days, he had been scrupulously careful to neither touch nor kiss this concubine-become-daughter, lest his motives be misunderstood—a thing that his sensitive soul could not have borne, so filled with repentance was it already. And, to a man to whom visible demonstration of love was an integral and necessary part of life, this torture was unbelievably severe. It could not last and it didn't.

By the third morning after the day-and-night-long chief-feast, most of the tribe had more or less recovered and camp-life had resumed near-normality. Aldora did not know how to ride and for one who was to be a horseclanswoman, this was a calamitous condition which could not be allowed to continue. So, mounted behind and clinging tightly to Beti, she arrived at the tribal horse-herd to choose and be accepted by two or three horses. As they drew near to the herd, they were mindspoken by a late-adolescent female cat, preening herself on a hummock, from which she was afforded a clear view of the portion of the herd to which she had been assigned.

"Greet-the-Sun, Cat-sisters. Have the two-legs at last recuperated from the sickness of cloudy minds and shaky legs and bad bellies?"

"Yes, we have all recuperated, sister-mine, and it only took two days. But if you make yourself any more beautiful, it will take *you* the best part of three moons to 'recuperate' from *your* 'bad belly'!" replied Beti, laughingly.

The cat gave vent to a shuddering purr. "Wind and Sun grant that *that* kind of sickness come quickly. Already poor Mole-Fur is nearly twenty-four moons, and she has no desire to die a maiden."

Beti's delighted laughter trilled again. "Small chance of that, Cat-sister." Then she cantered on around the outskirts of the wide-spreading herd.

At what appeared a likely spot, Beti slid from her mare's back and helped Aldora dismount. Then, after removing saddle-pad and halter, she mindspoke her mount and the mare trotted into the herd.

Bewildered, Aldora regarded the thousands of horses— whites, grays, bays, chestnuts, sorrels, roans, claybanks and blacks with occasional pintos, piebalds and that flaxen-maned and tailed variety of golden-chestnut known as palomino.

At last, she burst out, "But Beti, how can I tell which ones are Linszee, which ones belong to us?"

Beti smiled and patted the child who stood nearly as tall as she. "It is simple, Aldora. None of them are *ours*. No man *owns* a horse, not in this tribe. The horses are with us because they choose to be. Other races enslave horses. They have to because they're incapable of communicating with them. It has never been thus with us. Since first the Undying God came to the Sacred Ancestors, the horse has been our partner and equal. It is a partnership older even than that of the cat.

"Though not as intelligent as our cat-brothers and sisters, the horses have their own tribes and clans and, over all, a king-stallion. It was him that I sent Morning-Mist to seek. King Ax-Hoof will mindspeak you—he is far more intelligent than the bulk of his kind—and then conduct you through the herd, introducing you to those he feels would best suit your mutual needs and temperaments. I think . . . wait, here they come now."

Aldora looked to see Beti's long-barreled, short-legged little mare trotting back. Beside her was a huge, scarred, red-bay stallion.

Beti was first to mindspeak. "Greet-the-Sun, Horse-King. I am Beti, wife to Chief Hwahlis of Linszee. This other two-leg female is the adopted daughter of the Linszee and she has come to exchange the Horse Oath. None of your hellions, mind you, Ax-Hoof, this female is not born of the tribe and knows nothing of horses or riding."

The big, rangy horse stepped closer. "Do you mind-speak, Chief's daughter?"

"Yes," Aldora answered him. "I . . . I am called Aldora, Horse-King."

"And you fear me, little two-leg," stated the red-bay. "Why?"

"You're . . . you're so *tall*," Aldora replied. "So big and . . . fierce and dangerous-looking."

Morning-Mist snorted and stamped one hoof. Though she did not mindspeak, her amusement was discernible.

"Little black-haired female," said the Horse-King gravely, "I was foaled on the plains. For twenty years have I carried clansmen into battle. My forehooves are as sharp as a steel ax-head. They gained me my name and have sheared full many a helmet and the skull beneath. My teeth, too, know well the feel of man-flesh. But *man*-flesh, little one, only *man*-flesh. I am neither as bull nor bear nor wolf. I do not war on females and foals. You need fear neither horse nor man, not when Ax-Hoof the Horse-King is near."

With that, the speaker sank onto his haunches that Aldora might more easily mount him, bidding her not fear falling as, if fall she must, the grass was soft and thick and she would come to no harm.

When Ax-Hoof bore her, who was now his oath-sister,

back to where he had met her, it was settled. She had oath
with a presently-barren brood mare named Soft-Whicker—a
patient, easy gaited, motherly one Ax-Hoof felt would be a
perfect learning-mount for the gentle, likable little two-leg.
He had had her oath an as-yet-unnamed filly of his own line
as well, promising that if the filly had not finished her war-
training by the time Aldora had finished hers, he personally
would serve as her war horse until the white-stockinged sorrel
proved ready.

For Aldora, it had been a long and highly informative ride.
She had met, exchanged greetings and compliments and idle
chitchat with all of Ax-Hoof's wives and with a number of
the King-Horse's progeny as well.

Ax-Hoof and Aldora were within sight of the place they
had left Beti when an elderly male cat and two younger ones
raced up to them.

Without greeting or preamble, the elder cat addressed the
stallion. "Horse-King, keep your kind away from the hidden
portions of the east-flowing creek. It is possible that danger
lurks there."

"What kind of danger, One-Fang?" queried the horse.

"Lop-Ear, here," the cat indicated one of the younger
males—about twelve moons and all paws and head, but beginning to fill out—"became suspicious of a strange thought-
pattern and went to investigate. He found no creature, but he
did find a strong bad odor and some odd tracks. He called
me and I don't like the looks of it. Both the scent and the
tracks are too much like those of a very large Blackfoot to
suit me! I am sending Lop-Ear to Green-Walls to fetch the
cat chief and some two-leg cat-brothers with bows and spears.
So, warn your kind away from any place a Blackfoot might
hide."

The cat then mindspoke Aldora. "Have *you* bow or spear
or even sword, Cat-sister?"

"No," replied Aldora, "only a small dirk."

"Then," the cat went on officiously, "you, too, would be
well advised to keep away from streams or low, hidden
places; the Blackfoot tribe aren't choosy; meat is meat to
them."

As the three cats bounded off, the older and one of the
younger in the direction of the cut of the creek, the one
called Lop-Ear flat-racing for Green-Walls, Aldora asked

Ax-Hoof, "What does he mean, Horse-King? What is a Blackfoot?"

Ax-Hoof, who was now moving as fast as he felt he safely could considering the state of Aldora's horsemanship, did not answer in words, but the picture which reached her mind was of a furry—albeit, snaky-looking—body, about the color of dry dead grass, with four black feet and a black mask-like across its eyes. Its face looked like a cross between that of a cat and a fox. When it opened its mouth, she shuddered, for it was supplied with a plenitude of long sharp teeth. It was built low, so its height was unimpressive, but from nose-tip to base of tail, it was a good fifteen feet in length and the tail was close to five!

Then Ax-Hoof spoke. "That, Aldora, is a Blackfoot. Added to the fact that they are ever-hungry, they are as fast as a cat for short distances and strong enough to drag off a full-grown horse. And, they are very hard to kill. Years ago on the plains, I saw one so filled with arrows that he looked like a porcupine, and still not dead! None have been heard of since we crossed the Great River. Everyone had hoped that their kind did not inhabit this land."

By that time, they were up to Beti, who had seen them coming and was sitting Morning-Mist, waiting. "Well, Horse-King, what took so long? Did you have her horse-oath half your tribe?"

"No, Chief's-wife, she oathed only me and an old mare and a filly of my get," he answered her curtly. Aldora had discovered that he took all things seriously and had little sense of humor.

Beti's eyebrows rose. "*You* exchanged horse-oath with our Aldora? I thought that you retired after Chief Djahn of Kahnuhr was killed?"

"Djahn was my brother, Chief's-wife. So close were we that we might have been dropped by the same dam on the same day. Until today, I had never thought that there would be another two-leg for Ax-Hoof; but this one is different from most of you. Her mind is different. I have spoken but one other like it, so she is now my oath-sister; care for her well . . . or fear you my hooves and teeth!"

"Threats are unnecessary, Horse-King," Beti reassured the serious stallion. "She is as dear to her clan as to you."

When Aldora had slipped down behind Beti, the big horse advised both woman and mare. "Go not near the flowing

water. One-Fang fears that a Blackfoot is about. He and one
of the cubs smelled where it had been, below the lip of the
cut."

Smiling, Beti slapped her bow case. "Never fear, Horse-
King, though no longer a maiden, still I can draw a bow."

Though he was galloping toward a knot of young stallions,
he beamed back, "Be not oversure of yourself or the value of
your bow, Chief's-wife. You have never hunted the Blackfoot
as I have!"

14

Body to body, mind to mind;
Horse and rider shall be as one.
Close as blood, the oath shall bind,
Till death has come and life is done.
  —From *The Couplets of the Law*

At the very moment Beti had been first greeting the Horse-
King, Milo, Mara, the Chief of Mercenaries, Hwil Kuk and
Horsekiller were closeted with four other mercenaries of
Milo's following. It had taken days to find three of these
men, as Aldora's mind retained no clear image of them, and
the fourth—Djo-Sahl Muhkini—had, at the time, been too
drunk to remember to whom he had traded his Ehleenee
child-captive. Finally, after each and every man of one
hundred-fifteen had denied any connection with the incident,
Milo and Hwil became mildly exasperated and commenced
subjecting the mercenaries to the Test of the Cat. They so
tested twenty-eight before they struck pay dirt. Now they had
them all—Pawl and Deeuee Shraik and Hahnz Sahgni—three
northern barbarians from the Kingdom of Harzburk and
former troopers of the Theesispolis *kahtahfrahktoee*. Insepara-
ble, they referred to themselves as "The Triple Threat"
(though no man could remember ever having seen them in the
van of any charge or battle).

"Now heed me well!" Milo commanded. "Despite the fact

that when you swore oaths to me, you placed yourselves under the jurisdiction of tribal law, I'll not quote it to you here; there's no need to invoke it, as—so your chief informs me—in all lands, sexual abuse of children is as heinous an offense as it is with us. You must have known that what you did was wrong, else you'd not have lied when Hwil and I questioned you.

"My wife and Hwil would like to see your blood—here and now—but I am going to free you. On this table are four purses of silver, your wages for the time you have served me. You may retain your armor and gear and weapons, but not the war horses you now use. Outside are a number of horses and mules who are anxious to return to the dominion of man. They cannot stomach true freedom and slavery appeals to them. Of them, you may take your choice. By the time that the Sacred Sun goes to rest, I expect you all to be a long day's ride from this place."

Shortly, the four—secretly happy to have escaped with even their lives—clattered out of the Citadel-barrack and trotted their animals through the city streets. All were well mounted, even though the horses they bestrode were not war-trained, and Djo-Sahl led a fifth animal—a mule, on which were packed their food and waterbags, plus a small tent and cooking pot. Even the youngest of them had been a mercenary for nearly ten years and all had long ago learned to accept the bitter with the better, so no recriminations—self or otherwise—were voiced.

They left the city by way of the south gate, passed through the charred ruins of the outer habitations, and wove a way between the haphazardly located tents and wagons of the nomad encampment. When they were finally clear of the camp, they cut cross-country in a westerly direction, so as to strike the north-south Traderoad. All were familiar with the road, having often patrolled it as *kahtahfrahktoee,* and as they were headed for Karaleenos to enlist under Lord Zenos' green and crimson banner, it was the logical road to take.

After about a half mile, Djo-Sahl's mount began to limp. Cursing, the brown-bearded trooper dismounted and, finding a pebble firmly lodged between hoof and shoe, began to work at its removal, telling his companions to ride on ahead. It was for this reason that he was not with the three northerners when their path crossed that of Beti and Aldora.

· The Triple Threat—Pawl, Deeuee, and Hahnz—did not need to communicate, nor did they hesitate!

Only Aldora's frantic pleas had prevented the adventurous Beti from riding the creek bank in search of the mysterious animal. Grudgingly, the nomad woman turned back toward the camp. Nonetheless, she continued to grip her strung bow, a barbed hunting-shaft nocked and ready.

Morning-Mist had crested a low, rolling hill and was loping down its eastern face when the three scale-armored men came into view. Few of the nomads liked or really trusted any of Milo's renegade mercenaries, so Beti urged Morning-Mist slightly northward, out of their path. They had been riding abreast, but when Beti's course deviated, they extended their interval, cantering in file with the obvious intention of cutting her off.

Where another might have waited or even ridden on to see what the men wanted, Beti—nomad-born and bred and trusting nothing, especially a male not of the Kindred—whirled her little mare and galloped back to the crest she had just crossed. There, she turned her left side to the oncoming men and extracted two more arrows from her case, clenching them with the fingers of her bow-hand.

"Aldora," she said urgently in a tone that brooked no argument, "I will hold them here for as long as I can. Run! Back to the horses. Mindcall Ax-Hoof. He will protect you. Now, go!"

Obediently, Aldora slipped from the mare's low crupper and raced down the western slope, broadbeaming, without being aware of it, a mindcall for help.

Old Hari sat in a sun-drenched court of the Citadel. Beside him was a small brazier in which were heating a half-dozen short daggers. Horsekiller and Old-Cat were with him. Employing Old-Cat's eyes, the hot daggers, and a pair of tiny pincers, the bard was engaged in removing ticks from the Cat Chief's hide, having just done the like for Old-Cat.

With a ghastly yowl, Horsekiller suddenly leapt ten feet, his mind filled with language he had heard Milo's troopers use. Hari dropped the hot little knife, with which he had singed the Cat Chief, and he and the two cats raced toward Milo's suite.

At that moment, Milo was astride Steeltooth and trotting through the south gate, trailed by the faithful Hwil Kuk. Brave and battlewise his mercenaries might be, but Milo was sure that none of them had ever hunted or confronted a giant ferret. Even under the best of conditions, it would not have been an experience to look forward to; but, if it had to be, Milo wanted men around him who knew what they were doing. So he was riding to gather a group of middle-aged nomads, who had faced the sinister creatures on the plains and prairies.

When the mindcall came to him, he at once recognized the sender; and, as her call was directed at Ax-Hoof, the Horse-King, she must not be far from the herd. Shouting for a clear passage ahead, he kneed Steeltooth into a gallop and turned his head in the direction of the Linszee clan-camp.

Mole-Fur had not mindspoken with Aldora, so, did not recognize the source of the call; but it could only be a cat-friend in dire straits. She left off her preening and jumped down from her knoll and tore off for the source of the amazingly powerful call.

Ax-Hoof, three or four horse-chiefs and a dozen young war horses were trotting along the edge of the creek-cut, following the mind-patterns of One-Fang and his cub assistant, as they scent-trailed the Blackfoot creature upstream.

Two-Color-Tail—a six-year-old who was horse-oathed to a warrior of Clan Hahfmun—was nowhere as intelligent as Ax-Hoof or many of his peers, but his mind was such that cat-calls could range him much more easily than most of the other horses and men. So, though they were a good three miles from the vicinity of the herd, he received the call and communicated it to his king. Leaving the party in charge of Armor-Crusher, one of the horse-chiefs, Ax-Hoof took to a ground-eating gallop—the Horse Oath took precedence even over the excitement of a hunt.

By the time he reached the fringes of his herd, they were milling about and a thousand or so were trotting along the path that Mole-Fur had taken—they, like her, all-but-mind-blasted by the powerful urgency of the call.

When Hari and the cats reached her, Mara was just dropping her baldric into place.

"I *know!*" she said cutting them off abruptly. "*I* too have a mind, you know. I expect that every mind within ten square-miles has picked up *that* call. When next we council, Hari, you have my voice. Her mind has *got* to have training! Such power, uncontrolled, could be deadly."

As Milo and Kuk came within sight of the Linszee chief-tent, Hwahlis was just swinging leg over horse. His sons and nephew-sons were already mounted and, like their chief, armored and fully armed. When his seat was firm in his kak, Tsheri passed up his shield and Gairee handed him a heavy wolf-spear.

"You heard?" shouted Milo, reining up.

"Who didn't?" came Hwahlis' quick retort. "We—all of us—heard, even Kahl, and ere have the cats remarked him difficult to range. By my sword, that girl has power!"

"We may need more fighters than this," said Milo. "She's calling old Ax-Hoof, which means she's probably near to the herd; and One-Fang sent a cub in to say that he suspected a Blackfoot was nosing around out there."

Hwahlis' weathered face paled. "*Blackfoot*, you say? By Sun and Wind, I'd hoped I'd *never* hear that name again!" He turned to his eldest son. "Erl, raise all the clan, the maidens, too! Plenty of arrows, with spears as well, mind you. Then ride for the herd.

"Fil," he said to his second-eldest nephew-son, "my compliment to Chief Sami of Kahrtuh, tell him . . ."

"Tell me what?" Chief Sami drew up near them; at the edge of the clan-camp he had left a score of full-armed Kahrtuh clansmen.

As Milo and the two chiefs commenced to lead their contingent of Linszee and Kahrtuh clansmen through the other clan-camps, they found that their numbers were growing. Apparently the terror-stricken girl's mind-call had reached every nomad capable of receiving it. Most had no idea *who* was calling, but only one of their Kindred would call Horse-King, and Kindred never called Kindred in vain. They did not wait for their chiefs, they simply armed, mounted and rode. By the time Milo reached the edge of the tribal enclave, there were six chiefs and at least six hundreds of warriors behind him—and there would have been more, except for the fact that most of the horses were grazing with the herd.

"*This*," Milo thought wryly, "is going to be a Blackfoot hunt to remember!"

Beti stole a glance to be sure that Aldora was well on her way. As she looked back, one of the ironshirts was starting up the hill, the other two close behind him.

She raised her bow and hooked thumb ring to string. "Halt, money-fighters!" she shouted. "Halt, or feel an arrow from the bow of Beti, wife to Hwahlis of Linszee!"

Hahnz Sahgni experienced a brainstorm—or so he thought. Reining up, he said pleasantly, "Yes, they told us we'd find you out here. We are from Kuk's squadron, serving your war chief, Milo. He sent us to fetch you."

"Liar!" retorted Beti. "If the war chief desired to see *me*, he would send a cat-brother to my husband, the Chief. I warn you, lying ironshirt, come closer and you die!"

The three men had been slyly sidling their mounts closer. Now, Hahnz clapped spurs to horse-barrel and, bending low over pommel and neck, charged up the hill.

Beti's first shaft caromed off the scales of his hauberk's back, but her second skewered his right biceps; as his head came up, her third, an iron-headed war arrow, thunked solidly into his forehead between his bloodshot eyes.

Before she could get another shaft out, however, Pawl and Deeuee were upon her. A back-hand buffet of Pawl's iron-shod gauntlet knocked her from the mare's back, senseless.

15

Hear, oh Wind, the cry of a clan, bereaved;
of how Linszee mourns the loss of one held dear. . . .
                                    —Clan Linszee Death Chant

Aldora was panting up another of the rolling hills when she fell. In the second that she lay on the ground, it communicated a swelling vibration to her flesh. Then Mole-Fur bounded up and commenced to lick at her dusty face.

"What threatens, black-haired Cat-sister? Why did you mind-call?"

"Did I?" asked Aldora. "I must have done so unconsciously then."

"Indeed you did, Cat-sister," Mole-Fur affirmed. "And if *that* was an unconscious call, Sun and Wind preserve my poor mind from one of your conscious calls!"

Then Aldora recalled the reason and waved an arm in the direction from which she had come. "Oh, please, Mole-Fur, it's Beti . . . three men are after us and she's trying to stop them all alone, with only a bow."

Taking a layout of the topography of the area in which Beti was making her stand from Aldora's memory, the young cat raced to the rescue.

Djo-Sahl, having finally dislodged the stubborn pebble, had just remounted when he saw—at about a half-mile's range—Milo and his body of warriors.

"Gawdayum!" he ejaculated as he hurriedly untied the mule's leadrope. "I thought they let us go too easy! Now they comin' for us!"

Discarding his lance, he spurred off at a tangent to his original course, heading due-west. The Triple Threat were not really friends and he saw no need to warn them of the approaching nomads.

"The hell we'll kill 'er!" was Pawl's reply to Deeuee's stupid suggestion. "You jes' go down there an' get the silver off of ol' Hahnz. He ain't gonna be needin' it no more. I'll tie 'er up and get 'er on 'er horse. The both of 'em should bring right fair prices, down Karaleenos way."

By the time his dim-witted brother regained to the top of the hill—having relieved their former comrade's body of the purse, a couple of silver arm-rings and a handsome Ehleenee dirk—Pawl had Beti tied securely over Morning-Mist's back and had remounted his own horse.

As Deeuee mounted he called, "Which way'd the other one go?"

His brother shrugged. "I dunno, and it'd take too long to hunt 'er. Let's go."

"Hey," yelped Deeuee, "how 'bout ol' Djo-Sahl? We oughta wait for him . . ."

Pawl shook his head and hooked a thumb at their unconscious captive. "You wanta have to take thirds on 'er all the way down to Karaleenos, and then split her price three ways?

B'sides, he's prob'ly took off with the mule and stuff anyhow."

Deeuee was known to be quite a trencherman. Now, he looked as if he was about to cry. "But that means he's got all of the food. We'll starve!"

Pawl laughed harshly and slapped the two purses hung under his hauberk. "Damfool boy, I don't know why Pa didn' drown you, anyhow! You got no more brains 'n a houn'-dog. We gonna be trav'lin through farming country, 'tween our silver and our swords, we won't have no trouble fillin' our bellies."

They were half-way to the next fold of ground when, voicing an unearthly battle-screech, Mole-Fur came bounding toward them. Cursing mightily, Pawl couched his lance and charged to meet her. Mole-Fur avoided the glittering point easily. As the horse tore past her, her long fangs ripped through horse-hide and horse-flesh and horse-muscle. Screaming, the hamstrung gelding went down, pinning his stunned rider beneath his barrel.

Deeuee had never been very adept at the use of the lance, so he discarded his and unslung his ax, then dropped Morning-Mist's lead and spurred toward the inexperienced Mole-Fur who was attempting to get at his downed brother's throat. But just as he reined beside the young cat and whirled his heavy ax aloft, he was violently propelled out of his kak, to join his brother on the ground. He had time for but half a scream, before Old-Cat's fang-spurs all but severed his neck.

Old-Cat's borrowed armor rattled, as the venerable fighter shook his head forcefully in an attempt to clear the bad-tasting blood from the razor-edged steel. "Idiot!" he mind-snarled at Mole-Fur. "Had I not come when I did, the two-leg would've chopped you in half! Can't you remember your battle-training, stupid female? You did a beautiful job of hamstringing, especially, as you had no fang-spurs. But why in the world didn't you then go after the other one? With a crippled horse on his leg, this one is going nowhere."

Mole-Fur endured the mental tongue-lashing in silence; then, her eyes downcast, she replied humbly, "Mole-Fur is very sorry that she displeased so strong and handsome a fighter, and she is very grateful that so valiant a cat-warrior saw fit to save her worthless life. This stupid young female has never fought two-legs before, and . . ." She trailed off disconsolately.

Her unhappiness was very real and very apparent and, for some reason that he could not fathom, it disturbed Old-Cat. "Never mind," he told her gruffly, lightly nuzzling her shoulder (soft-furred and tinglingly delightful to the touch). "You'll remember this and learn from it. We always learn from our mistakes."

When she buried her velvety muzzle under his chin, Old-Cat felt anything but old. "Oh, Mole-Fur is *so* glad that she is forgiven. She could not bear to have so wise and powerful and virile a cat angry at her."

Old-Cat extended his tongue and licked the young female's neck, suppressing an urge to lightly bite it. None other of the females of Horsekiller's clan had aroused him like this. Perhaps the Ancient Wise One *was* right and . . . He shook himself and drew away from the seductive young cat; there was work to do. "Mole-Fur, there was a mind-call from Aldora Linszee. Have you seen her?"

"She is well and safe, brave one. I left her on the near slope of the next hill. The Horse-King and his fighters should be there by now. Does Mole-Fur's hero wish to kill this two-leg, or shall she?"

"Neither," he told her. "The ironshirt can't get away. Let him live. There are clansmen coming. It will be interesting to see what Chief Hwahlis of Linszee performs upon the flesh of this would-be female-stealer."

Walking over to Morning-Mist, he employed his left fang-spur to sever the thongs which held Beti on the mare's back and, carefully, he reared up until he could grasp the waist-rope of her trousers and pull her from horseback to ground. After he deposited the blond woman's limp form on the sward, he slashed wrist and ankle lashings, then turned her over and began to clean the blood and dust from her face.

When he had done all of which he was capable, he left Mole-Fur to look after Beti and loped over the hill to see to Aldora.

Djo-Sahl had not ridden far when, to his right, he saw a mounted nomad and one of the great, fearsome cats bearing down on a course which would cross his path. Sobbing with fear, he further lightened his mount's load by throwing off shield and ax and, digging spurs deeper, pulled the horse's head around and fled southward. As his hard-driven steed galloped across the face of a slope, he was all but deafened by the thunder of thousands of hoofs on the opposite slope, beyond the crest to his right.

Then, immediately in front of him, an unmounted nomad female suddenly rose from the grass. His lips skinned back from his teeth and, drawing his sword, he charged down on her.

Aldora had heard the horses coming and had mind-informed Ax-Hoof that she was well and safe. He had advised her to stand where the leaders of the thousand or so horses could plainly see her. But she had only just come erect, when a horse passed behind her, a bright object flashed in the periphery of her vision and, with paralyzing force an agonizing something sliced into the angle of her neck and right shoulder. As the grass rushed upward at her face, she felt the hot gush of her blood, then, nothing.

Just as the first horses came over the crest of the hill, they saw in ironshirt saber a female of the Kindred. Carefully avoiding Aldora, the herd swept down the hill, bowling over both horse and rider. When the herd had passed, they left only a pulpy, red paste behind them.

Milo and the chiefs reined up around Mole-Fur who sat beside the still unconscious Beti and snarled at the whimpering Pawl, straining to pull his leg from under his feebly twitching, almost-dead horse.

"Beti?" Hwahlis mind-questioned.

"She lives, Cat-brother," Mole-Fur reassured. "One of these ironshirts must have stunned her before they tried to carry her away. But she is uninjured. She will bear you many more fine kittens."

"What of the younger one, the black-haired female, Sister-cat?" queried Milo.

Mole-Fur began to lick Beti's face again while she answered. "The new cat—that handsome, older one, who came in from the Battle of the Black Horses—has gone to see to her. She is two hills west and was well when Mole-Fur left her, before she met these two ironshirts." Raising her head, she bared her teeth and rippled a low snarl at Pawl, who shuddered and moaned.

Hwahlis dismounted and strode over to the soft-gray cat.

Resting his hand on her head, he said, "Sister-cat, are you cat-oathed?"

"Oh, no, Cat-brother. Mole-Fur is only twenty-four moons and has not yet been battle-trained," she replied. "No clan would want so worthless a female."

Slipping his hand under her chin, between the sharp tips of her projecting fangs, Hwahlis raised her head and looked deeply into her eyes. "Trained or not, *my* clan will oath so fierce and brave a female, and will be honored to go to battle with her! So courageous an . . ."

Without warning, Mole-Fur interrupted, "God Milo, the black-haired two-leg female, she is where I left her, but Old-Cat says that another ironshirt has sabered her, and . . ."

Hwahlis heard no more. Spinning, he sprinted to and leaped astride his horse and, before Milo could shout the rest of the message to him, was over the crest of the hill. So disturbed was the chief, neither Milo nor Mole-Fur could contact him mentally.

Mara had just finished binding a strip torn from her shirt over Aldora's rapidly closing wound (mostly, to keep the flies off), when Hwahlis pounded up, leaped, running, from his lathered horse and raced to the side of his "daughter." Tears and sweat had mingled to plow shiny furrows through the thick dust covering his features. Mara tried mindspeak but the begrieved chieftain's mind was closed, so she spoke.

"Chief Hwahlis, Aldora will soon be . . ." But then she was aware that he didn't hear her voice either. He could only hear the voice of his own self-recriminations and his eyes only registered Aldora's closed eyes and pale face and blood-soaked shirt and the bandage only partially concealing the still-gaping wound.

Dropping to his knees, he gathered her, whom he thought dying, into his arms and covered her face with kisses, tears and dust. Then, sobbing, rocking back and forth, he raised a keening wail.

Aldora, who had simply been following Mara's instructions to lie quietly until the bleeding had entirely ceased and the wound closed, opened her eyes then and gazed up into Hwahlis' sorrow-twisted face.

"Mara, what . . . why . . . ?" She mindspoke.

"That doleful noise is his clan's death chant, child," Mara answered. "He thinks you are dying and grieves for you. I told you that he was a good man. This barbarian loves you, Aldora; not as a man loves a woman, but as a parent loves a daughter."

"So accept the spirit of her we love, oh Wind," Hwahlis sang, his eyes screwed shut, tears bathing his cheeks. "For she is of your people. Bear her smoke to Your home. . . ." He broke off at the sound of Aldora's voice, the touch of her hand.

She wiped ineffectually at his face. "Why do you weep, Father? I am not bad hurt. Lady Mara say soon well I will be. True father, who I love, weep no more. Please?"

16

Milo would not have allowed the tribe to tarry so long at Green-Walls had he been aware of the exact depth of High Lord Demetrios' dilemma. That unhappy man's father, the late Basil III, had left richly productive lands, a generally wealthy nobility and a well-stuffed treasury. But his son had squandered his patrimony as if gold and silver were about to become valueless. He had robbed his nobles, his people, the priests and everyone else within his grasp. What could not be immediately spent or converted to cash was mortgaged to the hilt—usually several times over. As the saying went, "He robbed Petros to pay Pavlos," and when Petros was stripped, the High Lord had hounding creditors quietly murdered, then seized their books and possessions to be held "in trust" until someone appeared to claim them. But the first few persons rash enough to register claims all either disappeared under mysterious circumstances or met with invariably fatal accidents; word traveled fast and no more claimants appeared.

Throughout most of his long reign, Basil III had conducted wars against the host of small barbarian principalities to his north and west and against his southern neighbor, Zenos VII, High Lord of Karaleenos. Therefore, a part of Demetrios' inheritance had been several thousands of seasoned, hard-bitten, veteran mercenaries and many times that number of experienced, disciplined Ehleenee spearmen. Many of these troops had worn the azure-and-silver and the crest of Kehnooryos Ehlas for half-a-lifetime. In addition, his estate included some few dozens of really effective Ehleenee staff and field officers, these latter being men who, over the years, had not been too pompously stiff-necked to learn from the professional soldiers with whom they had served. Within half-a-year of Demetrios' ascendency, these atavistic Ehleenee were to a man giving serious consideration to the elimination of their dangerously inept ruler and then sending back to Pahl'yos Ehlas for a warlike man of noble lineage who might help to restore them to their ancient glory. However, in his spy-ridden court, Demetrios soon became aware of these sentiments and moved first and quickly. Four and a half years later, the few atavars still alive were in exile or in hiding.

With the barbarian horde camped upon and about the shell of Theesispolis, the High Lord had but few of his father's powerful army remaining. Early in his reign, Demetrios had dissolved all save a tiny fraction of the spear-levies, sending them back to the mortgaged land to produce already sold crops. Despairing of ever collecting their back wages, many of the mercenaries had left to seek employment from a lord who payed in something more substantial than promises. The lives of others had been frittered away in ill-planned "campaigns," conceived and commanded by the High Lord's totally inexperienced but suicidally self-confident sycophants and favorites. Of the ten full squadrons remaining, seven had been lost with Lord Manos' ill-fated expedition and another virtually wiped out at what the nomads called the Black Horse Battle.

Now—in addition to the eight hundred ax-men of the city guard, who had originally been mercenaries, but who now were resident civil servants, having acquired wives and families in Kehnooryos Atheenahs over the years; and his personal guard of two hundred and fifty black-skinned spearmen—Demetrios had but two one-thousand-man squadrons to his name! The White Horse Squadron's lot was irrevocably cast with that of Demetrios, like it or not. They had treacherously deserted Zenos of Karaleenos at the crucial point of the battle some ten years before, having been bribed to do so by the present High Lord's father, and now they knew better than to seek employment elsewhere. They had not been paid in years and were, in effect, military slaves, who cursed the day that ever their greed had brought them into the clutches of the foresworn and dissolute House of Treeah-Pohtohmas.

Though the Whites were trapped, the Grey Horse

Squadron was more fortunate. When what was left of their Black Horse compatriots came straggling back to the capital, Demetrios—in the grip of one of the screaming, tooth-gnashing fits, which had possessed him since childhood whenever he was thwarted or disappointed—ordered the common troopers killed and the surviving noncoms thrown into his dungeon to await his pleasure. At that point, Sergeant-Major Djeen Mai, the actual commander of the Greys, once more presented a request for the back pay due for his men's services for six months, some eighty thousand ounces of silver. When two more weeks went by without even a token payment, the entire squadron packed, armed, mounted, and after freeing the Black Horse noncoms, rode out of Kehnooryos Atheenahs unopposed.

Demetrios raged insanely for three days after the desertion of the Greys and the aided escapes of the men he had been looking forward to having slowly tortured to death. Then, swallowing his overweening pride, he dispatched pleas for assistance to the other three Ehleenee High Lords of the mainland principalities.

If nothing else, the answers he received were prompt. Hamos, High Lord of the Northern Ehleenee, profusely and abjectly apologized for being unable to send either monies or troops, reminding Demetrios how closely pressed was the northern realm by the warlike Black Kingdom to its south and west. Ulysses, High Lord of the huge and fabulously wealthy land of the Southern Ehleenee, pled poverty. Zenos of Karaleenos did not deign to reply to his ancient enemy; he merely sent troops to seize and occupy all Demetrios' south and southwestern border themes—from the mountains to the Great Swamp—and tentatively probed farther north.

Even with the harvest in, the spear-levy was responding very sluggishly to their summons and, as for the supposedly loyal nobility, many were selfishly husbanding both resources and personal forces to defend their own cities. It was at that juncture that the harried High Lord realized that he had no option. He sent a message of appeal to the one remaining Ehleenee who might render him aid—the pirate, Pardos, Lord of the Sea Islands.

Portions of the domain of Pardos were said to have existed in the time of the gods, and the presence of certain ruins on the three southern islands tended to substantiate this supposition. However, when first the Ehleenee set foot on the Sea Islands—lying over one hundred sixty leagues due east of the Principality of Karaleenos—the only indigenous creatures were sea birds, seals, a few wild swine and goats, several varieties of lizards and some rats and mice. It was obvious to all that the central island and seven of the ten major outer islands had not been long out of the sea, most being still but bare rock, splotched with the lime of the birds; and the archipelago-to-be was still rising, each year the winter tides' point of furthest advance was a little lower on the beaches and the central, twenty by thirty-two mile lagoon now averaged nearly three feet shallower than it had in the time of Pardos' great-grandfather.

Demetrios' messenger had returned from the Sea Islands to say that Lord Pardos was willing to discuss the rendering of aid to Kehnooryos Ehlas; but that, since it *was* Demetrios' plea Pardos thought it meet that the High Lord come to *him*. Demetrios raged! He screamed, swore, foamed, slew three slave-boys and seriously injured a member of his court; he had the messenger sought out, savagely and purposelessly tortured and then crucified with an iron pot of starving mice bound to his abdomen. Shouting, he laid curses on all of Pardos' ancestors and the man himself, gradually broadening his sphere to include the whole of the world and every living thing in it. Toward the end, he commenced to tear at himself with teeth and nails, roll on the floor, pulling out handfuls of beard and hair, beating fists and head upon floors and walls.

At the same time High Lord Demetrios was raging, a meeting was taking place in the haunted ruins of another of the god-cities, Lintchburk.

Four men were seated in a small stone chamber. Outside, it appeared but a tiny hillock grown with grass and trees. Within, it was presently lit by odiferous, smoky fat-lamps and their wavering luminescence flung huge, distorted shadows upon the ancient walls. Imperfect as was the light, nonetheless, it was enough to have driven out the small, scuttling creatures of darkness who were this chamber's usual inhabitants, and who now crouched in crevices, voicing bitter complaints at this unwonted invasion of their territory.

Three of the chamber's occupants were barbarian mercenaries: Sergeant-Major Djeen Mai, captain of what had formerly been the High Lord's Grey Horse Squadron; his second-in-command, Normun Hwebstah; and a man that Milo and the other survivors of the hill fight would have recognized as he who had retrieved the standard of the Black Horse Squadron, former Sergeant-Major Sam Tchahrtuhz. Though they bore a racial similarity to the nomads, these men were bigger and heavier, and Hwebstah's dark beard and hair proclaimed more than a tinge of Ehleenee heritage.

Though the fourth man's hair and beard were snow white, his features and his black eyes proclaimed him pure Ehleenee stock. Aside from these and his dress, however, he bore as little resemblance to the mincing effetes of Demetrios' court as would a boar-hound to a lap dog. His arms had not been depilated in all his life and they and every other visible portion of his body were crisscrossed with old scars. His gaze was piercing, his bearing dignified and his voice firm.

"I am that touched, gentlemen. So you—all of you—knew precisely where to find me all these years, and you breathed no word of it. When last I'd word, Demetrios had placed a bounty of one hundred thousand ounces of silver on my head. Didn't that even tempt you?"

Sam spoke for them. "We swore Sword Oaths and Blood Oaths and God Oaths to you, Lord Alexandros. Though I have lived and fought more than twenty years among the Ehleenee, I have picked up precious few of their habits and customs. *I* have not the ability to swear falsely, to violate a trust, nor has Djeen or Normun. We are but crude, uncultured barbarians and, in our ignorance, were unable to acquire such sophisticated traits."

The old Ehleen hung his head. "Would that I could throw the lie at you, my dear friend. But all you say is true. The old values are dead and their memory is mocked, as memories of childish stupidities, among my race. Our ancestors would never recognize us, what we have become.

"Four hundred years ago, when my race came to these shores, the Hellenoi were a strong, fierce, hard, resolute people. Though all of a definite type, we did not then consider ourselves a race, being, as we were, Greek and Turk and Albanian and Italian and Sicilian and French and Moor and Spaniard. We landed in successive waves and, though our numbers were small, our courage and perseverance enabled us either to slay your ancestors or drive them into the swamps and mountains, even though their far greater numbers were augmented by the fact that they had horses and we did not. Despite repeated and savage counter-attacks by your ancestors—whose reckless courage very nearly equaled our own—despite earthquake and tidal wave and famine and plague, we retained our hard-won lands, because we were one and one in our purpose.

"Then, in the time of my father's grandfather, it all began to change. We had been too *successful* and, with success, had come decadence. War had been the delight and avocation of our people, now our young men found it beneath their dignity, unnecessarily dangerous folly and, above all, too uncomfortable for their pampered bodies to endure. The old religion, which had endured for thousands of years and had been brought here by our fighting priests, began to die, to be replaced by polytheism and the unnatural worship of monsters. As the pursuit of money took precedence over the pursuit of honor, our free-farmers were tricked and deluded into their present state—ruthlessly ground peasants, virtual slaves of the land, no longer decent material for soldiers as they have nothing for which to fight anymore.

"In our days of glory, Sam, the spine and body of our arms were the spear-levy, the head and limbs, the swords and axes of my class. Now, alas, three-quarters of the body has forgotten how to fight and nine-tenths of my class have become too soft and craven to risk life or limbs or pretty looks in the forefront of a battle. What was once an honorable relationship of brotherhood and love of warrior for strong warrior, has become a sick rapine of small slave-boys. The sacred quality of marriage has evaporated, and I would wager much that fully half of our women who bear children are unsure of those children's true paternity.

"For nearly one hundred years now, Sam, the bulk of the truly effective troops in the armies of the Ehleenee states has been of you and your kind. To your credit, your people have learned from us, learned selectively though. You have taken the good grain that we were and rightly discarded the poisonous chaff that we are become. Could your people but unite, you could easily sweep all this coast clear of the useless parasites called Ehleenee, regain your ancient holdings, and—pray God—prove yourselves better masters of land and peoples than those you dispossess. For long have I said that your folk needed but a strong and resolute leader, perhaps this man you name, this western barbarian with his uncanny battle-skill, he whom our friend Hwil Kuk now serves, is the man I have prophesied and you have awaited.

"In any case, I think that, can it be arranged, we four should quickly meet with him and decide for ourselves whether to enlist in his service."

The three mercenaries exhibited broad smiles. "You *will* join us then, Lord Alexandros?" queried Djeen Mai anxiously. "You will be our *strahteegos* once again?"

Lord Alexandros smiled. "Why, of course, I've been champing at the bit, since first I laid eyes upon you all again."

17

Within a fortnight of Lord Alexandros' fateful meeting with his three old friends, the god-haunted ruins of Lintchburk were beginning to come to life again. His ready acceptance of the proffered generalship had been all that was required to send messengers at the gallop north, south, east and west. Their guarded communications had been whispered into just the proper ears, ears which had been awaiting such a communication for nearly five years.

And the word spread like wildfire. In ones and twos and dozens and occasional scores, old soldiers—those who remembered and some who had only heard—dodged roving bands of Horseclansmen or probing patrols of Karaleenee to ride or tramp into the growing camp. But there were more. Before the new moon, Rahdnee, Prince of Ashbro, rode in with two hundred troopers, apologizing that he could not bring more, but the bulk of his fighting men were already contracted to the High Lord of Karaleenos and their contracts would not expire for six months yet. The next large arrival was that of a contingent of veteran mercenaries—one and one-half thousands of heavy infantry, the mercenaries of Djim Brawuh, dusty and tired from over two weeks of forced marches, which had brought them from the vicinity of Pitzburk. These were put to immediate work, training the spear-levy caliber peasants who kept wandering in—all having heard of Lord Alexandros' resurgence and drawn by the undimmed luster of his name and fame.

By the time that Hwil Kuk arrived to emotionally greet his old *strahteegos* and conduct him, Djeen Mai, and Sam Tchartuhz to Green-Walls and a meeting with Milo Morai, the well-built castra had become home to some thirty hundreds of foot and nearly eighteen hundreds of cavalry. The nomads with Kuk's escort were visibly impressed.

"Understand," said Milo, "that my last contact with the Ehleenee was some two hundred years ago, and that was with the North Ehleenee, not with these people. If I'm to deal with this man—and, along with Hwil Kuk, you seem almost in awe of this Alexandros, dear wife—I'll want to know as much as is possible about him."

Mara drew a puff from the stem of her jeweled pipe. "My love, before the chaos which resulted from the Great Earthquake, all these lands—from the barbarian kingdoms a few days' ride north of here to the very borders of the ill-omened Witch Kingdom—was one domain called Kehnooryos Ehlas; the Ehleenee with whom you lived were, even then, a separate state and the Sea Islands had not yet been settled.

"Though located upon the Blue River, the capital of this huge realm, Kehnooryos Atheenahs, was only some twenty miles from the sea. It was all but obliterated and thousands of its population died when the first huge wave struck in the middle of the night. Of the entire ruling family, only the High Lord and two of his sons survived the disaster—and they, only because at the time of the calamity, they happened to be campaigning in the mountains with their troops; his second wife and two younger sons, also, because they were in a villa near here.

"It was weeks before the High Lord and his forces could win back to the location of the capital. Passes had been partially or completely blocked, rivers had changed their courses, inland cities had been shaken down, and almost every coastal city had been drowned. Stretches of coastline had sunk many feet, creating the Salt Fens of today, and much of the richest and most productive farmland in the realm had been rendered sterile by saltwater. More than nine-tenths of the then sizable fleet was destroyed and the only army left was the twelve thousand or so who had been campaigning with the High Lord.

"Then in his early forties, Pavlos of the House of Pahpahs was a man of tremendous vitality and purpose and, had he lived longer, he might have held his shattered realm together despite all that had happened and all that was to come. He established his military headquarters in the relatively undamaged area some fifty miles up the Blue River from the ruins of Kehnooryos Atheenahs at the place where the river ceased to be generally navigable—the Kehnooryos Atheenahs of today occupies that same site. There, he began to gather together the salvage of this portion of the realm, began to reorganize the government and reestablish lines of communication with the other provinces.

"Most members of the hereditary ruling families of Karaleenos and the Southern Province had been extirpated along with their capital cities, both of which had been located on the ocean coast, lacking the relative protection of headlands and bays and rivermouths enjoyed by Kehnooryos Atheenahs. The disaster had taken place a month or so prior to harvest time, so—in addition to the chaos resulting from a total breakdown of the central authority and ever more punishing raids by the mountain barbarians—the gaunt specter of starvation was approaching with the winter.

"It only required some three months for Pavlos to restore some semblance of order to the capital and its province. When it was secured, he left it under the coregency of his young second wife and one of his ablest *strahteegoee*, Vikos Pohtahmas; he left them half his army, and he and his two sons marched south with the other half, reinforced by two thousand mountain barbarian horsemen—these being the first mercenaries ever hired by an Ehleenee lord—who were with his army not so much because he felt he needed them, as because he preferred to have them with him than behind him.

"He marched right through Karaleenos, leaving only Hamos, his youngest adult son and a thousand troops at Kehnooryos Theevahs to establish a temporary capital and do what they could to re-institute some semblance of order. This was necessary because the Southern Province—the largest and, formerly, by far the richest of his principality—was being severely menaced from two sides. Within three months of his arrival, Pavlos cornered and exterminated no less than five barbarian hosts, each as large as or larger than his own! By late winter, the Southern Province was secure in all ways and well along the road to complete recovery. So, he left Petros Eespahnohs, another of his *strahteegoee*, as trial-lord and marched back to Karaleenos.

"Once in Karaleenos, he discovered why he had never been sent a messenger by his son and why none of his messengers had ever returned. Hamos Pahpahs, twenty-two and headstrong, cocksure of Ehleenee arms and his own prowess and abilities, had over-ridden the advice and objections of older and wiser heads and allowed himself and his small command to be tricked into open battle against far superior barbarian forces and annihilated, less than a month after his father had left him. When Pavlos arrived, the few strong points still holding out were under constant and heavy siege by the barbarians and over most of the devastated province, Ehleenee were being hunted like rabbits by troops of whooping barbarian horsemen. Memories of this time is why barbarians, and especially horse-barbarians, are so hated and ill-used by the Ehleenee today.

"If his campaign in the south had been a whirlwind one, what he did in Karaleenos could be likened to the speed and destruction of a tornado! Not content with simply driving the barbarians back into their mountains and hills and swamps, he and his avenging army pursued them, slew them and their families, and burned or pulled down their hovels and villages and forts. Such havoc did they wreak that full many a barbarian kingdom or principality required two or three generations to recover and some never did! Only one of the nearer barbarian domains escaped—Ashbro, the principality from which Pavlos' two thousand mercenaries had been hired—and, seeing what had been done to his neighbors, the Prince of Ashbro was more than happy to sign a long-term treaty with this terrible Ehleen. Pavlos selected a site for a new capital for Karaleenos and left his eldest son, Philos, as regent, along with the survivors of his two thousand mercenaries and another thousand of his Ehleenee troops, leaving himself a force of just over two thousand veterans.

"He arrived back in the new Kehnooryos Atheenahs almost six months to the day from the date he had quitted it to find his wife about five months pregnant, conditions in Kehnooryos Ehlas even worse than they had been when he left, the army racked by desertions and mutinies, and the treacherous Vikos Pohtahmas to have decamped with all that was left of the treasury.

"The steadying influences of his and his veterans' arrival and presence settled the bulk of the army's problems overnight. It did not take him long to discover the paternity of his wife's bastard, and but a little more to learn that Vikos Pohtahmas was in Petropolis, attempting to repair and refurbish a partially wrecked ship in which to flee. With the speed of the swooping falcon, he and two hundred of his veterans were in Petropolis and had taken Vikos and his followers and the stolen treasury.

"Hardly had he and his prisoner returned to Kehnooryos Atheenahs, however, when he received word that three barbarian kinglets and their armies were in coalition and despoiling the northern themes of his capital's domain; whereupon, he had Vikos' eyes burned out and threw him into the new city's jail, had all his officers and men swear loyalty to the young twin sons his second wife had borne him before she became adulterous, then marched out to his death.

"In the fury of the first charge, a barbarian's arrow pierced his breast-mail, but few observed and he plucked it out with a jest on the lack of strength of barbarian bows. He led two more charges before he crashed from his chariot, dead. After completing the slaughter, his men marched back to Kehnooryos Atheenahs, bearing his body.

"When informed of his father's death, Philos, leaving his new wife in Kehnooryos Theevahs, rode to claim his patrimony. He was duly installed as High Lord and was on the point of sending for his bride, when he was mysteriously poisoned. At this, a clique of *strahteegoee* took over. Their first step was to have the blind prisoner, Vikos, strangled, then they imprisoned Pavlos' unfaithful wife in seclusion—they were loath to kill her openly, but fully intended doing so, should her bastard prove a son.

"Next, they designated themselves regents for Alexandros and Nikos, Pavlos' twin sons, then aged seven years, and right well they ruled. Philos' bride bore a son, six months after his death, him the regents confirmed as Lord of Karaleenos, despite his tender years and he was the direct ancestor of Zenos, the present Lord.

"Pavlos' widow's bastard was a female and so, rather than slaying her, the regents simply banished her and her spawn, regardless of her plea that the child had been gotten on her in rape. They felt that there was division enough in the empire without adding one more dissident element in the form of a girl, marriage to whom might give some ruthless and ambitious man ideas.

"When Alexandros was eighteen, he was confirmed as High Lord and the regents gracefully stepped back into the position of advisers. He was married to a female of the ruling house of the Southern Province, whose loyalty had become rather shaky after Pavlos' death. For all else that he was and was not, Alexandros was a first-class stud! By the time it became frighteningly obvious that he was too mentally and emotionally erratic to rule, he had sired three legitimate and the gods alone know how many illegitimate children, most of them sons. He was not quite twenty-three when he fell in a battle against the mountain barbarians.

"Now, Milo, allow me to explain something. Among the Ehleenee, inheritance is strictly by primogeniture, the oldest son, no matter how unfit he may be, falling heir to everything. Pavlos had had four sons: Philos, Hamos, Alexandros and Nikos. Hamos died before his father. Upon Pavlos' death, *Philos was confirmed as High Lord,* though murdered shortly thereafter; so, by law and custom, *his son,* not his younger brothers should have fallen successor to him. But the regents had—for a number of very laudable and highly practical reasons—circumvented law and custom some fifteen years prior to Alexandros' death.

"While Nikos—who wanted confirmation as High Lord, not simply as regent until the majority of Alexandros' oldest son, Pavlos, then aged three years—was disputing with the aging *strahteegoee,* who had been regents for Alexandros, a messenger arrived from Kehnooryos Theevahs bearing a communication which struck with the impact of a thunderbolt.

18

"When the Lady Petrina—she who had been the wife of the High Lord, Pavlos—had been exiled, all had assumed that she had journeyed to Kehnooryos Mahkedohnya in the north as she was a noblewoman of that land. Such, however, had not been the case. A branch of her house resided in Karaleenos and to them she had flown, to reside there for nearly fifteen years, she and her bastard daughter. Not quite a year before Alexandros' death, Lady Petrina took seriously ill and, when she realized that she was dying, she had her relatives send for Paiohnia, widow of Pavlos' son, Philo, and mother to Zenos—he who had at birth been confirmed Lord of Karaleenos by the *strahteegoee*-regents. In return for a promise that the Lady Paiohnia would take in and provide for her bastard daughter, Lady Petrina gave her certain information and swore her Death Oath as to its veracity. On the basis of this information, Zenos' mother dispatched agents to begin lengthy and exacting investigations in various quarters. Of course, as years had passed and men had died and records had been destroyed or lost, and Paiohnia and Zenos—whose mind had been that of a man, even while his body had still been that of a boy—were fully aware that any hope of success lay in the provision of overwhelming proof at the outset, and the received information must needs be sifted and weighed and placed in order. Some thirteen moons were required to effect their purpose. When all was collected and arranged, they entrusted copies of their documents to a noble of their court, a man but newly arrived from Pahl'yos Ehlas, Lukos Treeah by name. As he was unrelated to any of the principals, they felt that he would tend to make a better emissary than a member of any of the older families.

"When received privately by the *strahteegoee*, Lukos' skillfully delivered message—backed, as it was, by irrefutable proofs—first shocked and stunned, then overjoyed the driven-to-distraction old men. Harried by Nikos, who insisted that, as they had once set precedence over custom in the case of Philos' son, they not only could, but *should* do so again and set aside the claims of Alexandros' legitimate issue, in favor of confirming him, Nikos, to the position of High Lord. Furthermore, he had broadly hinted that should they be so unwise as to foil him, he was not above raising sufficient armed might to *take* what they would not give! The *strahteegoee* had, in recent times, oft repented their rashness in disinheriting Zenos, however good an idea it had seemed at the time. Now, Lukos Treeah had saved them.

"The painstaking efforts of Zenos and his mother and their agents had produced solid substantiation of one earth-shaking fact: Alexandros and Nikos had been born *bastards!* On her deathbed, the Lady Petrina had sworn that *never* had she conceived of her husband, Pavlos, and that the true paternity of Alexandros and Nikos had been the same as that of her girl-child—namely, the *strahteegos*, Vikos Pohtahmas. One of the strongest proofs of the brothers' bastardy was the fact that never—never in any living person's memory and never in any existing records—had a Pahpahs man or woman sired or produced twin offspring, and the same was true in the noble house of which the Lady Petrina had been a scioness;

on the other hand, four of Vikos' brothers had been twins, as had his mother, his maternal grandfather, and other near relations, and his father's father had been one of *triplets*. In addition, the Pahpahs stock had been mentally and physically sound, until Alexandros; but many of Vikos' ancestors were known to have been rather peculiar. Therefore, the *strahteegoee* commenced preparations to announce all this to the Council of Nobles and to pave the way for exiling all of the spurious Pahpahs and inviting Zenos—proved to be Pavlos' only legal heir—to assume his rightful status.

"But Lukos Treeah moved first! His initial lightning-maneuver was to marry the widow of Alexandros, then to have every one of the old *strahteegoee* murdered. As first one, then another of Alexandros' illegitimates met with a variety of fatal 'accidents,' Nikos saw how the wind was blowing and took certain measures of his own. When his attempt on the lives of Lukos and his wife and adoptive children failed, Nikos took his household and retainers and possessions aboard a speedy ship and fled.

"Now Zenos and his mother were unaware of the murders of the *strahteegoee* and the other developments in Kehnooryos Ehlas, so Lukos was able to continue putting them off for some little time—at least until all conditions were to his satisfaction. When at last he saw fit to apprise his erst-while employers of the radical changes he had effected, their foreseen reactions were such as to play directly into his hands.

"Lukos Treeah was gifted with a silver tongue. It is said that he could have talked a viper out of biting him and, after a few more minutes, have persuaded said animal to make him a present of its skin! So it was that, by the time Zenos and his mother awakened to the fact that they had been duped and bamboozled out of the game, Lukos had both the Council of Nobles and the army and navy solidly on the hip. When Zenos and his Karaleenoee marched across the border, Lukos had himself declared dictator, imposed martial law, and set about jailing or killing, as suspected supporters of Zenos, all those who had opposed him in his meteoric ascent to power. Feeling his position to be secured, he then led his troops to meet Zenos' advancing host.

"And this same Lukos, who had never before commanded troops, proved to be a military genius of the first magnitude! For nearly two weeks, he maneuvered his numerically inferior force—marching and counter-marching—until he had Zenos just where he wanted him; then he struck. In a six-hour battle, he soundly trounced the Karaleenoee. When his troops would have pursued, he held them back, re-formed them, and, after an all-night march, struck again. The orderly retreat of Zenos' army became, after that attack, a rout. At the head of his victorious forces, Lukos pursued to and across the border, turning back only when arrows and stones, shot from the walls of Kehnooryos Theevahs, began to fall among his vanguard.

"After *that* victory, there was no stopping him. By acclamation, the army proclaimed him High Lord and the cowed Council of Nobles could only add their own acclaim in compliance. At Lukos' death, Alexandros' eldest, Pavlos, succeeded him, as he had been childless. Pavlos had virtually worshiped Lukos—who had indeed proved a good ruler and had been the only father Pavlos could remember—so, at his own accession, he declared his surname to be Treeah-Pohtahmas, and his family and descendants have been so known.

"Never again in his lifetime did Zenos Pahpahs of Karaleenos—truly the rightful heir to the title of High Lord—attempt a full-scale invasion of Kehnooryos Ehlas, but, in the centuries since, the wars between this province and that have been frequent, bitter and intense, though never very rewarding for either antagonist.

"Then, about a century and a half ago, there was a fratricidal struggle in the House of Karaleenos. The losers fled to Kehnooryos Atheenahs, where they settled under the protection of the then High Lord, Petros Treeah-Pohtahmas. Since then, there has seldom been a time when a Pahpahs was not a high officer in the armies of Kehnooryos Ehlas.

"That Lord Alexandros who is coming to speak with you served the present High Lord's father, Basil, for nearly all his life. He was a tremendously popular *strahteegos*—not only with the Ehleenee, but with every manjack of the barbarian mercenaries, who seldom have any use for any Ehleenee officer. When Basil died, however, Lord Alexandros' luck ran out. Basil's son and heir, Demetrios, could not have been less interested in affairs military; in fact, everything in his domain was considered in value only as it was useful in the promotion of his personal pleasures. A covey of officers and high nobles, Lord Alexandros among them, commenced a conspiracy to replace Demetrios with a High Lord at once less hedo-

nistic and more militaristic. They were, in some way, found
out—some say that Lord Alexandros' own son betrayed them
on a promise of leniency for his father and family. If such a
promise was ever made, it certainly was not kept. Demetrios
had the would-be conspirators and their kin hunted down and
put to death with incredible savagery or immured under his
palace to be dragged forth and further tortured or maimed
whenever he became bored. Some few escaped, fled to Karaleenos or the barbarian kingdoms or oversea, and Demetrios
placed huge rewards for their capture and return to him—
alive. It had been generally held that Lord Alexandros was
dead, but now it seems that he never even left Kehnooryos
Ehlas and has indeed been in hiding within less than forty
leagues of Demetrios' very capital!

"As regards the man himself, he is a throwback, almost as
different from most of the Ehleenee of today as would be
Hwahlis Linszee or Djeri Hahfmun or any other of our
people. As a young man, at the court of Basil—who, though
infamous for his cruelties and dissipations, was all man, something his son is not—Alexandros Pahpahs stood out like a
sore thumb. He was ever the direct antithesis of the fop, af-
fecting plain clothing and unadorned, serviceable weapons
and gear. He is fluent in every language and dialect used on
this coast, and has a phenomenal memory for names and
faces and dates and events. They say that he never forgets
anything that he reads and he reads not only Ehleeneekos,
but Old Mehrikan as well. The numbers of his defeats may
be counted on the fingers of one hand and, though he is wont
to make quick decisions, they are invariably sound decisions.
Though he has been known to encourage or condone some
rather gruesome practices in warfare, in command he is fair
and eminently just. He is honest to a fault, brutally frank and
worships personal and family honor as a god. He is clean and
decent and his tastes are simple and natural. He is now sixty
or thereabouts."

Milo soon discovered that Mara had been right about Lord
Alexandros Pahpahs. He was so bluntly frank as to be almost
disconcerting. The moment that the amenities preceding their
private meeting had been attended, he launched into a series
of probing questions.

"My Lord Milos [from the start, he had Ehleenicized
Milo's name], for what possible reason did your people come

to this land? You are horse-nomads, you need plains and prairies, endless expanses of graze for your herds and flocks, and you'll not find them hereabouts. This is *farming* country. If your purpose is simply one of despoiling this land, then moving on to another, you'll find no ally in me; quite the contrary, sir. The rulers of this land and people have served my kin ill; but only the rulers, never the land or the people who live on it. The people are one with me. They are as my flesh and I shall defend them to the last drop of my blood! So, then, tell me why you are come to Kehnooryos Ehlas."

Milo told the old fighter as much of the truth as he felt he should know. "Lord Alexandros, for many hundreds of years has this tribe been nomadic, but no more. In the time of the gods, the Sacred Ancestors came from the sea—from 'the Holy City of Ehlai beside the shining sea'—and it was long ago prophesied that, in due time, they should return to the sea and rebuild their city. When the tribe comes within sight of the sea, they shall cease to be nomads. They will but wait there for a sign, a sign that will tell them where Wind, Who blew them here, wishes them to begin their rebuilding."

The old Ehleen nodded. " 'The Prophecy of the Return'? Yes, I've acquired some little familiarity with the customs and legends of the western peoples, Lord Milos. However, as I remember having heard, your tribe was to be *led* back to the sea by an immortal god. Are *you* then a god, Lord Milos?"

"No, Lord Alexandros," replied Milo. "I am but a man like you."

The *strahteegos* eyed him shrewdly. "What is your family name, Lord Milos?"

"Though I am clanless, in my capacity here," responded Milo, "my clan is Morai."

Lord Alexandros shook his head. "That is your name, among the nomads, Lord Milos. But *you* are no nomad, that much is obvious. For one thing, you're too tall and big-boned; for another, there's your coloring, had you a beard and civilized clothing, you could walk the streets of any city of this realm without drawing a second glance. It is quite clear, to me, you are an Ehleen! Judging by the idioms of your Ehleeneekos, I should say that you came from Kehnooryos Mahkedohnya and that you are noble-born. You have no need to feel shame for your present status, you know. Whatever dishonor caused you to leave your homeland has apparently been long expunged, for a stranger who lacked for honor could not have risen to your present exalted position among these people. I greatly admire the western nomads, Lord Milos. I admire their bravery, their honesty and their inflexible code of honor. These are qualities which my own ancestors possessed, which—to my shame—their descendants have lost. I could not watch this land despoiled and its people extirpated; but even a barbarian king could rule it better than the present kakistocracy. That the new ruler should be an Ehleen of noble lineage is even better. This is why I ask you your family name, Lord Milos."

It was Milo's turn to shake his head. "I reiterate, Lord Alexandros, no matter what I may appear, I am no Ehleen! I am Milo Morai, war chief of this tribe."

The old nobleman's features darkened and his lips became a tight line and the words which next issued from between them were clipped, short and sharp as a new-honed blade.

"I do not believe you, Lord Milos! For some cryptic reason, you wish to delude me. And you obviously take me for a fool. I am not! Until you decide to be candid with me, I can discern no point in continuing discussion of an alliance. Now, will you tell me your Ehleen name?"

"Oh, 'Lekos, 'Lekos, ever were you pig-headed! With a bone in your teeth, you're stubborn as a hound. I should have thought that age might have vouchsafed you *some* measure of wisdom," said Mara as she advanced into the room.

She was garbed as an Ehleen noblewoman, jeweled and cosmetized, her hair elaborately coiffed. Milo had never seen her like this.

But Lord Alexandros obviously had! He paled and rapidly crossed himself with a trembling hand. "Dear sweet God!" he whispered. *"Lady Mara!* Lady Mara of Pohtahmas! Am I mad? Was the wine drugged? Or are you a ghost out of the past, come to haunt me?"

19

It is told, that in the days
  When Gods bestrode this earth,
The Sacred Ancestors of our clans
  Did have their birth,
In the God-built city of Ehlai,
  By the blue and sunny water;
Whence they fled, when evil Gods
  Their own good Gods did slaughter,
In God-made wingless birds,
  They flew above the mountains,
To bide within the ancient caves,
  Until the fiery fountains
Had ceased to blossom, where
  The Gods' death-arrows fell. . . .
      —From *Song of the Beginning,*
          Clan-Bard Song

A half-smile curled Mara's lips. "No, 'Lekos, you are not mad." She glided to a point beside his chair, lifted his wine cup and took a long draught of its contents. Then she laid the warm palm of one smooth hand on his scarred, gnarled knuckles and gazing into his bewildered eyes, said, "Nor was the wine drugged, 'Lekos, nor am I a ghost."

Lord Alexandros' mind was whirling madly. He felt as if he had been clubbed. He shook his white-maned head vigorously. "But . . . but . . . Mara . . . my love . . . it . . . it's impossible! *Impossible!* You . . . not one white hair . . . no change at all . . . and . . . and it's been nigh to *forty years!* It's *impossible,* d'you hear me? You *cannot* be her!"

Her voice became tender. "Poor 'Lekos, I could not tell you then; so you do not understand now. 'Lekos, long years ago I gave you a token. It was a cameo executed in the milk-stone with the gem for its setting. In the gem, which is

139

an amethyst, is a tiny cavity filled with liquid. On the back of the stone was carved a single word."

"Remember," whispered Lord Alexandros with awe and reverence. "Then, impossible as it is, it must be. None other, even my wife, ever knew of that stone. Many years ago in a battle, the chain which held the golden case in which it was sealed was torn from my neck. After the battle, I went back and scoured the bloody ground until I found it. Something—horse-hoof or chariot-wheel—had crushed the case flat against a rock and ground the stone within to dust. Since then, my only links with you have been my memories and . . . my love."

Bending over him, Mara tilted back Alexandros' head and kissed his lips. Then, leaning back against the table, she said, "Oh, God, I had almost forgotten! I loved you so much, my 'Lekos, loved you more than I have ever loved another man in all the years of a long, long life."

"And I, you," replied Lord Alexandros. "And I waited, hoping against hope, long after all my old comrades were wed. At last, bowing to familial pressure, I married. For twenty years was I wedded to Katrina and, though I got children upon her and the fondness of familiarity inevitably developed, I never loved her. It was ever you, my love, you who inhabited my dreams or fantasies, you whose name I called in sleep or delirium. Oh, why, why Mara? Why did you go away? Why did you never return to me?"

She took his old hand again, and stroked it as she answered him. "Because I could not, 'Lekos. You'll never know how every fiber of my being wanted to stay with you. For years, each time I thought of you or heard of your exploits, I ached to be with you once more. But to have done so, 'Lekos, to have surrendered to my desires would have been wrong, terribly wrong.

"For one thing, 'Lekos, I could never have given you children . . ."

When he opened his mouth to retort, she gently placed her finger athwart his lips. "Wait, my love, hear me out.

"The second thing is this: I could not have borne watching you grow old and finally die, while I remained as I am; and I could not have left you a second time."

Lord Alexandros' eyes seemed to be bulging from their sockets. "*No!*" he gasped vehemently. "*No*, I'll *not* believe it! You? *My* Mara . . . one of the Cursed? No, there is nought of evil or devilishness in you. For some reason, you're *lying* to me! Can't bel. . . ."

Mara shook her head. "Milo, give me your boot-dagger and come around here to restrain him, if necessary. I'm going to have to give him proof that he *will* believe."

Before he rose, Milo drew his short-bladed *sgain dubh* and handed it to her, then came around the table to stand close behind Lord Alexandros' chair. The old man was wonderingly glancing at first one then the other of them.

Mara handed the Ehleen the small knife. " 'Lekos, assure yourself that this weapon is genuine, that it is sharply pointed and that the blade will not retreat into the hilt." Then, she set about dragging over another of the heavy chairs and placing it so that she could sit facing him. That done she held out her hand to Lord Alexandros.

"The knife, please, 'Lekos."

Taking the blade, she laid it on the chairarm and began to undrape the upper portion of her torso, not ceasing until her entire left side—shoulder to waist—was exposed. Then she picked up the *sgain dubh* and tested its point on her fingertip.

"You are satisfied that the knife is genuine, 'Lekos?" she inquired.

All but frozen by what he suspected was to come, the white-haired man could only nod dumbly.

Mara used one hand to lift her brown-nippled left breast, then placed the needletip of the little dagger in the flesh just below the breast's proud swell. Gritting her teeth and tightening her lips, she commenced to slowly push the short, broad blade into her chest.

"NO!" shouted Lord Alexandros, starting up. Only Milo's powerful hands, gripping the elderly nobleman's biceps, restrained him from his purpose.

When the guardless hilt was pressed against her skin, Mara said, "Dear 'Lekos, you were but twenty years of age when I fell in love with you; and at that time, I had lived over two hundred and fifty years already! Now, I am nearly three hundred."

Gathering a handful of the stuff of her gown, she held it in readiness as she slowly withdrew the steel from her chest, being careful not to cut the sensitive breast in so doing. When she was sure that the *strahteegos* had gotten a good look at the wound, she pressed the bunched cloth against it, nodded at Milo to release his hold and started to speak again in a slow, gentle tone.

" 'Lekos, I've no idea how that terrible myth originated— the 'Curse of the Undying.' For the only thing that makes our lives cursed is the unremitting persecution of us by those who believe that ancient fable. Fortunately, these Horseclansmen don't share that murderous misbelief and, for the first time in more years than I care to remember, I've been able to relax, be myself, let down my guard and live at peace with others of my kind. The tribesmen all revere us, you see.

" 'Lekos, now you see why I could not marry you, why it would've been so terribly wrong. I never married anyone until quite recently. When I did, it was to the god of these people, one like myself." She extended her right hand to Milo, who took it and came to stand beside her.

"So," Lord Alexandros nodded. "You did lie to me after all. You stated that you were not a 'god.' "

Milo shook his head. "I am *not* a god, only a man like yourself. That I differ from you, in some respects, is the norm, for in nature no two things or beings are or can be precisely similar. I did not ask to be what I am, nor did Mara, nor did little Aldora. Both of them were born as they are, perhaps I was, too, I don't know; I was born nearly six hundred and fifty years ago, which makes it difficult, sometimes, to remember. Until about two hundred years ago, I had thought that persons like me were a by-product of that man-made catastrophe of over half a millennium ago, which came quite close to exterminating man. Now, I am not so sure but what we are a superior mutation of man. We have probably been cropping up, here and there, since long before the catastrophe of which I spoke. But in a world of several billions we were not so noticeable as we are and have been in the more recent past. Too, it is logical that a larger proportionate number of us should have survived, where most of the races of man did not, for—as is well known—we are much harder to kill than our non-mutant Kindred—nature's recompense, I suppose, for the fact that we are sterile.

"You state yourself to be one flesh with the people whom your house should, by right, be ruling. I can understand this, Lord Alexandros, for I am as one flesh with the Kindred, my people, too. Hundreds of years ago—realizing that, in the world as it was then, a nomadic existence offered my people's ancestors the best chance of survival—I established among them the rudiments of their culture and way of life. Though rude and barbaric and cruel in some respects, it has been a good life for them. From a beginning of a few dozens of terrified, pre-adolescent children—the orphaned remnant, who were all that was left of a city which had died of all-consuming fire—the Kindred are become a strong, independent, self-reliant people.

"Because I knew that, without it, they had little chance even of life, I gave them the Law and taught them to reverence their gods. Although I was absent from them for over two hundred years, they never wavered in that reverence, and not even I could sway them from its path today."

Lord Alexandros had regained his composure. Both Milo and Mara were surprised at the speed with which he had done so, considering the severity of the emotional shock he had just undergone. Keeping his eyes fixed on Milo's face, he heard him out.

"You know, Lord Milos, strange as it may sound, I had never connected the 'Undying God' legends of the western barb . . . nomads with the well-known facts that certain persons existed who were all but invulnerable to most forms of death. Knowingly, I had never met one of you—your kind— and knew but little of you save what the priests say, 'evil, unnatural, creatures of the AntiChrist, agents of the Devil.' Truly, I knew not what to believe. Had you alone confronted me with your . . . peculiarity, I should probably have bade you a courteous farewell, promised to think on this matter of an alliance, then gathered my mercenaries and marched against you to crush your evil before it could spread.

"But, with Mara, too . . . Husband or not, I'll tell you, Lord Milos, that forty years agone, we were much in love and there was such between us that I know her as I know myself! No *army* of priests could ever convince me that there is aught evil or unnatural in her! So, by your leave, I'll put my questions to her."

After Lord Alexandros was satisfied, he, Milo and Mara came to an unofficial agreement. Then they and the two mercenary captains went before the Council of Chiefs.

Some seventy-odd of Milo's personal troop had agreed to assume the surname Kuk and had elected Hwil Kuk to be their chief, whereupon, the council—in session two weeks agone—had unanimously welcomed Clan Kuk to the tribe. So now, forty-three chiefs sat in council.

After a certain amount of orderly debate—which to Lord Alexandros, Djeen and Sam appeared to be a but barely controlled state of chaos and set them to nervously fingering their hilts, expecting a pitched battle to erupt at any moment, as furious rhetoric and deadly insults flew thick and fast among the chiefs—the agreement became official. Mara produced documents setting out the provisions of the alliance, in both Ehleeneekos and Old Mehrikan. Milo, Lord Alexandros, Djeen, Sam and five of the chiefs signed it; the other chiefs made their marks.

In partial payment for aiding Lord Alexandros to ascend to the throne of his ancestors, the tribe was to receive clear title to whatever site Wind chose for their city and its environs. In addition, High Lord Alexandros and his people were to render them every possible assistance in the construction of said city. While in no way subjects of the High Lord, the tribe willingly accepted the responsibility of continuing to provide troops for the High Lord's armies. These troops were to be armed and mounted at tribe expense, but to be paid regular wages by the High Lord or his paymaster. In the present campaign, the tribe's fighters were to function as skirmishers, shock-troops and/or a screening-force of horse-archers, while the Maiden Archers were to provide concentrated covering-fire where needed. Though the bulk of them were not to penetrate Kehnooryos Atheenahs when it fell (a wise precaution, both Milo and Mara agreed, as not even Milo himself could predict how the Horseclans-men would behave), they were to be paid their fair shares of whatever loot might have been taken, had the city been properly sacked— something Lord Alexandros did not care to countenance, knowing that only Demetrios and certain of the nobles were truly his enemies. Another provision was that, from the signing of the alliance henceforth, the nomads were to desist despoiling the countryside and killing or enslaving its inhabitants. Lord Alexandros saw no need in attempting to forbid them to fight, if attacked, but they were not to initiate hostilities in the future.

The moment formalities were completed, Lord Alexandros and his escort enhorsed for Lintchburk to begin preparations to move his camp and men to Theesispolis; as well as to dispatch certain trusted individuals to Kehnooryos Atheenahs, Petropolis, Nohtohspolis, Leestispolis and certain other ports and cities, to sound out the various elements of the population and place the word of Lord Alexandros' imminent arrival in the proper ears. Within a fortnight of Lord Alexandros' condottas' appearance at Theesispolis, Milo had the chiefs pass the word to break camp. All spies were back and had made favorable reports, all conferences were completed and it was time to begin the final advance.

20

As a gesture of good will, the Council of Chiefs agreed to free all their Ehleenee captives before the march began. Freed men were given the choice of joining Lord Alexandros' condottas or remaining at Theesispolis until the conclusion of the campaign; most chose the former. Freed women were given the choice of honorable marriage into a Horseclan or simple freedom; very few chose to leave the camp. Children were given no option, they were simply adopted into the clans which had held them. As Lord Alexandros seemed quite pleased by this unasked favor, Milo saw no need to persuade the chiefs to make any further reparations.

Of course, Milo did not free his own two prisoners, Lord Manos and Theodoros of Petropolis. He was unsure just what to do with them for they were useless as hostages. Milo had had a free trader pass on a communication regarding them, and the High Lord's answer had been short and blunt: So far as he was concerned, the two were already dead. The barbarians could hold them until they both sprouted long, gray beards, and they'd not see anything resembling a ransom for them! Both men were in a state of constant terror and had long since supplied Milo with detailed and carefully drawn sketches of the wall plans of Kehnocryos Atheenahs and Petropolis, as well as with copious notes on subjects relative to the cities' defenses and the plans of every level of the High Lord's palace.

Finally, during one of his last pre-march conferences with Lord Alexandros, he brought the subject up. The *strahteegos'* face became a grim mask and, from between clenched teeth, he said, "Suffer the swine to live a bit longer, I say. For there are those in the capital whose souls would rejoice at sight of them, living." Then, he adroitly changed the subject before Milo had the opportunity to question him further.

Having insisted that she be allotted a stint at guarding the cattle, as did all others of her age group, Hwahlis had had Aldora given a crash-course in the use of the wolf-spear and the sling. The morning of the day before they were to march, she was slowly riding her old mare along the section of perimeter which was her assigned area.

The mare mindspoke. "Oath-sister of the Horse-King, Soft-Whicker is thirsty and the water of the pond smells good."

Reining up, Aldora stood in her stirrups and waved her spear until she attracted the attention of Djak Kamruhn, a thirteen-year-old who had the next post west of her. When he waved acknowledgment, she mindspoke him. "My mare thirsts, tribe-brother. We are going to the pond to drink."

The boy, though he could receive, had not the mind-power to transmit, so he simply bobbed his spear up and down and ended by pointing it toward the pond.

When they got down to the water level, it was to find several dozen cattle clustering around the edges of the pond. Smiling, a nomad girl rode up, her spear, like Aldora's, slung diagonally across her back. When she was close enough, she spoke. "Tribe-sister, before these witless beasts are done, there will be more mud than water here. If you want a drink that you won't have to chew, you'd better ride up there." She waved her arm toward the debouchment of the creek which fed the pond.

Thanking her advisor, Aldora rode up to the clearer water, dismounted and led Soft-Whicker to the water's edge, then began to walk upstream along the creek bank. Finding that the wolf-spear had a tendency to catch on branches, she shrugged out of the sling and leaned the weapon against the bole of a tree before continuing on.

It was not until she had rounded the next turn, however, that she realized she was in mortal danger. Terrible thoughts beat against her mind. Without thought she mindspoke the source.

"But why? Why would you want to kill me, who would be your friend?"

For a moment, the thought-transmission ceased, then came the answer. "Because I am hungry. It is long since I ate. I am starving. My foot hurts and makes me too slow to catch deer. You look slow. I think I could catch you."

Aldora's heart went out to the starving, hurt creature. "Oh, poor hungry thing. It is bad to be hungry, but there's no need for you to kill me. Wouldn't you rather have a sheep? If you'll wait here, I'll bring one to the mouth of the creek and, after you have eaten, I'll see if I can do something to stop your poor foot from hurting. Would you like that?"

Her sincerity was easily discernible and, as her unseen "companion" had never really cared for man-flesh, anyway, he acquiesced.

Aldora rode to her adoptive brother, Sami Hwahlis, who was herd-master-of-the-day, and explained her promise to the hungry thought-source. He heard her out, then grinned and shook his head.

"Sister, your mind is a source of constant amazement. Though your 'friend' is probably a wild Tree-Cat—some of them *can* mindspeak, so I've heard—I'll give you a sheep. For one thing, promises should always be kept, no matter why they're made or to whom. For another, what with all the inferior stock we've captured, the herds will need some winnowing soon."

At his order, three boys quickly caught, threw, slew and skinned an old ram, which had been taken from some Ehleen farm. As soon as they had taken the horns, they wrapped the carcass in the hide and laid it across Soft-Whicker's withers.

"Mind you, sister," Sami told her, in parting, "the cat is more than welcome to that tough old carcass, but I'll be wanting the skin back."

As Aldora again neared the creek's small delta, Soft-Whicker shuddered and mindspoke urgently.

"Oath-sister, there is great danger here. I can smell it and feel it. I am not sure just what it is, but. . . ."

"It is what we have brought the sheep for." Aldora patted the mare, reassuringly. Then she mind-called, "Are you there, hungry one? I have a sheep for you."

There was no threat in the answer, only anticipation and respect for the provider of food. "I am here, two-leg. I can smell the blood."

"I will come as far as the horse can go," said Aldora. "I'll leave the sheep but after you've had time to eat, I'll come back and see what I can do for your hurt foot." So saying, she urged the mare to the fringes of the brush and laboriously off-loaded the bloody ram. Before she remounted, however, she remembered her spear. Sighing, she walked the few paces to where it leaned against the tree. As she did so, there was a crackling of the brush and, out of the corner of her eye, she saw a something—huge and dark-colored—fade back into the brush.

She returned about two hours later. The sheep carcass was gone and there were no marks to indicate its being dragged. Whatever had taken it, had carried it clear of the ground. What might have been huge tracks had now filled with seepage-water and were undefinable depressions in the soft ground.

"It was good, two-leg," the formerly hungry creature mindspoke from the wooded area. "Do you think that you can now do something for the hurting in my foot?"

"I can try," replied Aldora. "Come out here, where the sunlight is good."

The creature beamed a strong negative. "If I do, I will frighten you. You will make loud noises and run, if you see me. All other creatures do, when they see or smell me."

"No," said Aldora. "I won't. Why should I? Aren't we friends? I cannot help you, if I cannot see you."

"I do not truly know what means 'friend,'" said the creature, wonderingly. "All things either fear or hate me. Even those who used to feed me, feared me. And those two-legs who trapped me and took me from my swamp and brought me here, they both feared *and* hated me. When you see me, you, too, will fear and hate me."

"Why should I fear you?" queried Aldora. "There is nothing of threat to me in your mind."

"Then, you will hate me!" stated the creature. "For I have killed many two-legs. I was so hungry that I *ate* the last ones."

Aldora indicated the negative. "I cannot hate you for that. You did what you had to do to stay alive. I cannot remain here long, I must get back to the herd, it is my duty. So, come out, so that I may see to your foot."

After a few moments, she could see the shadow of a low-slung bulk, just beyond the fringe of the copse. Then it stopped.

"Do you promise," the creature queried, "that you won't try to hurt me with the long thing you carry?"

"Wait," came Aldora's reply. Walking quickly over to her mare, she slipped the ferrule of her weapon into the lance-socket and looped the rawhide sling around the pommel to hold the spear erect.

"Now," she begged. "Please come out."

Lutros did! With a scream of pure terror, Soft-Whicker quitted the proximity of the pond, at a hard gallop. Her scream panicked the cattle near the pond and they, too, pounded up the slope in her wake.

Only because she was prepared for a shock, Aldora did not scream. Her only movement was to extend her hand toward Lutros, reiterating her request that he come and allow her to examine his injured member.

Lutros was truly awe-inspiring! To some extent, he resembled Ax-Hoof's description of the dreaded Blackfoot, though he was larger—his body being about eighteen feet long and his thick tail adding another six feet—more chunkily built and his fur was a uniform dark-brown color, becoming a few shades lighter on his underparts. He was possessed of relatively short legs, which bore his heavy body low to the ground. His rear toes were webbed. His head, too, was carried low, on a comparatively long neck, and the highest part of his body—just forward of his rear legs—was about at Aldora's eye level, some five feet above the ground. A thick fringe of light gold-brown whiskers graced his sharp muzzle and his stubby claws were shiny black. He exuded a strong, musky odor.

As he slowly approached, he asked, "How is it, two-leg, that you can understand me and I, you? You are not of my kind."

"I have been told that my mind is different from most, stronger in some ways," was Aldora's reply. "I am become sister to many four-legs."

"Stop my foot from hurting," Lutros stated, "and you will be sister to me, too."

When she examined the foot, Aldora soon saw what was causing the creature such agony. He had been shot with an arrow, a barbed-head arrow. The shaft had obviously been deflected or almost spent, for only the head had penetrated. But it lay lodged between the metatarsals, inducing pain whether the foot was in use or not. He had managed to bite off the shaft, but, due to the barbs, extraction of the agonizing point had been beyond his abilities.

"I can get what is hurting you out of your foot," she mindspoke him. "But I am going to have to hurt you to get it out."

"If I let you hurt me and you get it out, will I be able to get food?" he asked.

"After a few days, I think you will. Tonight, before I go, I'll see that you get another sheep, too. Do you want me to take it out?"

"Yes," Lutros affirmed. "Go ahead and hurt me, I promise I won't bite you."

Cutting with her sharp little knife only when she had to, Aldora soon had the arrow-head free. Immediately she informed her "patient," he plumped down and fell to licking the injury.

After renewing her promise of another sheep, she climbed up the slope toward the herd. At the top, she stood in wonder, watching a score of fully armed clansmen gallop toward her. They reined up at the rim of the depression.

"Wind save us!" exclaimed their leader, pointing at Lutros, who was zipping back into the woods. "Did ever you see one so big?"

Rapidly, he nocked an arrow and drew.

"*NO!*" screamed Aldora. Leaping, she grasped his extended bow-arm and his shaft *sished* into the depths of the pond.

The tribesman regarded her with amazement. "Are you daft, child? Though oddly colored, that was a *Blackfoot*—a damned big one, too! How in the world did you ever manage to escape him? They're fast as lightning and vicious as snakes."

Aldora stamped her foot. "He is *not*! He was hungry and hurt. I gave him a sheep and this"—she hurled the arrow-head against the man's cuirass—"I took from his poor foot. Lonely and scared, he is; and bad men, who hated and feared him, took him from his home and brought him here. And he was so afraid that I would fear him too and run from him, the way that silly mare did, or try to hurt him with my spear. He wanted to be my oath-brother, and now you've scared him away! Shame!"

The nomad cased his bow, dismounted and picked up the arrow-head. Bits of flesh still clung to its wicked barbs, and it was obvious that the inch or so of shaft had been bitten through, not cut. "Child," he said, gravely, "do you mean that you cut *this* out of that beast's foot?"

"He is *not* a beast!" Aldora stated, vehemently. "He can mindspeak. And he is not a Blackfoot. From plains come the Blackfoots; *he* came from a great large swamp. The only reason he stayed here was because men fed him. No more now do they feed him, and he hungers. I promised him another sheep and told him it would hurt to get that thing out of him and not to bite me. He promised and he did not and he wanted to be my oath-kin and *you* tried to hurt him more! You are a terrible, terrible man!"

The man leaned against his mount's withers and shook his head several times, hardly able to believe what he had heard. Though silent, the other men exchanged wondering glances.

"Child," the dismounted leader said at last, "I have seen nearly fifty winters and never have I heard of man or woman mindspeaking other than man or woman, cat or horse. Your mind must be of such a power as man has never dreamed. Even to be able to mindspeak such as that Bla. . . ." Stopped by the angry flash of Aldora's black eyes, he corrected himself. "That big, brown creature. Who are you, girl? What is your clan?"

Aldora drew herself up, proudly. "I am Aldora, daughter to Hwahlis, Chief of Linszee."

The nomad whistled softly and there was a rumble of muted comment among the mounted men. He nodded sagely, then stated, "Indeed? Then you certainly have such a mind as what you did would require. Some of us here," he gazed around his group and chuckled, good-naturedly, "have had some small experience with the power of your mind."

It was at that juncture that Hwahlis, four of his sons and a couple of other Linszee clansmen pounded up, ready for action.

"You're all right, Aldora? Ax-Hoof sent one of his sons, Clear-Talker, to find me. He said you'd been attacked by a Blackfoot."

When she had explained matters to him, Hwahlis, too,

shook his head. "Has ever a clan been gifted with such a fine and rare daughter? Furthermore, I think you may be right. The animal you describe sounds little like a Blackfoot. Except for the size, I'd say, an otter would be more what you dealt with, but I've never seen one longer than about four feet, including the tail. Is he still around? Can you range him?"

"Hungry one," she broad-beamed. "Can my thoughts reach your mind? Are you still here?"

"I am hidden, two-leg," came the response. "Have you got another sheep? I am getting hungry again. Have the bad two-legs with the sharp, hurty things gone yet?"

"They are not really bad," she tried to reassure Lutros.

"They *are*!" he insisted. "I could feel their hate, and one of them sent a sharp thing at me, I heard the noise that it made."

"They were mistaken and are now sorry, brother," soothed Aldora. "There is a very bad creature that looks a little like you, and they thought you were one of his kind and would hurt me. Please come out, my father wants to see you."

Lutros' answer was flat and frightened. "*No*! He will hate me and try to hurt me!"

"Ask him," suggested Hwahlis, when she had explained the creature's quite understandable fears to the chief, "if he wouldn't rather have a steer. There's a sick one we passed on our way here. In his condition, he'll never last a day's march and the Law states that sick animals are not to be slain for food. We could drive the beast down to the pond and kill it. Then, after we've taken the hide and horns and hooves, your acquaintance could take over."

When she queried Lutros, he waxed enthusiastic at the prospect of several hundred pounds of meat; even so, he was still reluctant to show himself, so long as the men were about.

Telling her not to press the issue, Hwahlis had her brothers go out and drive the sick steer to a point near the upper end of the pond. With skillful speed, they butchered and flayed the beast and, after removing horns and hooves, rolled them into the hide and rejoined the group of horsemen on the crest of the slope.

Hwahlis dismounted, tossed his reins to Erl Linszee and his spear to Gairee, the youngest of his sons. Then he slung his target on his back and, retaining only saber and dirk, followed Aldora down the slope, toward the steer's bloody carcass. Arrived, they took a stand, facing the woods, and Aldora mind-called.

"Here is your steer, brother. Won't you please come out now, so that my father may meet you? He would be your friend, too. It was he who provided the steer."

Gradually, foot by foot, with soothing words and comments on the excellence and quantity of the proffered meat, Aldora managed to coax the reluctant monster out of the protection of the trees and brush. Slowly, taking mincing steps, Lutros timidly forsook the brush and approached the wet, shiny carcass and his two benefactors.

"It smells *so* good!" he mentally drooled. "Even better than the sheep. You were right, the other two-leg does not smell of fear or of hate, either. You are good two-legs. The other two-legs only brought me goats. Will you bring me cattle often?"

"I am sorry, brother," replied Aldora. "But we cannot, for we are leaving this place tomorrow."

Hwahlis had never had much difficulty in mindspeaking the cats or most horses, but found that communication with this huge creature lay beyond his powers. At last, he spoke to Aldora, aloud.

"You were right, daughter-mine. Though obviously of the same tribe as the Blackfoots, he is clearly of a different clan. From those webbed hind feet and the shape of his tail, I'd say that he is truly a water animal. Of course, his smell is much akin to the Blackfoot, so I can see why he panicked your mare."

Aldora had walked over to place an arm around the creature's neck. At length, she said, "Father, he is sad because we are going away and there will be no one to feed him and there are but few deer left hereabouts, and in his lake no fish swim. He wants to go with us. May he?"

"Aldora," replied Hwahlis, "well-meaning or no, the sight and smell of that creature would stampede our cattle and sheep and goats clear back to the plains; the horses, too, probably! No, I'm sorry. If I should allow it, the other chiefs would flay me alive."

"But, *Father*," wailed Aldora. "The poor thing will starve!"

Hwahlis thought for a moment. In a way, the girl was right. Between the tribesmen-hunters and the cats, any game larger than mice had been virtually exterminated within two-

days' ride of Green-Walls. Also, he doubted not that a creature of this one's size required a goodly amount of meat to
keep body and soul together. But wait, there might be. . . .

Hwahlis, along with the other chiefs, had done extensive
scouting of their projected line of march, as well as of a
number of leagues to the north and south of it. Now he
squatted in the dust—which was all that the teeth and churning hooves of the cattle had left at the edge of the pond—
and, with the tip of his dirk-sheath, began to sketch a rough
map on the ground.

"Child," he addressed Aldora, "watch and listen. Then see
if you can make him understand. This little creek and the
ponds along it are all that remains of what was a true river,
which joined an even greater river some day's ride southeast
of this place. If this creature will but follow the creek and the
old riverbed, he will soon come to the big river. Tell him that
there is much game along this river and many fish and water
beasts in it. That big ring-tail, whose pelt Neekohl is teaching
you to tan, came from the edge of that river. Tell him, also,
that some say that extensive swamps flank the mouth of this
river. Perhaps they house others of his kind."

He stood and replaced his dirk on his belt. "It is the best
that I can do for him, daughter. It were rankest folly for him
to follow us, for he wears a fine coat and winter is coming
and, did I not know he could mindspeak, I myself might be
tempted to try to kill him for that fur."

Leaving her to communicate as much of the idea as she
could to the splendid creature, Hwahlis started back up the
bank toward his horse and followers. He had wasted enough
time today; there was much to do and little time to do it.

Aldora repeated herself until she was sure that the big
creature understood her; then, bidding her new friend farewell, she rejoined the men of her clan.

Below, Lutros commenced to tear the steer apart.

Few slept in the camps around Green-Walls that night.
Though all had been preparing for weeks, still were there
things which needed doing. The oxen which drew the wagons
and the huge, wheeled lodges of the chiefs, had to be driven
in and paired and yoked; war horses must be brought in and
saddled and armored, then picketed in readiness; here, an
axle was discovered to have developed a crack within the last
week, and it had to be removed and replaced; there, slaves of

the Cat Clan and a few nomad volunteers were seeking out strayed kittens and loading them into one of the several horse-drawn wagons which would convey them; between the new moon and the thousands of fires and torches, the camps were almost as bright as day and the light glinted from steel and leather and brass and silver, as the warriors armed; there was an almost steady *thrruumm* in the air, as men and maidens tested bowstrings, and the shrill rasp of blade on stone, as a last honing was imparted to the edges of saber or ax. An unending caravan of men and horses wended through the splintered city gates, to return with bulging water-skins, filled at the city's fountains—though the country they were to travel through was well-watered, old habits were hard to break. The odors of cooking breakfasts mingled with those of smoke and dust and dung and sweat and wet hide and grease and tallow and resin.

Two hours prior to dawn, the drums and fifes and trumpets of Lord Alexandros' army joined in the cacophony and, with the first rays of the sun, the seasoned *kahtahfrahktoee* trotted out of the castra followed by serried ranks of infantry, then the baggage. By the time the first of the nomads' wagons lumbered onto the stones of the road, the condottas were two miles east: infantry stepping a mile-eating pace to the tireless beat of their drums; cavalry at van, rear and flanks; and, ahead of all, a rough crescent of nomad riders fanned on either side of the highway; a little behind, Horsekiller and his clan.

Unaware that the old man had always detested such contrivances as effete and anachronistic, Milo had presented the late Lord Simos' best chariot to Lord Alexandros. On the march, it rolled along midway the column, loaded with water-skins. Lord Alexandros, astride a fine, chestnut gelding, rode with the knot of mercenary officers, exchanging jests and rough banter and swapping yarns of shared campaigns in times past.

21

The tribe made nearly eight miles the first day and Milo and the chiefs felt pleased. But not so Lord Alexandros. Unannounced and unaccompanied, he galloped the chestnut up, slammed out of the saddle before the animal was fully halted and stormed into Milo's wagon-lodge a couple of hours after dusk.

Seated, cross-legged, around a bowl of wine on the thickly carpeted floor, were Milo, Mara, Blind Hari, Chief Hwil of Kuk, Chief Bili of Esmith, Chief Rahsz of Rahsz and Chief Djimi of Peerszuhn. Hari was flanked by Old-Cat and Mole-Fur, and Horsekiller crouched between Milo and Mara, now and then taking a surreptitious lap out of Milo's cup (he had developed an unadmitted fondness for the resinous Ehleen wine).

Milo rose smiling. "Welcome, Lord Alexandros. Your presence honors my tent and our gathering."

Exerting his iron control the *strahteegos* forced himself to sit and accepted a cup of the wine (and the fact that it was part of the loot of Theesispolis did nothing to improve his frame of mind).

Still smiling, Milo spoke. "All the clan smiths are hard at work, tonight, my lord. They will continue to be every night of the march, too. By the time we reach the vicinity of Kehnooryos Atheenahs, I can promise you that each and every one of your peasants will be armed, after a fashion—even if it's only with spear, shield and helmet."

Lord Alexandros took a deep draught of the contents of his silver cup. In a tight, restrained voice, he asked, "And how many days do you think it will take this . . . this 'column' to reach our objective, Lord Milos?"

Though the old nobleman possessed a mind-shield which made the reading of his thoughts impossible, even for Milo or Mara, the very restraint in his tone betrayed the force of his anger. For the nonce, however, Milo chose to ignore it, going on in the same friendly, conversational tone.

"Oh, ten days to two weeks, I should say, sir. The former,

certainly, if we continue the same fast pace and make as good time as we did today."

The last statement was too much. Lord Alexandros slammed his scarred knuckles into the carpet before him and sparks shot from his eyes. "My *God*, man! You call this good time? The outskirts of *your* camp are less than eight miles from where it was this morning! Why, I expect even fully armed *infantry* to make twenty miles a day—and God knows, I've the reputation for driving my men no harder than is necessary!"

So *that's* the bone in his craw, thought Milo. He said, "Lord Alexandros, were none but our warriors involved, they'd have been nigh on to Kehnooryos Atheenahs, *this* night! But such is not the case. This is not—no matter how you may wish it were—a purely military movement. It is a migration! In addition to your troops and the tribe's warriors, there are nearly eight thousands of women and children, well over a dozen hundreds of wagons, more hundreds of tentcarts, some twenty thousands horses and nearly twice that number of cattle, sheep and goats. It is because of the latter, principally, that our advance is—by your lights—slow. Cattle and sheep and goats can be driven just so far and just so fast."

"Then I suggest they be left here or driven back to their original pasturage," said Lord Alexandros shortly. "As I expect us to be under the walls of Kehnooryos Atheenahs in no more than three days."

Chief Bili opened his mouth to make a sizzling retort. "No, Bili," Milo mindspoke him. "Let me handle this."

"Lord Alexandros," he said to the white-haired Ehleen, "your baggage wagons carry the grain and vegetables which are your troops' accustomed diet. *My* people are accustomed to a diet which consists to a large extent of dairy products, therefore the herds are *their* rations. You'd ask them to leave their rations behind?"

"Being without milk for a couple of weeks isn't going to *kill* them!" snapped the *strahteegos*. "There's always hard cheese or jerky, you know."

"Babes and very young children, too?" questioned Milo gently. "Or aged persons, who lack teeth?"

"Well, dammit! Let them camp here," was the old man's tart rejoinder. "This is warfare, Lord Milos, serious business! Non-combatants have no place in it!"

"In such case, my lord," Milo informed him, "you'd march on alone, on your own. My warriors would not leave their families camped, unprotected, in hostile territory."

"Then . . . then . . . then let them go back to Theesispolis! They'll be safe behind its walls."

Scouting a column's advance was hard, dirty, dangerous work; this Lord Alexandros knew well. It was very comforting to know that it was being done—and done well—by troops he felt no responsibility for, and he had no wish to lose the services of these expendables, simply because they felt obliged to stay with their squalling brats and their smelly women.

Milo felt it might—at this point—be impolitic to mention how little safety those same walls had afforded the former inhabitants of Theesispolis. "No," he said, shaking his head. "I could, of course, convene the Council of Chiefs, and put the question to them, but there's no need, I can tell you their answer now.

"The tribe is migrating toward the sea. Kehnooryos Atheenahs lies in that direction. It would've been necessary to move the camp soon, in any case, as the area of Theesispolis is all but grazed out. If the warriors and the maidens go with you, the tribe goes with you. If the tribe goes with you, the herds go with you. It is that simple, Lord Alexandros!" Milo drained his cup and dipped it into the wine bowl.

Nonetheless, Milo did see that as little time as possible was wasted on the march. The second day, the tribe did nearly ten miles and the third saw a bit over ten covered.

By the sunset of the fourth night, they were almost halfway to the capital and, as the tribe halted, Milo passed word that the chiefs were to council before his lodge within the hour. It was a short meeting and was in the process of adjourning, when Lord Alexandros arrived. He was not alone this time. In his wake trotted a hundred fully-armed *kahtahfrahktoee*. His features were grim and the blaze of the fire before Milo's lodge was no hotter than the glare from the old Ehleen's eyes.

"Had I known you wished to attend our little conference," Milo addressed the glowering noble, "I'd have seen that you were apprised of it, my Lord."

Chief Hwil of Kuk strode smiling to assist his old *strahteegos* in dismounting. "You are right welcome, Lord Alexandros. Will you not honor my tent before you depart?"

By pressure of knee and rein, the old man danced his mount away from Kuk, saying, "*Foresworn!* You have sold out to these howling savages! Now you are no better than they, if ever you were. So, I'll thank you to keep your gory hands off my horse and my person!"

"Shocked and abashed, Kuk could but stutter. "But . . . but . . ."

Amid an ominous muttering from the chiefs, Milo stepped forward. "My Lord, I know not what is *now* troubling you, but perhaps, if you were to dismount and come in to my lodge, we . . ."

He got no farther. Leaning forward, over the hands crossed on his pommel, Lord Alexandros said, "I only dismount to converse with *equals*, barbarian! I came not for conversation. I've heard more than enough of the yappings of you and your pack of curs, thank you! I came for justice and I mean to have it!"

At that moment, Old-Cat—patrolling the fringes of the camp—mindspoke Milo. "Friend Milo, all the Ironshirts are spreading around the camp. The archers have arrows on strings and most of the others are lighting torches. The minds I have been able to enter are filled with thoughts of burning the camp and slaying the Kindred!"

Milo mindspoke Mara in his lodge. "Mara, it would appear that your former lover has had some change-of-heart. His cavalry are in the process of surrounding the camp at this moment, and he is raging and ranting about justice. Go out the back and raise as many warriors and maidens as you can. Fortunately, he was stupid enough to ride in here with only a hundred men. No matter what his orders to them were, I don't think his troops will attack, knowing that his life would be the first taken—not as much as they idolize him."

To Horsekiller, "Call up your clan, Cat Chief. Be ready to attack, but only at my word."

But, from Lord Alexandros, Milo withheld the bulk of his knowledge for the moment, saying only, "If my Lord would deign to let me know what he is raving about, perhaps we could get to the bottom of it. However, I'll have to request that you cease to insult my chiefs; you're not High Lord, yet, sir, not by a long shot!"

"And, you imply," said Lord Alexandros acidly, "that I'll not be, without the help of you and your red-handed butchers? Is that it?"

Milo was playing for time. "I implied nothing of the sort, sir. However, since *you* did bring up the matter, know this: We are a loose confederation of blood-related clans. Should a chief be sufficiently provoked, there is nothing to prevent him and his clan from wreaking *personal* vengeance, where and on whom he sees fit!"

"Including," snarled the *strahteegos*, "helpless, innocent peasants! You see, I have been apprised of your treacherous, bestial infamy, you supposedly civilized pig!"

Milo hooked thumbs through his dagger-belt and shook his head. "*I* do not anger easily, Lord Alexandros, so insulting *me* is pointless. I am beginning to surmise that you have taken leave of your senses. It is quite obvious that you are highly incensed in some way; but you seem disinclined to bring your reasons into the open."

"Milo, love." It was Mara, mindspeaking. "There are about a thousand warriors, maidens and matrons ringing your lodge area now. Their bows can drop every one of the soldiers, whenever you say; but don't hurt 'Lekos, unless he gives you no choice, please. More clanspeople are forming a 'reception committee' for those troops now outside the camp, and Horsekiller has the most of his clan there or on the way."

When Milo spoke to the Ehleen again, an edge had come into his voice. "Lord, you accuse *me* of treachery, of infamy! What, may I ask, do you call your own conduct? Is surrounding and preparing to attack the camp of a supposed ally not treachery? At this moment—as you well know, *sir*—your *kahtahfrahktoee* are in the process of moving into attack-positions on our camp perimeter. Should they be so unwise as to attempt an assault, they—and you—will find us well prepared for them, and they will take heavy casualties!

"Now, before this 'meeting' gets any more unpleasant, I'll ask you once more: What possible justification have you for this night's actions? What brought you, frothing at the mouth, to my lodge, to insult me and my chiefs?"

"You know why I am here!" hissed Lord Alexandros. "I want the culprits dragged before me immediately, or my men attack! There can be no excuse for the actions of the criminals you are sheltering, and I'll not rest until I see them impaled—as they so richly deserve! I know what is right and just, and I have the troops to enforce my will."

"Should you be sufficiently stupid to throw them against this camp, you blathering old doddard, you'll not have them long!" declared Chief Djeri of Hahfmun, having taken all he could stomach. "The tribe will make the same hash of you and yours that we did of the last Ehleen jackanapes who tried to attack us!"

Turning to his hundred, Lord Alexandros waved an arm in Chief Djeri's direction. "Seize me that grunting hog! He's probably one of the very swine we came for; if not, he'll do as hostage for their delivery!"

Warily, four troopers dismounted and started toward the gray-haired chief. With a wolfish grin, Chief Djeri drew both saber and dirk and, in the twinkling of an eye, Sami of Kahrtuh, Bili of Esmith, and Chuk of Djahnsun had their own steel out and were ranged beside him. Even without armor, they obviously felt themselves more than a match for the four clanking *kahtahfrahktoee*.

At a pre-arranged signal from Lord Alexandros, the bugler raised his instrument to his lips, but found he was unable to force air past the shaft of the arrow which had suddenly spitted his throat! And that was the end of the battle. The troopers were not fools and, as they became aware that at least ten bows were trained on each of them, their lances came clattering to the ground and their scabbarded swords quickly followed.

Milo advanced a few paces closer to the still-mounted Lord Alexandros. "I'll *ask* once more, my lord. Will you dismount and come in and discuss this matter of contention? I have no desire to shed the blood of any more of your men, though many of my people would be overjoyed to muddy this earth with their blood."

For a long, long minute, the Ehleen sat his mount, staring venomously; but, at length—bowing to the inevitable—he stiffly, correctly, dismounted. When Milo turned, the old noble followed him up the stairs and into the war chief's lodge.

Even unconscious, it required strenuous and concerted efforts from both Horsekiller and Old-Cat to force a breach in Lord Alexandros' formidable mind-shield. When, through the cats, Milo and Mara and Hari had entered, their shock and agreement were simultaneous.

"Someone or *something* is controlling him!" stated Milo flatly. "Placing thoughts in his mind, overriding his will."

Mara nodded. "I *knew* that that man out there was not

'Lekos. How long, do you suppose, has this entity been forcing him to *its* evil will?"

Milo shrugged. "No way of telling, really. Days, weeks, who knows? Days, certainly. I *thought* that that business, the other night, was damned odd, come to think of it. Because, in one of our early conferences—do you recall, Hari?—he made the remark that it was regrettable that he would have to retard the advance of his column, or something like that. . . ."

"Yes," affirmed the aged bard. "I, too, thought of that when he came storming in here that night. He knew, well beforehand, that the tribe's average day's march was something less than two leagues."

"Then it must have taken him within the last week," decided Milo. "So, we know *when*. What we must now determine is *how* and *why* and precisely *what*."

Once more, the three humans and two felines entered the Ehleen's mind and vainly strove to probe farther. At length, Milo sank back, perspiration beading his forehead.

"It's no use! Even with the cats, we just haven't the mental force necessary. That thing is unnaturally strong."

"Milo, Hari," Mara asked hesitantly. "How about Aldora? True, she's untrained, but we're here to guide her and she *has* demonstrated fantastic strength and ability . . ."

When Aldora entered, she was still dangling her loaded sling and a pouch of stones for it hung around her neck. "You mind-called, Lady Mara."

"Yes, child," Hari answered. "We have need of your powers."

22

When it was finally over, Aldora looked at them wonderingly. "There is much that puzzles me. This man or being, this Titus Backstrom, he *thinks* in Ehleeneekos, but he thinks of strange places and unbelievable things and he is surely no Ehleen. And, too, he thinks, sometimes, words and phrases and names that are framed in a language of utter strangeness. It is like to our tongue—of the Horse-people, I mean—but oddly different. It . . . it must be terrible to be as he is . . ."

"What do you mean, dear?" prompted Mara.

"Being someone that you are not for so many years, inhabiting another's body and . . . and now . . . not even fully inhabiting that. He . . . he can only withdraw from this body," she indicated the inert form of Lord Alexandros, "if it is conscious, you see. He expected it to be killed, knew that that would be dangerous to him, but he had done such things before and had planned to withdraw whilst it was dying, but still conscious. As it happened, he was only able to retrieve but little of his mind, before it became senseless and the way was closed. Now, he is terribly frightened that you will slay the body, without allowing it to regain consciousness, in which case, his mind can never re-enter the body—which, while not his own, he has become accustomed to. And if he cannot return in the body he has been using, to the place where is his own real body, he cannot return to *it*, when his work is done . . ." Aldora trailed off, seeming to but half-understand what she had said.

"Hari," asked Milo urgently, "is there *no* way that I can project through her?"

Blind Hari shook his head. "No. Not even I can. There are many differences between her mind and ours."

Milo turned back to Aldora. "Child, is it possible for you to ascertain *where* the controller's body—the one he left to enter this old man's, I mean—is located now?"

After a moment, she said, "In the camp of the Iron-shirts, War Chief Milo."

Rapidly, Milo gave Mara and Hari instructions on how to keep Lord Alexandros unconscious, without either killing or waking him, then helped them to move the old man into the rear of the lodge, onto a sleeping pallet. Striding back to the lodge entrance, he stuck out his head and called for Hwil Kuk and the commander-of-hundred, who had accompanied Lord Alexandros' escort.

Shortly, the escort-commander hurried out, mounted, and spurred toward the outskirts of the camp, escorted for his mission by Horsekiller.

When Milo had finished speaking, Djeen Mai slammed his big right fist into his left palm, then nodded slowly. "Witchcraft! I should've known. My lord has been strangely unlike himself these past few days, but I thought it was something else."

"What?" demanded Milo. "What untoward has happened?"

Mai looked around self-consciously. "Well," he said hesitantly, "I promised I'd tell none other, but . . . Well, nearly a week ago, just before we left Theesispolis, a man who had once, briefly, served my lord drifted into camp. He brought word that Lord Sergios, my lord's only living son, is a gravely wounded captive of the infamous pirate, Pardos, Lord of the Sea Islands. My lord told me this in confidence, ere he went back to his tent to talk further with the man, Titos. What he was told then must have been ill indeed—or so I thought—for he has behaved oddly since."

Milo's eyes narrowed. "Where is this man, this Titos, now?"

"He is in our camp," replied Mai. Then, his brow furrowing, he added, "And that, too, is odd, devilish odd. He took sick on the same night he spoke with my lord. He has remained in a swoon since then. I was for leaving him behind, but my lord insisted he be brought with us. He lies, now, in that wagon which carries him on the march."

Titos was lifted from the wagon, tightly bound and placed in a horse-litter, then conveyed back to the War Chief's lodge. Inside the front section of the lodge, he and Lord Alexandros, also bound, were placed side-by-side on the carpet. Then the group—Milo, Mara, Kuk, Hari, Mai, Sam Tchahrtuhz, Aldora, and the two cats—waited for one or both to regain consciousness.

Milo was well into his second cup of wine before he noticed that the muscles of Titos' bare arms were straining against the bonds; all at once, they relaxed completely; and, shortly after that, Lord Alexandros opened his eyes.

"Hari, Aldora," Milo mindspoke hurriedly. "Is there any way to force Titos back to his own body?"

Hari "conferred" briefly with the girl before he "spoke." "Yes, Milo, I think so. If we could but put the body in sufficient peril, I think that Titos would 'voluntarily' return, for—as has been said—he can only return to his own, real, body—wherever it may be—from the body of Titos."

"Why," snapped Lord Alexandros, "am I bound? If you savage pigs mean to kill me, get it over with! And what is your purpose in dragging my poor, sick former servant here?"

On a hunch, Milo said, "Don't try to con us, Backstrom. Don't put us on. We've got your number! Furthermore, we're gonna cool you, baby, liquidate you—both of you—*per-manently!*"

He had the satisfaction of seeing "Lord Alexandros" momentarily pale. Then the *strahteegos* growled, "If you *must* speak to me, you savage dog, bark in a dialect I can understand!"

Milo switched back to Old Mehrikan. "Oh, you understand me well enough, Mr. Backstrom. Also, I'm beginning to remember some things and I think I understand a bit more about you." Then, addressing himself to all in the lodge, Milo said, "Before The Great Catastrophe—as the Ehleenee so aptly name it—Kehnooryos Ehlas was but a part of one of the states of a gigantic nation which stretched for thousands of leagues—east to west and north to south. Though the civilization of that pre-catastrophic era was far higher than anything in existence today, those who inhabited the world then, and benefited—or suffered, as the case may be—from that civilization were not gods, or anything resembling them. They were but men as yourselves.

"The search for knowledge of the universe and everything in it—which was called 'scientific research'—had advanced quite far in all conceivable directions. One of these was the search for immortality and, since the 'scientists' as they were called, had been unable to go very far along the road of true physical immortality, they had commenced a search for ways to make at least the mind immortal. One of these ways, as I remember, was a process in which the mind of an aged person could be transferred to a younger body. When knowledge of these experiments—which had been financed by the nation's government with funds which had been taxed from all its citizens—accidentally became *public* knowledge, it was labeled 'scientific vampirism' and so heatedly did the great masses of the citizens object, that the project was, supposedly, dropped.

"This all occurred some two or three years prior to The Great Catastrophe and details of this devilish enterprise were fairly well known in some circles. That is how I came by the following facts: Although some sort of mechanical contrivance was necessary to effect the initial mind-transfer, subsequent transfers and re-transfers could be accomplished by the parasitic mind alone, under certain unalterable conditions. To transfer, the parasite's brain must be conscious and the prospective host's unconscious; to return or re-transfer, the parasite's true brain must be unconscious, while the host's parasite-occupied brain was conscious. This is why Mr. Backstrom, here, could not quit Lord Alexandros, until he had been allowed to regain his senses.

"I know my statements to be truth for this reason: When first he regained consciousness and I spoke to him, I addressed Lord Alexandros/Titos Backstrom in highly idiomatic American English *and he understood!* Though this tongue was the direct ancestor of Old Mehrikan and the other Mehrikan dialects, it differs markedly from anything spoken today and too few books have survived half a millennium for any to have been able to learn, even were they, by some miracle, capable of reading them. Therefore, we can only surmise that we are dealing with a pre-Catastrophic mind."

"Unless," said Mara aloud, "he is like us . . ."

"That, Mara, is what I mean to ascertain," Milo stated. "As all know, we Undying may suffer terrible wounds, but we never die of their effects, due to our bodies' regenerative abilities; so, one of the surest tests for detecting one of us is to open an important artery or large vein and wait to see if the wound closes before the suspect bleeds to death. That is what I intend to do here.

"We will untie Titos/Titus' body's hands. After tying the body of Lord Alexandros, quite immovably, on the other side of the lodge, I shall open the other body's left femoral artery. I shall place materials, from which tourniquet and bandages may be fabricated, near to the hands of the wounded body. Then, we shall wait. We shall just wait, Mr. Backstrom. The next move will be up to you."

"You're all insane!" snarled Lord Alexandros, as Milo and Hwil Kuk lashed him to the wooden wall of the lodge. "If you murder my old friend, you'll live to regret it!"

When the carpets were turned back, an oiled skin was placed over the floorboards and the Titos body was untied, unclothed and laid upon it. Mara prepared several strips of cloth and folded a couple into thick compresses. Milo laid them, a pair of rawhide thongs and a foot-long wooden stick neatly beside the body's right hand. Then, with the blade of his *sgain dubh,* he stabbed the inside of the thigh, halfway between knee and crotch. The withdrawal of the knife brought a spurt of bright red blood:

Arising, he returned to the others and, with them, sat sipping wine and studiously ignoring the virtual litany of curses, threats, orders, imprecations and, finally, pleas, from Lord Alexandros' lips. As no one heeded any of his utterances, the *strahteegos* at last fell silent.

All at once, the naked body sat up, hurriedly tied one of the thongs between the wound and the body on the hairy thigh, inserted the stick and began to tighten it. When the rawhide was biting deeply into the flesh and the bloodspurts had slacked to a trickle, he attempted to hold the stick and apply a compress at the same time. He failed at both. The tourniquet unwound and, when the blood recommenced to spurt, he panicked, addressing Milo in the ancient vernacular.

"Oh, God damn you, you dirty bastard! Help me, I can't do it alone. I'm not one of your blasted mutants! This damned body's about to bleed to death; it's already getting weaker."

"It must have been whilst I was out talking to Djeen that night, that the swine slipped something into my wine. For, when I wakened—if you can call it that—he was *there*, within and in complete control of me! Though I knew all that he had my body say and do, I was helpless. What is he? Why did he do it?" asked Lord Alexandros.

"I don't know why yet," replied Milo grimly. "But I will, soon! As to *who* he is, he is a hundreds-of-years-old mind, that remains 'alive' by invading and usurping the bodies of others—God alone knows how many human beings he's victimized, since he began his noisome career. But he'll tell us that, too, before I'm done with him!"

Milo mindspoke Chief Djeri, issuing certain instructions, then he addressed Titos/Titus.

"There are some things I'd know of you, Backstrom. If you'll be cooperative and give me truthful answers to my questions, we can remain civilized. If not, I suppose we'll just have to see how much punishment that body of yours can endure."

The captive's answer was short and couched in ancient Anglo-Saxon words.

Hwil Kuk and Mai hustled the naked man out of the lodge and held him fast until the chiefs had completed the preparations. While a half dozen of the chiefs were engaged in secur-

ing the struggling man to the heavy, wooden frame, Milo
called Hwahlis of Linszee over.

"Take or send Aldora back to your lodge, Hwahlis," he
told the chief. "I've the feeling that this one will be long and
hard. In any case, it won't be pretty and there's no need for
the child to see it."

Nodding in agreement, Chief Hwahlis turned his daughter
over to one of the Linszee clansmen, before he rejoined the
knot of chiefs near the fire.

Milo conferred, for some little time, with Lord Alexandros—who seemed still a bit dazed—and Djeen Mai, then
strolled over to talk with some of the chiefs. At last, he came
to stand before the spread-eagled captive.

"Backstrom," he said slowly, "we are born of the same era.
I suppose you are—or were—some variety of scientist. As
such, you must realize that any human body is capable of
sustaining just so much pain, then it will die; its heart will
cease to function. Over the centuries, I have unfortunately
found it necessary to torture a number of persons, also I have
watched expert professionals perform the functions of their
unpleasant trade. I don't know whether or not *you* suffer *with*
this body, but I assume that you probably do.

"Many of the people of our age were soft, Backstrom.
I, too, was soft—once. But I'm not soft anymore! Furthermore, I despise you and everything for which you stand. Because of my extensive experiences, I believe myself capable
of keeping this body alive for a long, long time—as long as it
takes to get some answers from you at least. Because of the
fact that you are a despicable creature, I shall probably enjoy
what I'm going to do to you, enjoy it so much, in fact, that I
may find it difficult to make myself stop, even when you start
to talk.

"Therefore, I implore you—for your own sake or, at least,
for the sake of this body which houses you—to reconsider
your previous, somewhat temerarious, reply."

"Up you!" Titos/Titus sneered. Then he spat at Milo.

23

When the spear blade was hot enough—when it glowed a pale-pink, held away from the fire—Milo had four of the wiry chiefs hold the prisoner rigid, while another removed the bloody bandages from the deep gash in the thigh. Then the war chief wrapped a scrap of wet hide around the blade's tang, turned, grasping the nearly white-hot metal, and walked over to the man on the torture-frame.

Titos/Titus' wide eyes never left Milo as, without another word, he clapped the hot blade onto the area of the wound! Had it not been for the lashings securing ankles and wrists, the four chiefs could never have held the prisoner. Grimly, they hung on, half-deafened by the screams which tore from between Titos' writhing lips, or splattered by the mucus which gushed from the tormented man's nostrils.

Milo held the iron in place for the space of five heartbeats, then removed it and, without even looking at his victim, walked back over to the fire and thrust the blade back into the embers. Fishing another bit of hide from the water bucket, he selected another spear blade and holding it before him, went back to confront the sobbing, gasping, shuddering captive.

"Well, Mr. Backstrom," he said conversationally, "now you are aware that I mean business. May I say that I have seldom done a better job of wound-cauterization. But, medical matters aside, where would you prefer me to apply this iron? The left eye, perhaps?" As the blushing blade-tip approached his face, the prisoner, moaning in horror, bent his head back and back, screwing his eyelids tight-shut. That was the moment that Milo chose to lay the red-hot blade in his subject's hairy arm-pit, a maneuver which evoked a very satisfactory response from said subject.

For nearly two hours, Milo and the chiefs and Lord Alexandros and Djeen Mai kept up the grisly task. Between screams, Titus/Titos sobbed prayers and curses, the like of which Milo had not heard in more than half a thousand years. At length, just before midnight, the broken, blackened, bloody thing indicated its willingness to answer Milo's question and the war chief had it cut down from the charred frame.

Milo hunkered beside the wreckage that had been called Titos and poured a trickle of wine down the screamed-raw throat. Then, setting the wine cup down between them, said, "All right, you parasitic bastard, *talk!* What were you up to, anyway, in taking over Lord Alexandros? It appeared you were either trying to get him killed or precipitate a pitched battle between his people and my tribe. Or, could it have been both?"

Milo had to strain to hear the hoarsely gasped answer.

"Either would've . . . been ac . . . acceptable, both better," came the reply from betwixt the Titos thing's chewed, charred lips. "Water . . . or . . . or wine? Please . . . ?"

Milo picked up the cup, holding it before Titos' remaining eye. "When you tell me this, you mental leech, *why*. Who put you up to it? The so-called High Lord?"

"No, not De . . . metrios. 'S part of . . . plan. Th' directors were . . . 'fraid Lord Alexandros . . . unite bar . . . barbarian indigenes 'n Greeks, b'fore we ready. Maybe even Black Kingdom, too . . . make one . . . whole Atlantic Coast . . . dangerous f' us. Then . . . found out you mu . . . mutant, from twentieth cen . . . tury. Had to . . . move fast . . . c'd'n fool you. Y'd *know* . . . science, not witch . . . craft. No time . . . lay groundwork . . . communicate, 'bout you . . . get help. Drink? Pl . . . please?"

Milo bent and lifted the hairless, mutilated head and held the cup so Titos might drink. He allowed the tortured hulk two swallows, then took the cup away.

"Okay, Backstrom, next question. Who are you?"

Titos' one-eyed gaze shifted. "You . . . you know . . . a'ready. 'M Titus Backstrom."

Milo drew his dirk, found one of Titos' fingers that still retained a fingernail, and jammed the dirk-point far under said nail. When, after a while, Titos' last moans had subsided, the war chief remarked, "Don't get cute with me, you son-of-a-bitch! It would only take one word from me to have you back up on that goddamn frame, you know. And the next time around, I won't take you down so soon. I'll give you another swallow of wine. Then I'll ask the question again. One more facetious remark, and you'll spend the next few hours where and how you spent the last two. Get me?"

Driving his blood-tipped dirk into the ground, he once

more lifted Titos' head and allowed him two more swallows. "Who are you, Backstrom? Whom do you represent? Where are these 'directors' and of what are they directors?"

"Titus Backstrom . . . really m' name, Doctor of Science . . . psychologist. Was Research Assistant . . . AMIR Project J & R Kennedy Science Center. Project never really stopped . . . went underground. Shelters . . . whole Center . . . fallout . . . lived through it. D'veloped vaccines . . . fight plagues . . . pigmentation viruses, too. Kept Center area sealed . . . years . . . finally let 'nough outsiders in . . . form breeding stock . . . new bodies, f' minds worth saving . . . scientists, others . . . chosen by directors."

Milo gave the wreckage another drink and continued his interrogation.

"Now, then, the sixty-four-dollar question, Backstrom. What are you damned vampires up to down there? You said you weren't ready yet. Ready for what?"

Before Titos could answer, there was the thunder of pounding hoofs and six nomad riders burst into the space before the war chief's lodge. All were bleeding, their armor hacked and shattered. Three were leading horses; on one, an ashy faced warrior reeled in the saddle to which his comrades had lashed him. Another of the horses bore a tied-on, dead clansman; the third, the arrow-bristling corpse of a prairie-cat.

Their leader, a sub-chief of Clan Pahtuhr, had lost his helmet. Half his scalp flapped with his movements and that side of his head and neck and face were crusty with dried blood. A soggy red rag was tied around his right biceps, the ends of it knotted to the cut stump of arrow-shaft protruding from the arm. He slid from the saddle of his foam-flecked mount, took one step, and pitched onto his face, to lie unmoving.

Gentle hands lifted the stricken sub-chief and others, equally gently, assisted his companions from their saddles and unhorsed the bodies. After a great quaff of wine, the sub-chief insisted that he be taken to the war chief. Hearing, Milo came to the wounded man, beckoning Lord Alexandros and Djeen Mai to accompany him.

"It is obvious, Tribe-brother, that you and your clansmen have fought hard," Milo said gravely. "But, then, never were warriors of Pahtuhr craven or lacking of honor. What are your words for me, man of valor?"

Despite his weakness and the pain of his wounds, the sub-chief smiled and glowed at the praise. "We were many hours' ride north and east of the river that the Dirtmen name Suthahnah, when we came upon strange Ironshirts, all as fair as the Kindred. As there were but less than a score, I decided to take one as captive, that it might be known how many they were and from whence, for they were as no Ironshirts I have seen. We ambushed them and slew most with arrows, but, as we rode off with their chief, who was only wounded, more came upon us. Hard pressed we were—fighting more than three score Ironshirts—but the brave cat-brother was far-ranging and heard and came to smite the Ironshirts from their rear. He panicked their horses and slew at least two men. In the confusion we fled. Though they did not pursue, they shot many arrows after us and one such killed our captive. I am sorry, War Chief, but as all of us were wounded, it would have been certain death to go back for another."

Lord Alexandros knelt on the other side of the nomad and laid a hand on the breastplate of the man's shattered cuirass. "Any could see that you and your brave companions did your best. Tell me, what colors did they wear?"

The nomad shook his head. "Again, am I sorry, Chief Alexandros. It is hard to distinguish colors by moonlight and . . ."

The old lord patted the nomad's shoulder. "Never mind," he soothed. "You said the captive was killed. What of his horse?"

Djeen Mai strode over to lead back the spent horse from which the dead cat had been unloaded. The animal's saddle was covered with the skin of a lynx—the fur now crusty-brown with blood of man and blood of cat—and the saddle-cloth was of a dark shade of green, its scalloped edges worked with black thread and silver wire.

At sight of the horse-trappings, both Lord Alexandros and Djeen Mai swore sulphurously and Mai burst out. "King Mahrtuhn of Kuhmbrulun by damn! So the eater of dung couldn't keep out of it! I wonder if he's hired out to Demetrios or just come to scavenge what he can? The latter sounds more like him, but . . . What think you, my lord?"

"I think it's an old game he's playing, Djeen." The *strahteegos* smiled tiredly. "He is as much aware as we of Demetrios' weakness. It's been advantageous to him to have a weak High Lord, one disinclined to warfare. The last thing he wants to see is someone like myself on the throne of

Kehnooryos Ehlas; but I don't believe him to be in Demetrios' pay. For one thing, he knows he'd play merry hell in
collecting—in coin, anyway. For another, even a thing like
Demetrios is, after all, an Ehleen and, as such, I don't believe
he would willingly ally himself with any of the barbarian
principalities or kingdoms.

"No, I think Mahrtuhn is playing himself a little game of
'king-maker.' He'll wait until we attack the city, then he'll attack *us* in the rear with an overwhelming force. When we've
been cracked between his army and Demetrios', he'll extort
some kind of settlement from the perverted child-bugger.
Those will be the kinglet's actions, if we allow his plans to
mature."

Milo was about to interject a question, when the mental
communication entered his mind.

"Now, you'll not hurt this body anymore, you goddamn
mutant bastard. Your day will come, you sonofabitch, heed
me well. When we're ready, your day wi—"

"Backstrom!" Milo shouted suddenly in alarm, furiously
thrusting his way through the press of men.

By that time, of course, it was already too late. Somehow,
despite broken bones and mangled, hideously maimed hands,
the Titos/Titus thing had managed to pull Milo's dirk out of
the ground and thrust the weapon's wide, sharp blade deep
into its own throat, just under the jawbone's angle.

Lord Alexandros ordered his troops back to their camp to
get as much rest as they could for what remained of the
night. Ahead of them went a galloper, whose mission was
that of fetching back the *heeroorgos*—surgeon—and his as-
sistants and wagon to tend and care for the members of the
patrol. Milo offered blood-price for the slain bugler, but both
the *strahteegos* and Djeen Mai brusquely refused to accept it.
They did accept, however, the War Chief's offer to cremate
the dead soldier on the same pyre which was to bear the
bodies of Pahtuhr clansmen and the dead cat. The body that
Titus Backstrom had inhabited was dragged a few hundred
yards and dumped in a patch of woods—an unexpected feast
for the animals of the night.

And, while the scavengers gorged themselves, Milo and the
Council of Chiefs and Lord Alexandros and his staff sat in
conference until the first light of the sun was paling the
eastern horizon, and it was time to break camp and recom-

mence the march. Results of that conference were not long in coming. By the time camp was pitched the next night, mixed patrols of nomads and *kahtahfrahktoee* had already garnered three prisoners. Two were mercenaries, natives of the Kingdom of Eeree, north and west of Kuhmbrulun, who proved only too happy to transfer their allegiance to the redoubtable Lord Alexandros (after all, they had already collected King Mahrtuhn's coin) and impart all that they knew of the barbarian kinglet's projected strategy. The third was an entirely different case. Captain Beem was a nobleman, third son of the Count of Frahstburk. He was twenty-eight years old and, though a bit dull-witted, honest as the day is long, honorable and not in the least craven. He had only been taken alive because the sling stone which had deeply indented his helmet had failed to crack the skull beneath, and this capture was a source of chagrin to him.

At Captain Beem's courteous but, nonetheless, flat refusal to impart them an iota of information regarding his liege, King Mahrtuhn, or aught concerning him or his army, one of the chiefs suggested that they build a fire and construct a torture frame. Lord Alexandros shook his head. "That man possesses every bit the courage that you and your people do. You might take him apart, bit by bit, and—ere he allowed the agonies you inflicted to render him false to his word— he'd bite out his own tongue and spit it in your faces! I know his breed of old; they are honorable and worthy opponents."

So, they drugged his wine and Milo—through Horse-killer—entered his mind. This exercise filled all the gaps in the information which the mercenaries had supplied. It was quite evident that Lord Alexandros did not entirely approve so dishonorable a method of obtaining intelligence, but he and his staff were quick to compile and begin to evaluate it, albeit.

It seemed that King Mahrtuhn had laid his last ounce of silver on this one throw of the dice. He had virtually stripped his own personal lands and cities—even to the extent of cleaning out prisons and offering amnesty in return for military service in this venture. He had squeezed his vassals as hard as he dared and hired every condotta he could contact. Furthermore, he was leading his army—huge to the point of being a bit unwieldy—himself! His heavy and light infantry numbered some five thousands—the heavy being mercenaries and the light being well-equipped, but mostly ill or untrained jail-scrapings and impressed civilians. He had hired eight thousand mercenary dragoons (*kahtahfrahktoee* to the Ehleenee) and these, with the armed nobles and their personal troops, gave him a force numbering something over sixteen thousand men. In his haste to reach the vicinity of Kehnooryos Atheenahs before Alexandros and the nomads, he had recklessly divided his forces and Milo and the *strahteegos* immediately came to agreement on a way to give the kinglet cause to regret his rashness. "Divide et Vincit!"

24

Count Normun was seething with suppressed anger and felt himself to be much put-upon. It was most unfair, he felt, for his cousin, King Mahrtuhn, to go galloping off and leave him in nominal command of the foot-troops and baggage-train. Realizing that anything vaguely resembling honor or glory or loot would be over and done long before he and his "command" came up, and sulking in consequence, he had allowed the interval—originally about a day's march—between the head of his column and the tail of the bulk of the cavalry to nearly double. The heads of the drums were covered and the troops sauntered along the roadway at whatever pace suited them. Their pikes were carried slanted at every angle and, as the weather was quite warm, many had removed their helmets and unlaced their brigandines. The lack of any semblance of discipline or order was contagious and was even beginning to spread into the ranks of Captain Looisz Klahrk's twelve hundred mercenary heavy infantry.

Count Normun sat slouched in his saddle, one knee crooked around the pommel. He was discussing various aspects of the hunting of deer with Captain Klahrk, who—though the younger son of a younger son and, consequently, landless—was nobly born and spoke the same "language" as his titular commander.

Although his own hard-bitten troops—despite the best efforts of their brutal but effective noncoms—were commencing to break ranks and straggle in emulation of the light infantry, Klahrk felt little cause for worry. The two columns of cavalry, which had preceded this one, were sure to have gone through this country like a dose of salts and any living human beings left in their wake were probably still running. Seasoned campaigner that he was, he had taken certain precautions, ordering three tens of the hundred dragoons, originally detailed as baggage-wagon guards, to position at point and flanks, and yet another ten to remain several hundred yards behind the last of the lumbering wagons and the gaggle of camp-followers.

Captain Klahrk was in the process of regaling Count Normun with the story of an exceptionally exciting shaggy-bull hunt in which he had taken part some years before in the Principality of Redn. All at once, both his horse and the count's screamed and reared. Klahrk managed to retain his seat, but the count was hurled onto the stones of the roadbed and only his helmet saved him from a fractured skull.

As Klahrk fought to control his maddened mount, the woods on both sides of the column began to resound the deadly *thruuummm* of bowstrings and the air was abruptly thick with hard-driven arrows. Twenty-five yards back, a pair of huge-boled trees crashed down on the already disordered infantry, squashing them like bugs. And the arrows continued to *ssiisshh* their song of death, coming in on a flat trajectory and—seemingly of their own volition—cunningly seeking out every gap of unlaced brigandine, every helmetless head or unprotected throat, skewering arms and legs and faces. No sooner had Klahrk brought his arrowed horse under control, than the poor beast was struck again. At that point, Klahrk gave up, slipped his feet from the stirrups and leaped onto the roadway. There, he drew his sword and, seemingly heedless of the feathered death hissing around him, commenced to try to whip his troops into a formation of sorts, to repel the cavalry charge which was sure to follow the arrowstorm.

Impelled by his valiant example, those of his sergeants still on their feet emulated him, and soon the familiar curses and threats lulled the men's panic somewhat. Shortly, his condotta had begun to form—their twelve-foot pikes properly slanted and faced toward the south, the only feasible route for an attack of cavalry. As the fire of the arrows abated to some degree, the kneeling front rank announced that they could feel the vibration of many hoofs, transmitted by the road-stones; Klahrk and his non-coms redoubled their efforts, for the more depth the formation possessed, the better their chances were of stopping the horsemen.

Soon everyone could feel the thud-thudding of the approaching attackers. Then, war cries became audible and the veteran pikemen braced themselves, their earlier panic dissipated. The horses and their shouting, screaming, cursing riders drew closer and closer and, at any moment, Klahrk and his condotta expected to see the first fours come galloping around the bend in the road. They waited, every man's nerves drawn tight as a bowstring. Then came an unfamiliar bugle call.

It was the crackling and crashing in the dark, roadside woods that first announced to Klahrk that he was about to be flanked.

"*Porkypine!*" he roared to his underlings. "Column one, right, *FACE*. Column ten, left, *FACE*. Columns one and ten, *KNEEL!* Columns one and ten, low slant, *PIKES!*"

And the discipline of drill-field and battlefield did the rest. In short order, the survivors of Klahrk's condotta presented a facade of bristling pike-points, very reminiscent of the animal the formation emulated. But it was all in vain, for—when at last delivered—the charge was not against Klahrk's dangerous veterans, but, rather, against the milling, all but helpless light infantry, who clogged the road behind them.

The heavy-armed Grey Horse Squadron wreaked truly fearful casualties among the already terrified amateur soldiers. Hundreds went down under the dripping swords and those who did not ran squalling in every direction—pursued relentlessly by the grim, iron-scale-armored men on the big gray horses. Discarding everything which might, in any way, retard them, the fugitives ran northward toward the comparative safety of the baggage-train.

Some reached it, only to discover that they had fled the fangs of the wolf and escaped into the jaws of the panther! For, by then, the nomads had already slain the wagoneers and their guards and most of the camp followers, had looted what they could carry, and were commencing to set fire to what they could not transport. They fell on the light infantry-men with gusto!

Pinned down as he was by the recommenced arrow-fire, Captain Klahrk had made no attempt to go to the aid of the light infantry. Besides, he had rationalized, what good would it have done, anyway? Who ever heard of infantry attacking mounted cavalry? He had—at great personal risk—strapped a body-shield to his back, run out, and dragged the semi-conscious Count Normun back—only to have an arrow kill the nobleman as he was lifting him over the forwardmost file of pikemen. Doggedly, he held his impregnable formation, even as the rising billows of smoke announced the firing of the wagons.

Then, all around his porkypine, bone-whistles shrilled and the arrows ceased to fly. Down from the north, trotted a column of disciplined—if somewhat blood-splashed cavalry—dragoons on gray horses. They halted at a hundred yards' distance. More of the ominous crashing indicated that additional cavalry were within the cover of the woods. Around the bend of the road, from the south, appeared the vanguard of what seemed to be a sizable number of light cavalry—western nomads, from the look of them.

Klahrk was of the opinion that he was about to fight his last battle and was mentally framing a stirring address to his doomed command when, out of the dragoons' ranks, a vaguely familiar man rode forth, to rein up just beyond the pike-points.

The rider—by dress, obviously an officer—lowered his beavor and shouted, "By God, you bastards are professionals or I'm a bit of mule's dung! Whose fornicating company is this?"

Klahrk shouldered his way through the ranks of his men. "Mine!" he shouted. "Looisz Klahrk's. Who wants to know?"

Then he saw the horseman's face at close range. "Djeen!" He grinned, hugely. "Djeen Mai! Why you old boar, you! I'd have thought that the law-keepers, somewhere, would have caught and hung you long since; if a jealous husband or vengeful father hadn't beaten them to it. If *you* engineered this ambuscade, my compliments, it was beautifully designed and executed. King Mahrtuhn'll be excreting red-hot pokers when he hears of it. You cost *me* a good three hundred killed and wounded. But I've still enough to take a fair toll of . . ."

Djeen raised his hand. "Hold on, hold on, old friend. I've no desire to *fight* you! Tell me, has King Mahrtuhn paid you?" At Klahrk's nod, he went on.

"I'm in service to Lord Alexandros of Pahpahs, who means to make himself High Lord of Kehnooryos Ehlas—all of it, as it was three hundred years ago, if I know my lord—and think of the pickings of that!"

Klahrk frowned and shook his head. "Djeen, if you're hinting that I change sides—foreswear my oath to save my hide—forget it. I swore King Mahrtuhn three months service and took his gold and I'll not go back on my word to him. As well as we know each other, in fact, I'm surprised that *you* would suggest such a thing to *me!*"

"Well," Djeen sighed, "it was just a thought. But there are different ways to serve an employer, Looisz. For instance, there're a goodly number, I doubt me not, of wounded back there." He hooked his thumb northward. "They're in serious need of attention. They really *should* be gotten back to Kuhmbrulun. What of your stores we didn't lift, will be burned to the axles by the time you get to them, and you're going to play pure hell, trying to march on without them through a countryside the dragoons have already picked clean! Then, too, I'd not be at all surprised but what the Prince of Fredrik was very interested when our messengers informed him that damned near every mother's-son in Kuhmbrulun was deep in the heart of Kehnooryos Ehlas. Yes, Looisz, there're many, many different ways of serving one's employer."

Djeen reined half around and extended his right hand to grip that of his old friend. "I lost half a dozen troopers," he said in parting. "I'll leave their mounts for you and your sergeants. You needn't fear for the safety of any messengers you should decide to send south—if you do so decide; they'll be passed, never you worry."

While they had been conversing, the nomads had clattered off, headed south and west. When Djeen rejoined his command, the squadron left the littered, blood-splotched road and were soon lost to sight, in the forest.

By the time Klahrk's men had done what they could for the wounded and salvaged what little they were able to salvage of the stores in the merrily blazing wagons, the mercenary captain had come to a decision. He carefully drilled one of his sergeants, until the man could repeat the message word for word three times running. Then he gave him one of the gray horses and sent him southward at a gallop to seek out Duke Herbut, commander of the main contingent of dragoons.

The nomads had driven off most of the horses and oxen and mules, but a few had been unavoidably slain; these,

Klahrk had his men flay and butcher; then set them to cooking the meat, ere it began to spoil.

Remembering the topography of the country they had traversed, he and his condotta—bearing with them the wounded and such supplies and equipment as they possessed—withdrew a half-mile up the road. There, on a meadow which was near to an adequate source of water, they ditched and mounded the outline of a castra in which to spend the night. Early in the morning, they set about palisading it with logs, hewed in the nearby forest and snaked out by men and the five horses.

When, nearly three days later, Duke Herbut and some six thousand cavalry arrived, it was before a stout little emergency fort. After he and captain Klahrk had conferred briefly, the duke detached two squadrons to escort infantry and wounded on their trek north, then he and the other four squadrons spurred hard for Kuhmbrulun.

When word was brought to the council, the chiefs roared and hugged each other and danced joyfully. Djeen Mai and Sam Tchahrtuhz beat their thighs and howled their merriment. Even undemonstrative old Lord Alexandros allowed himself a broad smile of satisfaction at this unqualified success of his brain-child.

"So," commented Milo, when the hubbub had died down, "they swallowed it, hook, line, and bloody sinker! Well, deduct six thousand *kahtahfrahktoee* and deduct the thousand or so who survived the ambush and deduct the four thousand casualties that Djeen estimates we inflicted, and your remainder is about five thousand cavalry. They're completely unsupported and they've lost the bulk of their supplies; they're nearly forty leagues deep in basically hostile territory with a ravaged countryside behind them. I shouldn't think they'd present any appreciable danger to us, not unless the others come to realize the deception when they arrive in Kuhmbrulun, and hotfoot it back to reinforce. Barring that, we should be able to crush or scatter this kinglet's troops at will."

But Lord Alexandros shook his white head. "I beg pardon, my Lord Milos, but I must disagree with you; furthermore, I implore you not to underestimate King Mahrtuhn's abilities, for he *is* quite an able *strahteegos*. He rode ahead with the bulk of the nobility, not for personal glory, but because they are the most effective and formidable men that he has. Like your nomads, these men are, from the very cradle, *bred* to war and most are masters of every conceivable weapon. They are courageous and hard fighters, possess a strict and highly complex code of honor, and are altogether worthy and dangerous foemen. Djeen, here, is nobly born, being a nephew of the Duke of Pahtzburk; so, too, is Sam Tchahrtuhz, the natural son of the former Count of Zunburk.

"Noblemen, generally speaking, sire huge broods and this is very necessary, for they tend to kill each other off at a prodigious rate. Their states are small, inherently hostile to each other, and voraciously land-hungry. It is probable that, within the last three hundred years, there have been but few twelvemonths that did not see a conflict—of greater or lesser magnitude—*somewhere* within the north-barbarian states!

"As the land has been warred over for so many years, it is nowhere near as productive—in the senses of agriculture or husbandry—as even the border themes of the Ehleenee lands; but, for all that, most of the so-called barbarian states are well-off, if not wealthy. The reason for this is that every city and, frequently, town has its shops and manufactories. Prior to the arrival of the tribe, I would, for instance, have felt it safe to say that fully eighty of every hundred swords swung from the South Ehleen lands to the North Ehleen Republic had blades produced in the Kingdom of Harzburk, or the Kingdom of Pitzburk or the Grand Duchy of Bethlemburk! Those three and their neighbors also produce a plethora of metal products—tools and utensils as well as weapons, not to mention the best and most modern of armor—not this heavy, clumsy, old-fashioned loricate, or jazeran, mind you; but brigandines and cuirasses very similar to those of your people. But where yours are of leather, theirs are of steel! Also, the statelets produce glass, work gold and silver and fabricate jewelry.

"All in all, they are truly a gifted people and little deserve the appellation of 'barbarian.' Considering their technical skills and their military abilities, if they could stop fighting amongst themselves and present a united front, they could soon be the masters of all the Ehleenee lands and the Black Kingdoms as well.

"No, Lord Milos, do not underestimate the danger that King Mahrtuhn and his nobility represent. I thank God that our ambush and the trick which followed it were successful. For, had they not been, we'd have been wiped out, had we been sufficiently stupid to stand and fight!"

But as it developed, the confrontation Lord Alexandros so dreaded did not come to pass, not that year. On the receipt of certain information, King Mahrtuhn and his nobles and men cut cross-country to the Traderoad and spurred for Kuhmbrulun as fast as horseflesh could bear them, not even taking time to loot the areas through which they passed. Mahrtuhn could no longer afford to interfere in an Ehleenee civil war, as he and his retinue now had one of their own to attend. His informants had brought the sad news that his brother, Duke Herbut, had gathered what few nobles remained in the kingdom and overawed or bought them. However it had been accomplished, he had usurped Mahrtuhn's throne, declared Mahrtuhn and his chief supporters outlaw, and was busily hiring troops and fortifying the capital city. It seemed that Mahrtuhn had not only lost his stakes, but the dice as well!

25

From village and from cabin,
Rushed those loyal to our Lord.
And, fitting scythe to pike-shaft,
Joined our column, at his word.
And the High Lord's spies did tremble,
As our numbers swelled and soared.
When we marched east from Theesispolis.
                              —Ehleenee Marching Song

Something less than two weeks after Demetrios' tantrum, his understrength navy boarded its three best ships, scuttled the others, and beat their way downriver, bound for the sea. With them went the High Lord's last hope of escape.

His retinue of former sycophants took to avoiding his company as much as possible, for all who knew him expected the knowledge that he was trapped to drive him over the edge into true madness. But it did not. Oddly enough, the realization that he was doomed did what his father and the *strahtee-goee* had never been able to do—it made a real man of him. At the eleventh hour, the Demetrios-who-should-have-been belatedly emerged from the gross, debauched cocoon which had held him for so many years. And that perverted, self-seeking coterie who had influenced and guided him were stunned to discover that no longer had his High Lord need or use for them, no longer could they control or even predict his actions.

The first to meet—to his sorrow—this *new* High Lord, was Teeaigos, Lord High *Strahteegos* of Kehnooryos Atheenahs, a languid creature a couple of years older than the High Lord. He had attained the position by flattery, and "performance" of "duties" had made of him a fabulously wealthy man. On the day of his downfall, he was impatiently listening to the justifiable complaints of Sergeant-Major Mahrk Hailee, commander of the White Horse Squadron, concerning the all-time low quality of the rations just issued his troops—weevil-crawling flour, three-quarters rotted vegetables and stinking, overaged meat, and not one ounce of oil or wine.

When the non-com's flow of heated words had ceased, Teeaigos waved his white, gilded-nailed hands negligently. Though his painted lips smiled, his eyes were cold and uncaring. "If your barbarian swine don't like the good food—really, far too good, for the likes of them—that my quartermaster issues, let them eat their horses; after all, what good are the smelly beasts, pray tell."

The occupants of the headquarters included Teeaigos, his two secretary-clerks, Sergeant-Major Hailee and his adjutant, and two representatives of the civil guard who were awaiting a hearing. None of them had noticed the quiet entrance of another figure. The newcomer was half-armored—helmet of ancient-Ehleenee design, breast-and-back and articulated pauldrons of finest Harzburk steelplate, scale-back gauntlets secured to tight-fitting vambraces of watered steel; the kilt was of blue-dyed canvas brigandine and fell to the knee; and on his left hip was belted a heavy, cut-and-thrust sword, while a dagger with wide, leaf-shaped blade jutted its hilt over his right hip. Not one trace of cosmetic remained on his face and, under the cheek-plates, his beard had been shaved, its last remnant being a blue-black spike, which jutted from his chin.

Even when the figure strode across to stand before the
Lord High *Strahteegos,* he went unrecognized until he spoke.
In a deceptively soft tone, he said, "Teeaigos, do you no
longer arise when your superiors enter; or has this office,
which I stupidly gave you, so swelled your head, that you feel
yourself to *have* no superiors?"

Teeaigos lumbered to his feet. "My . . . my lord!" he
stammered, nonplussed by sight of an armed and armored
Demetrios. "I . . . I did not know, my lord. Pardon, but . . .
but as sensitive as is my lord's skin, isn't he *terribly* uncomfortable in such barbaric attire?"

Not one whit so uncomfortable as you soon will be, my
false friend, thought the High Lord. But he said, "Discomfort
is of little consequence, when the city and its people lie in
such danger. Tell me, Teeaigos, if the White Horse Squadron
are to help defend this city, why were they served up with
such shoddy fare?"

Teeaigos squirmed uneasily; then, putting on a bold front,
said, "My lord must **know**, the war chest is all but empty.
The quartermaster purchased what he could afford, I am
sure. Food prices are astronomically high in the city and
country. Furthermore, most merchants and farmers are insisting that they be paid in gold, and we have only silver."

Demetrios extended a gauntleted hand to lift and weigh the
heavy, golden chain whose flat links rested across Teeaigos'
narrow shoulders. "There *was* gold in the war chest,
Teeaigos. Gold from Theesispolis. What happened to it? Did
it go into your new chain and armlets, perhaps?"

"Why . . . why . . . why, *of course* not, my lord,"
Teeaigos spluttered, his face chalky under the rouge and
paint. "My *personal* fortune . . ."

"Was dissipated," Demetrios cut him off, "long years before you wheedled this sinecure out of me! Here." He
brought up his other hand and, with both of them, lifted the
chain over Teeaigos' head. Then he turned and handed it to
Sergeant-Major Hailee.

"Perhaps, with the value of this useless bauble, you can
procure decent food for your squadron." He smiled. Hailee
was too shocked to answer and, as he continued silent, Demetrios frowned. "Not enough, eh? Well, take his armlets, too,
then. I'll find replacements for them."

Demetrios beckoned to the elder of the two civil guards.

When the man stood before him, he asked, "What is your name and rank, sir?"

Standing at stiff attention, the fiftyish guardsman snapped his answer. "Szamyul Thorntun, Senior-Sergeant of the southeastern quarter, and it please my lord!"

The High Lord turned to Mahrk Hailee. "Is this man trustworthy and loyal? Do you feel him to be a good commander of men?"

Hailee, though still a bit numb, had recovered to some degree. "Why . . . why, yes, my lord. Yes to both questions."

Demetrios nodded. "In the presence of you three men," he waved his arm to include Hailee, his adjutant, and the other civil guard, "I, hereby, declare Szamyul Thorntun elevated to the post of Governor of the Prisons and Grand Commander of the Civil Guard. As well as partaking of all the rights and privileges of that office, he is to faithfully discharge the multitudinous duties entailed. His predecessor and this other traitor," he pointed at Teeaigos, "the lord governor is to have stripped, fitted with the heaviest available chains and manacles, and immured in the lowest, dankest, foulest cell in the prison; there, to await my pleasure."

"Hai . . . Hailee, Kwinsee, quick," shouted Teeaigos frightenedly, "seize him, bind him! He . . . the High Lord has finally gone mad!"

Hailee didn't budge. "High Lord Demetrios sounds very sane to me, Lord Teeaigos. Saner, by far, than any other noble in this city." Then he snapped to attention.

"Has the High Lord orders for me?" he questioned Demetrios.

"Yes, sir," Demetrios answered gravely. "Though not truly orders. I have forfeited any right to order you by the disgraceful ill-treatment I've afforded you and your men. After the last five years, there is no understandable reason why you and your squadron should retain any trace of loyalty toward me; but, I pray that you do, for I have great need of you.

"You see, *someone* must replace Teeaigos, as Lord High *Strahteegos* of this city and, sad to say, all of his peers-in-rank are of his ilk—useless, treacherous, self-seeking, and false. I need a man who knows the city and its needs and its soldiery and their needs. I need a man of *your* caliber, Mahrk Hailee; but the city is doomed to fall in any case, so I cannot order you to assume the post. I can only ask you. I would consider it an undeserved, personal favor, if you would consent to become Lord High *Strahteegos* of Kehnooryos Atheenahs. Will you, please?"

When Teeaigos had been bereft of his finery and hustled out by the new prison governor and his deputy, bound for a whipping and a cell, Lord Mahrk spoke. "My Lord Demetrios, as to a new commander of the Squadron, I . . ."

Demetrios waved a gauntleted hand. "I defer to your judgment, of course, Lord Mahrk. I freely confess that I know nothing of military matters." He shook his helmeted head sadly. "I don't even know the basic elements regarding the use of the weapons I bear. This much, at least, I should like to try to remedy, before I die. Do . . . do you think that one of your troopers could find it in his heart to consent to teach me a little of sword-play? I . . . I'd not ask it, but . . . but, you see, I mean to take active part in the fight for my city and . . . and I'd not like to give too poor a showing in this, my first and last battle."

The changes which altered Kehnooryos Atheenahs in the ensuing weeks were sweeping. Teeaigos and his cell-mate soon had company in the lower tier, a great deal of it and almost all Ehleenee nobles, Demetrios' former cronies, one and all. In fact, such were the numbers of the new prisoners, that Lord Szamyul found it necessary to have all the former inhabitants of the lowest areas brought higher to make room for this influx of once-powerful personages. Appalled at the conditions of the starved, much-tortured, rat-chewed wretches—some of whom had not seen daylight in four and one-half years—the prison governor applied to the High Lord for permission to—insofar as was possible—restore them to health. He found Demetrios—clad in brigandine and plain helmet and weighted buskins, and gripping a double-heavy practice sword, with a huge, convex body-shield on his left arm—trading hard blows with the White Horse Squadron's weapons-master. There was a shallow scratch across the High Lord's right cheek and his chin-beard was stiff with dried blood, his features were uniformly red and sweat-streaked; too, he seemed to have lost a bit of weight.

When the High Lord spotted Lord Szamyul, he caught one more swipe on his shield, then stepped back and saluted the weapons-master, saying, "You must pardon me, for a moment, good friend, duty calls." Thrusting the metal-shod wooden sword through his belt, he walked over to Lord Szamyul, smiling. The prison governor noticed, at closer range, that, though the ruler's eyes showed weariness, both skin and eyes were amazingly clear. Demetrios looked healthier than Lord Szamyul—or anyone else for that matter—could ever remember having seen him!

Courteously, the High Lord heard his appointee out. Then he gave Lord Szamyul leave to do as he saw fit, complimented him on his recent activities and achievements and, with equal courtesy, excused himself to return to his session with the weapons-master.

The city was crowded with refugees from the countryside and their straits were desperate. When the new Demetrios was apprised of their plight, he immediately ordered the barracks, which had once housed Djeen Mai's squadron, opened to them. As this proved insufficient, he moved his black spearmen into the palace proper, and opened their barrack, as well, to the refugees.

As the threatening army neared Kehnooryos Atheenahs, the prices of food were driven up and up, until starvation grimly stalked most quarters of the city. In their sumptuous residences, however, the nobles still feasted on hoarded delicacies. At least they did until the new Demetrios was informed of the situation. Then the feasters discovered that Demetrios-in-the-right could be just as swift and ruthless as Demetrios-in-the-wrong! Without warning, his soldiers swooped down, between midnight and dawn, on the quarter of the nobility. By right of the sword, they ransacked homes and cellars and out-buildings. Everything edible was carted back to the palace warehouses. Throughout the next day, the confiscations were carried out in all quarters and, shortly, the courtyard of the palace had become a stockyard—packed with lowing, bawling, excreting, cud-chewing, food-on-the-hoof. Then Demetrios outlined what he wanted done. Soon, notices were being tacked up for those who could read. For those who could not, brazen-throated criers ceaselessly repeated that: In future, until the threat to the city had abated, all food was become the property of the High Lord and would be evenly rationed, twice each day, to all persons, citizen or no, equally.

The palace cooks had been put to cooking for the refugees,

so Demetrios began messing with the officers of the White Horse Squadron; and, now and again, the common troopers would find the High Lord—bowl and cup in hand, still garbed in his sweat-soaked brigandine—bringing up the rear of their own slop-line. (After the first of these incidents, the preparation of the food mysteriously improved!)

The High Lord took to appearing—armed and armored, but usually unaccompanied—on the walls and on the streets at all hours, day and night. He amiably chatted with noble and soldier, citizen and refugee, man or woman or child. The first question he put to any was always the same one: What could be done to improve their lot?

To all adult, male slaves, who were capable of and would swear to bear arms for the city, he granted freedom and citizenship. Of course, the nobles howled. Those who howled too loudly and too threateningly found themselves prevailed upon to partake of the High Lord's "hospitality" which was being enjoyed by Lord Teeaigos among others. After the incarceration of the loud-howlers, none others of the un-jailed nobles saw fit to even appear to question any of the High Lord's actions.

As all his advisors and high-ranking civil-servants had been imprisoned—most charged with a whole plethora of offenses against individuals, the state, or both—Demetrios, to all intents and purposes, ruled alone. But it was not as difficult an undertaking as one might have thought, for—with the sole exception of the bulk of the nobles, whose numbers were too small to really matter—the inhabitants of his city were solidly behind him and, if they had not had the time to come to love him, they respected him. To the men of the White Horse Squadron, their High Lord was become one of themselves, and they adored him.

So matters stood on the bleak, November day that saw the appearance of the vanguard of the army and allies of the outlawed *Strahteegos*, Lord Alexandros Pahpahs.

26

Lord Alexandros' eyes goggled at his visitor, Lord High *Strahteegos* Mahrk Hailee. At last, he shouted, "Has all of the world gone suddenly *mad*? He wants to meet *me*? There *must* be trickery somewhere! That spineless, quivering tub of flab . . ."

"My *Lord!*" *Strahteegos* Hailee cut him off, coldly courteous. "My dread sovereign, Demetrios, High Lord of Kehnooryos Ehlas, has bid me offer you honorable combat. This combat is to be of a personal nature and is to be fought in clear sight of the opposing forces." Hailee began to recite the rote. "Such an offer denotes courage and honor and battle-prowess, though deep respect for one's enemy is indicated in such willingness to accept a death—if need be—at his hands." He returned to a normal tone. "My lord realizes that he has earned your antipathy."

Lord Alexandros snorted and, glowering, started to snarl a reply. But Hailee raised his hand. "Please, my lord, have the courtesy to allow me to finish."

"Courtesy!" yelped Lord Alexandros. "Who are *you* to demand courtesy from me?"

Hailee drew himself to stiffly formal attention. "Lord Mahrk Hailee, High *Strahteegos* of Kehnooryos Atheenahs and, presently, War-Herald of my puissant Lord, Demetrios Treeah-Pohtahmos!"

"Oh, sweet Jesus Christ!" Lord Alexandros threw himself against the canvas back of his folding camp-chair. "The world that I knew has turned upside down and no mistake! What have we here? A barbarian is Lord High *Strahteegos* of an Ehleenee city. Another is commander of that city's civil guard and governor of its prison. Three quarters of that city's adult, male nobility are imprisoned. The fact that most of them have deserved at least that for years has no bearing upon the present issue. And ninety percent of the adult, male slaves have been declared to be free citizens of the city and are bearing arms in its defense.

"I arrive before city walls that I had expected to be all-but deserted, to find them literally bristling with spearmen. For five years, this city has been misruled, as has all of Kehooryos Ehlas, to the benefit of certain unscrupulous noble families; yet, who are the first persons who come to me begging asylum and protection from their benefactor, but representatives of these same rapacious noble families! As late as two moons agone, Demetrios was almost universally hated. He had well earned the hatred of slaves, foreigners, citizens, soldiery, all the minor nobles, and many of the greater, especially those of the older houses; but, who comprises the group which comes to me, but representatives of all these classes, warning me that they and those that they represent will fight to the death, that I will have to pull the city down, stone by stone, to unseat their well-*loved* High Lord! *I*, who came to free them from the domination of a half-mad tyrant, am given the greeting of a foreign invader!

"And now, this! To add insult to injury, a gross, loathsome creature, whose only accomplishments consist of wine-swilling and buggery, sends me a so-called war herald. A thing who is Ehleenee only by accident of birth, who doesn't know one end of a sword from the other and who probably can't even lift a shield, challenges *me*—Lord Alexandros Pahpahs, the foremost *strahteegos* of the age—to *personal combat!* Pah! On those rare occasions Demetrios is not besotted, he's so hung over that he'd have great difficulty in finding his posterior with both hands! *I'll* not take part in such a farcical non-combat. It would be pure butchery and would dishonor me. Tell your piggish lord: *No*, I'll not fight him!"

"*My* Lord," said Lord Mahrk, "in full realization of your advanced years, with their attendant physical debility, bade me inform you that he would as willingly face any surrogate you saw fit to choose, so long as he be Ehleenee and nobly born. My lord desires that all things be equal and he would not take unfair advantage of an age-weakened, old man."

"*WHAAT?*" Lord Alexandros, livid, sprang up so suddenly and violently that he sent his chair flying and all but overturned his table. "That. . . that . . . that swinish young . . . that arrogant pup! Old man, am I? Age-weakened, eh? I'll cut him in half! I'll split him, like a goddam mackerel, from crown to crotch! I'll . . . I'll. . . ."

Lord Mahrk suppressed his smile. "I take it, then, that you accept my lord's offer."

With an effort, Lord Alexandros regained control of him-

self. After a long moment, he chuckled, shook his head ruefully. "I fell directly into that one, like a panther into a pit!
Tell me, did the High Lord of Perverts really frame those
words, or were they *your* extemporaneous invention?"

"You have my word on it, Lord Alexandros," Lord Mahrk
assured him. "Each word and nuance of phrasing originated
from my lord. It is what I was to repeat, should you see fit
to refuse his honorable offer."

Lord Alexandros shrugged. "Though your word means
little or nothing, of course—you and all your cursed condotta
are well known, up and down this seaboard, to be foresworn—nonetheless, I do believe you. Demetrios chose just the
proper words and tone to obtain the reaction he desired;
Basil, his father, couldn't have done it better!"

It was decided and arranged. The combatants were to en-
gage along the lines of a formal Ehleenee duel and were to
meet and exchange the customary greetings and toasts at a
spot to be one hundred paces from the city walls and one
hundred paces from the lines of Lord Alexandros' army.
Each was to bear one javelin—unbarbed and not to exceed
one meter in length or one kilo in weight. Each was to be
dressed and armored in the style of the Old Ehleenee: tight,
white, cotton shirt with short sleeves; cotton trunk-hose of
any color; high-laced, leather buskins; stiff, white linen kilt;
quilted canvas cap. Their armor, too, was to be of the Old
Ehleenee pattern: the jazeran—knee-length, leather hauberk,
to which were riveted overlapping iron scales; brass or iron
rerebraces; elbow-length, leather gauntlets, lined or scaled
with metal; molded greaves, with knee-cop; unlined steel helmet, with cheek-pieces, but no nasal, visor or beavor. In addition to the javelins, their armament was to consist of: a
double-edged sword of the ancient *Thehkahehseentah* pattern—a cut-and-thrust weapon with the blade ten centimeters
wide, immediately below the cross-guard and tapering to a
point, along a blade sixty centimeters long; a convex-surfaced
body-shield of hide-covered wood, one and one-half meters
high by one meter wide (when measured around the curve of
its outer surface), bossed and banded and edge-shod with
iron; style and numbers of daggers, dirks and/or throwing-
knives, left to the discretion of the individual combatants.
Each was to be conveyed to the scene in a chariot and, in addition to the chariot driver, might bring three attendants.

These attendants might bear sidearms only and were to take no part in the contest.

The fight, it was understood, would be to the death: the victor, automatically becoming or remaining High Lord. There was quick agreement as to the fate of the city. Lord Alexandros had never intended to allow a sack or to execute reprisals against the bulk of the city's population. Most of those Lord Alexandros had intent to avenge himself upon, Demetrios had already jailed; therefore, they would not be difficult to find. It was agreed that if Lord Alexandros should win, the civil guard and White Horse Squadron would be retained in their present positions—the sole exceptions being Lords Mahrk and Szamyul, as Lord Alexandros felt Ehleenee should fill their current posts. It was further agreed that those slaves Demetrios had freed and enfranchised should remain free citizens. Many, many smaller but no less important issues were agreed upon as well. The only request that Demetrios made, which could in any way be construed as personal, was that the tombs and remains of his parents and ancestors remain inviolate.

When Demetrios descended to the palace courtyard— fully-armed, shield slung on his back, javelin and throwing-stick in his right hand and helmet in the crook of his left arm—it was to find, not only his chariot and driver and the three horsemen who were to accompany him: Lord Mahrk, Lord Szamyul, and M'Gonda, leader of his Black Spearmen, but the entire White Horse Squadron. The officers and men were mounted, armored, and fully armed.

Clapping on his helmet and snapping down the cheek-pieces, the High Lord strode over to where his escort sat their horses. "What means this, Lord Mahrk?"

The *strahteegos* dismounted and said, "My Lord, those western nomads of Lord Alexandros' love to fight. I will ask once more, let us request that this battle be between opposing forces of equal strength? There are nearly eight hundreds of the White Horse. . . ."

"And," interjected M'Gonda suddenly, "ten times twenty-three of my people. We are all yours. Let us fight with you."

Choking, Demetrios grasped each man's hand in turn. "No, I cannot. Such would be certain death for far too many of you."

"What, my lord, do you think this madness is?" Lord Mahrk burst out. "In weeks past, you have become a middling swordsman; but Lord Alexandros is a past-master! His age means nothing; he has the muscles and wind and stamina of a man of forty. The only possible way for you to survive this, is to down him with your javelin. Barring that, you go to your death!"

"I know, Mahrk," said Demetrios softly. "I have known from the first that Alexandros would slay me. I so planned it, for I have committed crimes which only my death can expiate. All my life, excepting the past few weeks, I have lived as a swine. I wish to die as a man."

So saying, he walked back to and mounted the chariot. "Let us go, Agostinos," he told the driver. "It would not do to keep your new High Lord waiting."

Lord Alexandros was first to throw his javelin. Demetrios surprised even himself by adroitly turning the missile on his shield. Then, remembering everything that M'Gonda had told him, Demetrios hurled his own. By some fluke, the *assegai* pierced the hide of Lord Alexandros' shield and sunk deeply into the wood and the older man freed it only just in time to take Demetrios' sword-cut on the shield and, slamming its iron boss at the High Lord's face, fend him off long enough to draw his own weapon.

They circled each other warily, Lord Alexandros talking to himself under his breath. "By God, the bastard came far too close to getting me that time! Whoever taught him to cast a dart knew what he was about. He doesn't look as fat as I'd remembered and there's strength in his sword-arm, too. He really looks much like Basil, his father. That barbarian who calls himself Lord Mahrk was right. He is more a man, now, than ever he has been. He's the kind of fighter, the kind of ruler, he'd have been if his father had taken the time to see to the proper rearing of him. Now, let's see . . . *HAAGGHH!*"

Lord Alexandros leapt in, down-slanted shield held before him, and delivered a vicious, backhand slash at his opponent's neck. Demetrios easily caught it on his own sword and the iron-shod edge of his hard-swung shield slammed agonizingly into Lord Alexandros' exposed right side. Disengaging his blade, Demetrios hopped backward just in time to avoid the uprushing shield of his adversary. With a speed which was astounding for one of his girth, Demetrios chopped up with the inner edge of his shield, catching Lord Alexandros' and forcing it even higher, at the same time, stabbing at the spot where the elder man's hauberk stopped, an inch or so above the knee.

This time it was Lord Alexandros who hopped hurriedly back, thinking, "Sweet Jesus, the boy's fast as a greased pig! What a fighting High Lord he'd have made. Saints above, with but a few weeks training, he's come close to killing me twice over!"

After two more attacks, producing nothing more rewarding than lightning counter-attacks from Demetrios, Lord Alexandros settled to a routine of hack and slash, forehand and backhand, high and low, figure-eight and circle; but never did his edge contact other than shield or parrying sword. When he had established an attack pattern and felt the time to be right, he feinted an upslash and ended in a high thrust for the face; Demetrios beat the thrusting weapon against its owner's own shield, then capped the sword-sandwich with his own close-held shield, immobilizing his opponent's blade, while his own remained free.

No one of the watchers took breath. Lord Alexandros was momentarily defenseless and all realized it. Demetrios could drive his point into face or back of neck or through the lacings of Lord Alexandros' jazeran with impunity; and that would be that!

The men's strained, flushed, sweat-streaked faces were bare inches, one from the other. "Well?" panted Lord Alexandros. "Get it over with! You tortured and butchered the rest of my family. Why do you stick at me?"

"You . . . good fighter . . . good man!" gasped Demetrios. "Too bad . . . couldn't . . . been friends. Be great honor . . . die by . . . your hand."

Alexandros started. "You *want* me to kill you?"

"Many sins . . ." Demetrios went on. "Heavy . . . must pay. Sat and . . . sipped wine . . . laughed . . . when your daughters . . . grandchildren . . . tormented to death. You have . . . dirk. Use it! Had many . . . things . . . done to . . . your kin." He went on to haltingly describe the gruesome and incredible brutalities which his torturers had inflicted upon the old nobleman's family until, foaming with rage, the *strahteegos* let go his hilt, drew his dirk, and plunged it into Demetrios' neck, just under the left ear! Hilt-deep, he drove the wide-bladed dirk, so that it transfixed the High Lord's thick neck—a good eight centimeters of the blade protruding from the opposite side.

Demetrios half-screamed at the bite of the steel. Dropping his sword, he wrenched Lord Alexandros' hand from the dirk. Stepping back, he saluted his slayer, then crumpled to the ground, eyes closed, lips smiling up at the sun.

Demetrios' descriptions had been accurate and revolting and Alexandros was still half-berserk and the smile further infuriated him. Furiously, he kicked at the dying man's face, then, picking up his sword, used its edge to sever the shoulder-strap of his shield, slipped free of the arm-bands, and dropped the buckler. Stepping to his fallen foe, he kicked off Demetrios' helmet, tore away the padded cap, and, raising the High Lord's head by the hair, he lifted his sword with the obvious intent of decapitating the body.

"NO!" shouted M'Gonda. With unbelievable swiftness, the black quitted his saddle, snatched a javelin from the holder on the side of the chariot, and fitted it to his silver spear-thrower. Just as Lord Alexandros' blade commenced its hard-swung descent, M'Gonda took three running steps forward and made his cast. The use of a throwing-stick imparts tremendous velocity to a javelin and such was the force of this cast that the entirety of the seventeen-centimeters of blade length penetrated the *strahteegos'* exposed right side, the needle-point tearing into his mighty heart!

Seconds after he had thrown his javelin, M'Gonda's body was pin-cushioned with arrows.

For a long, long moment, there was no movement, in any quarter—all knew that one untoward motion would surely precipitate a pitched battle. Then, above the stillness, sounded a clattering-clanging thud, as Lord Mahrk dropped his round buckler. With his gauntleted *left* hand, he drew his broad-sword and, grasping it by the blade-tip, waved it above his head before casting it down beside his shield. This done, he toed his white charger forward, to rein and dismount beside the bodies of the two Ehleenee. Shortly, he was joined by Milo, Mara, Djeen Mai, and Lord Szamyul; and the watchers relaxed, starting to breathe again.

Lord Alexandros Pahpahs was dead, though a trickle of blood was yet running from one corner of his mouth. Djeen

Mai set his foot against his slain lord's armored side and withdrew the imbedded javelin, then closed the glazed eyes and wiped the blood from the old *strahteegos'* chin. Wordless, Mara looked down on this dead, old man, trying to visualize the vibrantly alive boy she had loved so long ago.

Sadly, Lord Mahrk bent over Demetrios' body and, as gently as possible, pulled out Lord Alexandros' dirk. All at once, he straightened and reeled back, his face ashen, the dirk dropping from suddenly nerveless fingers.

"He . . . my Lord is not . . . *he is still alive!* He . . . he *moaned* when I took out the dirk!" The Lord High *Strahteegos* gasped, half-unbelievingly.

Milo bounded over to the downed High Lord and hastily ascertained that he was, indeed, yet sentient, not even truly unconscious. Then he noticed something else.

EPILOGUE

"As nearly as I can calculate, it is mid-December of the six hundred and fifty-second year of my life, 2593 A.D. It is now six hundred thirteen years since man's own folly plunged this world back to a cultural level of barbarism. What ancient man was it who said that World War IV would be fought with spears and clubs?

"Well, at least mankind will be spared that for a while yet. There just aren't sufficient people on this earth to man a world-wide war. I've no way of determining how many were left after the last of those terrible plagues had run its course; but, on the basis of what I've heard and what I've seen during my travels and such calculations as I've made, I'd say that even now—more than six hundred years after World War III—there're still far less than half a billion human beings on this old planet.

"I wonder if ever I will find the island and, if I do, what it will be like to live with none save others of my kind. What sort of government have they, I wonder—a democracy like the North Ehleenee or a kingdom like the Karaleenee and the South Ehleenee and most of the barbarians; a loose confederation like my people or a representative republic, such as we helped Demetrios to set up; or is it a dictatorship like that which Backstrom described.

"And, speaking of Backstrom, that's another project which I must see to. I've the feeling that those malicious bastards will never leave us in peace. God help this world if they and their kind ever gain control of any sizable portion of it. And I think that that's what Backstrom was hinting at when he spoke of their 'not being ready, yet'!

"We'll have to get established here, first, of course; and I'll have to get my hands on a ship of some sort and some experienced mariners and do some exploring. At one time, I had a fair, Sunday sailor's knowledge of these waters, but that damned earthquake so rearranged this coast that it's barely recognizable. Demetrios has offered every assistance and building materials to help us build a city here—hell, he's even named it already, calls it Thahlahsahpolis—but we're going to have to either drain that bloody swamp or build a road through it first. Maybe not, though; maybe we can barge cut stone down the river. Besides, although the ones aboveground are too weathered to be very useful, maybe, if we dig, we can find stones on the spot.

"Getting sleepy, so I guess I'd best call it a night. I'll have my hands full at first light, what with apportioning no more than twenty square-miles of high ground among forty-three clans. It's odd that the point of this peninsula rose, while the center sank; but that's nature for you.

"Took me twenty years to bring these people to the culmination of their dreams. God willing, a couple more hundred years will see their descendants helping me to the culmination of mine. Nonetheless, tomorrow will mark the first day of a beginning."

—From the Private Journal of Milo Morai

At last, after a migration which had consumed nearly twenty years, The-Tribe-That-Will-Return-To-The-Sea had done so.

Milo and Mara Morai, Blind Hari of Krooguh and the chiefs of all the clans sat their horses on the narrow thread of beach which marked the very tip of the peninsula, surf-foam lapping at the forehoofs of their mounts. Before them, as far as the eye could see, the blue-gray water heaved ceaselessly; the tide was at flow and each curling wave broke closer to the shore. The early-winter sky was overcast and gray as the tumbled, weathered stones of the ancient ruins, which brooded on the hill above the beach. Miles behind, the tribe was still toiling through the swamps, guided and assisted by Ehleenee, who were familiar with the treacherous fens.

No communication, vocal or mental, was exchanged, as the nomads remained stock-still, their eyes drinking in the reality which their dreams and numberless generations of their ancestors' dreams were become. Milo's eyes, too, stared, but not at the sea; he strained to see beyond the horizon, hoping past hope to espy that half-mythical island, the search for which had once taken him from these people for two hundred years.

"Now," he thought, "at the end of this phase, is the beginning of the real task: to mold these fine men's descendants into sea-rovers, rather than plains-rovers. I must remember to encourage intermarriage between the Clans-people and the Ehleenee, for the latter already possess *some* tradition and knowledge of seamanship, trading even with Europe. It'll probably take a few hundred years to do it right, but then, the four of us—myself and Mara and Aldora and Demetrios—have that much time and more.

"Of course, we may be delayed for a bit, here and there. Demetrios has become a real fire-eater, since he got a taste of warfare. He hasn't said as much, but it's obvious that he wants to conquer Karaleenos and, since Zenos seems to feel that lack of aggressiveness indicates weakness, I suppose we'll have to either openly annex his lands or eliminate him and put a puppet on his throne. It would probably be as well to invest a few years in subjugating the peoples to our immediate north and west as well; do to them what we know they'd do to us, but do it first."

"God Milo?" mindspoke the Cat Chief, Dirktooth (brave Horsekiller's smoke had resided in the Home of the Wind since the Battle of Notohspolis, some six months agone). "Soon, the lowest section of the way that we came will be completely covered with this bitter water. I am not as many of the cubs, *I* do not enjoy immersing myself in water. Can we not, now, return to the higher ground?"

Steeltooth snorted and stamped the wet sand and transmitted his agreement. "Steeltooth say go. Wind and water are cold on his legs."

"We have seen and will see for the rest of our lives," Milo

broad-beamed the thought to the long line of chiefs. "Let us return and speed the clans, that they, too, may see."

Then he gave the palomino stallion his head and Steel-tooth's big hooves spurned the sand as he trotted in the wake of the bounding Cat Chief.

ABOUT THE AUTHOR

ROBERT ADAMS lives in Seminole County, Florida. Like the characters in his books, he is partial to fencing and fancy swordplay, hunting and riding, good food and drink. And when he is not hard at work on his next science-fiction novel, Robert may be found slaving over a hot forge to make a new sword or busily reconstructing a historically accurate military costume.